DINNER WITH MILLIE

"Do you think your aunt is really going to start serving suppers?" Henry asked quietly.

Millie sighed. "No more than you believe that it's Vern's birthday."

"So we agree this was a setup?"

She nodded.

"Do we stay or go?" he asked. "It's up to you."

"Don't make me—"

Henry stopped her words, laying one hand on top of hers where it rested on the table. "I'm leaving it up to you because I want to stay. I want to have this dinner with you and more. If I'm truly being honest, I believe I want to have every dinner with you for the rest of our lives, but I know—"

"You mean that?" she asked. Tears filled her eyes. Hormones, she told herself, but she knew she was not fooling anyone. She was dangerously close to falling in love with Henry King, but she didn't want to be in love alone. But if what he was saying was true . . .

"With all my heart," he promised.

Books by Amy Lillard

The Wells Landing Series
CAROLINE'S SECRET
COURTING EMILY
LORIE'S HEART
JUST PLAIN SADIE
TITUS RETURNS
MARRYING JONAH
THE QUILTING CIRCLE
A WELLS LANDING CHRISTMAS
LOVING JENNA
ROMANCING NADINE
A NEW LOVE FOR CHARLOTTE

The Pontotoc Mississippi Series
A HOME FOR HANNAH
A LOVE FOR LEAH
A FAMILY FOR GRACIE
AN AMISH HUSBAND FOR TILLIE

The Paradise Valley Series
MARRY ME, MILLIE

Amish Mysteries
KAPPY KING AND THE PUPPY KAPER
KAPPY KING AND THE PICKLE KAPER
KAPPY KING AND THE PIE KAPER

Published by Kensington Publishing Corp.

MARRY ME, MILLIE

AMY LILLARD

ZEBRA BOOKS
KENSINGTON PUBLISHING CORP.
www.kensingtonbooks.com

Chapter One

"Who's that?"

At her aunt's question, Millie Bauman stopped pouring water into the little foam cups and gazed out across Thomas Kurtz's yard. She didn't see anyone she didn't recognize and immediately went back to her task. The sermon had been long and her back was aching. She was ready to finish her chore and find somewhere to rest for a bit. With or without a plate of food, she didn't care. She might be six months pregnant, but with the added weight she'd attracted recently, rest was quickly becoming more important than food.

The six-month mark had been strange for her. It seemed as if everything had shifted. Her balance was off, she got tired more easily, and with the growing heat there in central Missouri, she was decidedly crankier. Not that she let her change in attitude show. She did her best every day to be as even-tempered as possible. And that was not always an easy endeavor. Which seemed to wear her out. And then the whole process started all over again.

"I don't see anybody new," she said.

"You didn't even look," her aunt protested.

"I did. I saw Thomas Kurtz talking to Vern King and Christian Beachy. That's not exactly big news around here." After all, it was Thomas's house where they had just held their church services. He and Christian were both widowers in their small community of Paradise Springs, and Vern . . . well, Vern seemed to always be around somewhere. Not in a bad way, but it was as if he was always in the thick of things. There was another man, but she couldn't see him well enough to decipher who he was. Christian was blocking her view. Maybe that's who her aunt was talking about.

"That's Henry King," Lillian Lambert said, sidling up behind them.

The line had slowed and Millie had several cups already poured for the next people who wanted them. She got one for herself and took a long drink, studying the men across the yard. Then Christian moved and she saw him, this Henry King.

"He's handsome," Sylvie said offhandedly. A little too offhandedly.

"Sylvie, no," Millie protested. This was a new development in their relationship. Sylvie had taken it into her head that Millie needed to get married again. It was ironic, she supposed. The very reason she had moved to Paradise Springs, one of the two settlements in Paradise Valley, was to avoid that very thing. The rest of Millie's family was in Adrian, just a short distance away. Millie would have been there too, had her husband not died in a freak construction accident, leaving her alone and pregnant. Though, at the time, she'd had no idea that she carried a child. When she realized the truth, she decided she didn't want to get married again, so she sold everything she had and moved here to Paradise Springs to help her aunt with her business, the Paradise Springs B&B.

"You don't think he's handsome?" Lillian asked, brows raised till they almost met her hairline.

"She doesn't think who's handsome?" Elsie Miller picked that time to saunter up. She took up her own cup of water as she waited for Lillian to continue.

"Joy's cousin."

Millie quickly did the math. Joy Lehman was Vern King's granddaughter so, *jah*, that would make her and Henry cousins or siblings. Though it didn't matter how handsome he was—and he was handsome, rust-colored hair and dark eyes—she wasn't interested.

"I didn't think we were supposed to care about such trivial things as looks," she said with a sniff.

Lillian laughed. "Name me one woman who doesn't think their man is handsome."

"Frannie Lambright," Sylvie said emphatically.

They all laughed, though Millie wished she had curtailed her own humor. Leroy Lambright might resemble a donkey at times, but he was a good and godly man. Father of eight, grandfather to who knew how many, deacon to their district, and all-around beautiful man. On the inside. Where it counted most.

Frannie herself was something of a saint. Millie knew that most people would take it for granted that Frannie would see after her brother-in-law's new baby. After all, it had only been a couple of months since his wife died having the child, but Frannie was almost sixty years old. She was past the time for toting around an infant, but Benjamin needed her, and she had stepped up. To Millie, it sounded a tad crazy, but commendable all the same.

"And then Frannie and that baby," Lillian continued, echoing Millie's thoughts. Lillian shook her head, as if that explained everything. Actually, it did. They all knew it was quite an undertaking to accept the responsibility for such a small child to the benefit of another. Even Sylvie, who had never had any children of her own, understood how much time and care a newborn demanded. Frannie was on the cusp of her golden years, working toward the time when she could merely bounce her grandchildren on her knee and wait for others to provide most of her care. Instead, she wagged that baby to work with her at the Lambrights' meat market in town—Paradise Meats—and watched her and the counter all day. Benjamin's other children went to stay with his mother-in-law while he worked the dairy farm he shared with his brother, then onto the meat market, where they took turns manning the cutting blades each day.

"He's not going to be able to keep this up for long," Sylvie said with a small shake of her head.

"It's already been two months," Lillian pointed out.

"Doesn't matter," Sylvie continued. "He's going to have to remarry soon, even if he's in mourning. Those babies need a mother."

Maybe Sylvie was on an everyone-needs-to-be-married kick or something. Which was strange, seeing as how she had been a widow for as long as Millie could remember. Maybe even before she was born. And Sylvie pretty much ran the Whoopie Pie Widows Club, so it didn't seem like she was thinking about marriage anytime soon.

The Whoopie Pie Widows Club. So that wasn't the exact name of the group. It was something like Paradise Springs Widows Group or some such, but no one called it that. To most all of Paradise Springs—and neighboring rival, Paradise Hill—the group of widowed women were known as the Whoopie Pie Widows Club.

From what Millie had learned in her time in Paradise Springs, it had all started when Felty Lambright's wife, Sue, was diagnosed with cancer. The widows got together to do a bake sale for a fundraiser, but it just so happened that they all made whoopie pies. Millie figured someone fell down on their job in organizing a variety. At any rate, the ladies made exotic flavors of the traditional, well-loved dessert, and before anyone could turn around, the nickname had stuck. Not that anyone called them that where any of them could hear. But still, they were most definitely the Whoopie Pie Widows Club.

"He came into the store yesterday," Lillian said, drawing Millie out of her own thoughts.

"Who?" Millie asked.

"Henry King," Lillian explained with a small frown. Clearly she was disappointed that Millie was not keeping up with the conversation better than she was.

"The variety store?" Millie questioned, still a bit behind. Lillian's father-in-law owned and operated a variety store. Lillian had gone to work there several years before when her own husband had died. So it would make sense that was the store she was talking about.

"Of course." Lillian's frown deepened a bit. "He seems like a real nice man. A perfect match for one of our younger women."

"If he stays," Elsie said. "Betsy told me that he was only here for the growing season. Once fall comes, he's going back to Oklahoma. That's where he's from."

"Betsy would know," Lillian said sagely.

Betsy Stoll, also a member of the Whoopie Pie Widows Club, owned and ran the Paradise Apothecary. She sold herbs and home remedies to everyone in Paradise Springs and had a strong finger on the pulse of the community.

"Maybe," Sylvie said. "I know who would really know." She let out a low whistle and waved to Joy Lehman, Henry's cousin.

Joy nodded to the people she was talking to, then made her way over to where they stood at the water station. "Honestly, Sylvie, whistling at church?"

Sylvie returned Joy's look unabashedly. "It was a low whistle and everyone has eaten."

Joy shook her head. "You'll bring the bishop down on you in a quick minute if you don't behave yourself."

A few of the women snickered. That was the one thing that surprised Millie when she moved to Paradise Springs, the bishop. Zebadiah Miller might take his duties seriously, but he was not out to police his community. If no one complained, he didn't bother. And Millie was certain no one complained much. It made for a smooth-running district, even if they were a bit . . . unorthodox.

"Can I have a turn now?" Sylvie asked.

Joy rolled her eyes, but the action was a bit playful, Millie noticed. "What is it?"

"Millie was just asking about your cousin," Sylvie said.

"I was no—" Millie stopped. Denying it sounded worse than if she had actually asked. Which she hadn't.

Joy smiled. "He's a good seed," she said, then her expression grew dark. "But I think he's up to no good." She pressed her lips together before starting back up. "It's not his fault. It's Dale's . . . my uncle," she continued when no one responded.

"Oh." The ladies nodded in unison.

"He wants Vern to come to Oklahoma and live with him. Says he's getting forgetful and needs to be around his family. So I asked Dale what did that make me? He said I didn't count."

The ladies gasped.

"Not in so many words," Joy backpedaled. "But that was the gist. Then he offered to let me come down too. Not sure where he thinks I'll live. Not in the *dawdihaus* with Dat, that's for certain." She gave a small harrumph.

"What's in Oklahoma?" Elsie asked.

Joy gave a delicate shrug. "Most of the family, I guess. But when they all moved down there—to use the tractors, you know—Vern and my Rudy decided they wanted to stay here."

And then Rudy died. Joy had lost her income, so she leased her farmland and opened a bakery in her basement. After all, she had four children to care for.

That was one thing Millie could say about the widows in Paradise Springs: They were made of stern stuff. She laid a protective hand over her belly. She hoped some of that gumption would rub off on her. She had a feeling she was going to need it once her baby was born.

"What's the matter?" Sylvie asked, noticing Millie's fingers splayed across her bulging midsection.

"Nothing." Millie smiled to reassure her aunt.

"Did the baby kick?" Elsie asked, reaching a tentative hand toward Millie, but not quite touching her.

As near as Millie could figure, Elsie was at least fifty, but she had never had any children of her own. It was strange to Millie how such things came about. Elsie seemed like she would make a kind and loving mother, whereas Lillian seemed to be counting down the days until her youngest daughter and last child left home, got married, and moved out. Lillian had five kids total. Esther, the youngest, was promised to marry Mark Esh this December. And then that would be that.

But Millie knew that this child she carried—a little boy or a little girl, she did not know—would be her only child. She was never marrying again, so it only stood to reason. But she was fine with that decision. She had made peace with it, and with God.

"Maybe you should sit down," Sylvie said. "Out of the sun."

"Good idea," Elsie said. She grabbed a lawn chair off the side porch and carried it under the shade of the nearby oak tree. "Come sit, Millie."

What could she do but comply? Especially after the action had been carried out just for her. Still, she thought as she settled into the seat, it was good to get off her aching feet and to rest her aching back. No one ever talked about how painful pregnancy could be. There were days when she was certain even her hair hurt, but she wasn't complaining. One look at Elsie's sparkling eyes every time she caught sight of a sweet child was enough to have Millie thanking God for the blessings she had. She knew it was arrogant and prideful to believe that she would carry the baby full-term and have a healthy child to raise, but she still thanked God every chance she got.

"You just sit there and rest," her aunt said, patting her on the hand in a gesture that Millie was pretty sure was meant to show support.

Despite her aunt's overly considerate tone and the fact

that several people were coming up to get drinks, Millie decided to do just that.

Sylvie Yoder cast one last, quick look at her niece and started across Thomas Kurtz's yard.

Millie might not be able to see the truth for what it was, but Sylvie could. And the truth was, Millie needed to get married again.

Don't get it wrong, she enjoyed having her niece there at the B&B, helping take some of the workload from Sylvie's own shoulders, but Millie was only twenty-four. She needed more from life than dirty diapers, baking muffins, and changing the sheets for strangers.

Not that it was a bad life. Well, maybe the dirty diapers, but Sylvie had never had any children of her own, so she couldn't say for sure. Only that it *seemed* that way. But in truth, running a B&B and seeing to the needs of her variety of guests was Sylvie's calling. Just after her husband, Andrew, died, Sylvie pooled all her money together, marched into the bank, and demanded a loan. *Demanded* might be too strong a word, but she did ask very sternly, hoping her strong attitude would convince them not to turn her down. It must have worked, because they gave her the loan, she bought the old, run-down Davidson B&B, and turned it into the quaint overnight stay it now was.

She had worked hard and sacrificed a lot to make her dream come true and she was proud of what she had accomplished. But not in a bad way. In the absolute best way possible. But the life wasn't always easy, and she didn't want it for Millie and the baby she carried.

It was a boy, Sylvie thought. Maybe Millie would name him after her Andrew. They could call him Andy. Andy Bauman. That had a nice ring to it. Or maybe Andy King . . .

There he was!

Vern King. Just the man she was looking for.

"Vern," she called, resisting the urge to whistle at him as well. One whistle a church Sunday was plenty, she supposed. Zebadiah might be an easygoing bishop, but that didn't mean he had no backbone at all. No sense pushing it.

Vern turned when he heard her call his name. He smiled and shaded his eyes as he watched her draw near. She wasn't sure why he did that. He was wearing his hat; all he had to do was pull the brim a bit lower and wait for her to catch up to him. But no, he shaded his face with the back of one hand and watched as she approached.

"Sylvie Yoder," he said, a smile in his voice and still on his lips. "What can I do for you today?"

"I have a leaky sink," she said, the idea coming to her even as she said the words. "Can you come take a look at it this week? The sooner the better," she added.

Vern stroked his hand down his beard and thoughtfully checked the sun, as if that was where the week's schedule was written. "I suppose."

"It needs to be seen about before it gets worse," she pressed him.

"If you're in that big of a hurry, why don't you call a plumber?"

Sylvie propped her hands on her hips. "Because I don't want to pay that much. You know some of these English plumbers are worse than pirates." Well, at least the ones in Paradise Springs were. She couldn't say the same for certain about Paradise Hill, but she supposed if she tried to call one of them, he would leave a bigger mess than what she had started with. Which was none. There was no leaking faucet, but she needed an excuse to get Vern King and his grandson—especially his grandson—to the B&B this week.

"I suppose." Vern nodded, still stroking his beard. "Might there be a home-cooked meal involved in this transaction?"

"If you manage to come into town and actually look at the faucet, I'm sure there will be."

He dipped his chin approvingly. "And some whoopie pies . . ." he prodded.

Sylvie beamed him her brightest smile. "Of course."

Stroke, stroke, stroke.

"I'll pay you," she finally said. What else did she have to do to get the man to agree?

"Oh, no. No," Vern said. "The meal and whoopie pies will be enough. Sometime this week, eh?"

"The sooner the better,"' she said, still pushing, though Vern seemed intent on taking his time approving their plans.

"I suppose I can manage that," he finally said.

Sylvie wanted to jump for joy. This was it. The start of something big. For Millie anyway. "That's good," she said with a very controlled smile. She didn't want to give too much away. What were those card players who came to the B&B always saying? She didn't want to reveal her hand, or some such. She supposed that fit in this situation. She didn't want Vern to know how much she was counting on him coming to fix a sink that wasn't broken.

"Hopefully Wednesday," Vern continued. "Will that be okay?"

Sylvie gave a quick nod. "Perfect,'" she said, then she turned on her toes and started back to where the women waited, no doubt wondering what the two of them had been talking about. Well, let them wonder. She turned back to face Vern as if she had forgotten to tell him something important. She hadn't forgotten anything. "And bring your grandson," she said, before spinning back around and leaving him standing in the middle of the yard all alone.

Chapter Two

"It's because of Johnny B's accident," Sylvie said as they trotted home in their shiny black buggy. Unlike the Swiss Amish over in Seymour, the Amish in Paradise Valley— both Paradise Springs and Paradise Hill—rode around with buggies that had tops. Millie would be especially happy about that come the wintertime. It got cold in Missouri.

"What was that?" Millie asked. She had been listening to her aunt, but Sylvie had a tendency to jump from one subject to another without warning.

Her aunt sighed. "Johnny B's accident."

"*Jah*." Millie nodded. Johnny B was Joy Lehman's oldest son. He had fallen out of the hayloft earlier in the year and bruised all the muscles in his back. For the time being he was in a wheelchair. According to Joy, the doctors weren't sure if he would ever walk again. Only time would tell how deep the damage went.

"Johnny B had been helping Vern in the fields, but because he's hurt, Vern's son, Dale, sent Henry up to help him."

"So what's because of Johnny B's accident," Millie asked, not sure where she had lost the thread of the conversation.

Sylvie sighed. "That's the reason Henry King is in town."

"Oh." She nodded, though she was still a little confused. Not why or how Henry King came to be in Paradise Springs, but why her aunt was telling her this. No, that wasn't it either. She knew why her aunt was telling her all this; she wanted to keep Henry King in the forefront of Millie's thoughts. But she was confused as to why her aunt was telling her this *now*.

But Millie didn't ask. She loved her aunt, but sometimes inviting yourself into her thought process was an iffy endeavor.

Sylvie pulled their mare into the short drive at the side of the house and hopped down.

"Do you want me to take Daisy down to the stables?" Millie asked as she climbed down a bit more carefully than her aunt. All the extra weight being in the front had tipped her balance forward. It was hard to go slow and take her time when all her life she had been used to getting up and doing without thinking about it.

"I can do it," her aunt said, making her way to the front of the horse. She started to unhitch her from the buggy. "You need to rest your feet."

"Honestly, I would rather walk her down than try to put up the buggy." It wasn't that it was all that heavy, but it was awkward getting it turned around and into the carriage house without bumping it on the side walls.

And the stables weren't very far away. Jason Stoll, one of the members of their church district, had opened a stable there at the edge of town where he housed horses for townie Amish and English alike. It was so much better for the horses to be allowed both inside and outside time.

The land that the B&B had that could accommodate the horse for pasture time had been taken up in parking for the guests. So it was perfect for them. The horse was cared for during the week and over the non-church weekend. She got to be around the other horses, which Millie knew made horses happy, and she and Sylvie could concentrate their attention on their business without worrying about Daisy.

Sylvie shook her head. "I'll do both. You go inside and rest."

Millie opened her mouth to protest, but Sylvie shook her head once again, her *kapp* strings swinging around her shoulders. Sometime during the ride home, Sylvie had untied them. Slightly rebellious in their district, but it was better than cutting them off, like Millie had seen some of the younger girls do.

"Don't argue with me. Things are going to get harder and harder for you now. At least that's what Imogene told me."

"Imogene Yoder?"

Sylvie stopped unbuckling the horse and looked at Millie sharply. "You know any other Imogenes?"

Millie sighed. "No. But she's only been pregnant once, and with twins. Of course her balance was off." At least Millie suspected that was the reason. This was her first baby too, and it wasn't twins, so she could guess, but she couldn't say for certain.

"Stop being so stubborn and accept some help," Sylvie admonished as she went back to her chore. It was only a heartbeat later that she held Daisy's reins in her hand. She eased the horse around. "Now get inside and get off your feet."

Millie shook her head and smiled. She hated being treated like an invalid, but now was not the time to assert her independence. Her time with her aunt had taught her that she had to measure each situation and pick her battles. "Okay," she said on a sigh. "But be careful walking Daisy down to the stables." It was Sunday, and even though all the Amish businesses in town were closed, there always seemed to be increased automobile traffic. Englishers headed here and there, out to enjoy the beautiful late spring day.

"I will." Sylvie led the horse to the end of the drive, then stopped. "And we may have some guests coming by. I told them check-in's at four, but you know how that goes."

Millie did. People tended to get overexcited when they vacationed and had a habit of showing up early. Which was the exact reason that Millie and Sylvie left the church service with the others who had cows and such to tend to.

"It's almost three now," Sylvie continued. "When they get here, put them in the Lavender Room."

All the rooms in the inn were color coded. There was the Lavender Room, the Red Room, the Blue Room, and the Green Room, along with the Sunshine Suite, which was, of course, decorated in shades of yellow. All either had an adjacent bathroom or one close by. Something Millie was learning was extremely important in the business.

"I thought they were staying in the Green Room." It had the best view of the backyard and the edge of town. The Green Room was always booked.

"The bathroom has a leak," Sylvie explained. "So we need to put them in the Lavender Room."

The Lavender Room also faced the back, but the Green Room was on the corner, so it had a better view all around.

"We need to call a plumber, then." They couldn't have the Green Room out of commission for long. They were almost at capacity now. Millie started toward the door of the B&B, intent at doing just that, but Sylvie's voice stopped her.

"I've got Vern King coming to look at it this week."

Millie resisted the urge to roll her eyes or otherwise show her displeasure. It was her aunt's choice after all, but it seemed sort of silly to wait around to have Vern fix it when they could have an English plumber out before sundown.

"I know what you're thinking," Sylvie said. "But there's no rush."

Millie crossed her arms. "I disagree. The Henleys will be here on Wednesday and won't have a place to stay if the Green Room is out of commission because of the leak."

"The McCarthys are checking out on Tuesday. That gives us time to clean their room and get it ready for the Henleys."

Millie sighed. She hated arguing with her aunt, but as far as she was concerned that was cutting it a mite close. "What happens if the McCarthys decide to stay another day or two?" It had been known to happen.

"Stop borrowing trouble," Sylvie admonished.

Millie dropped her arms and carefully eyed her aunt. "I'm not trying to borrow trouble. I just don't see the need to have a room out of order until Vern King decides he has time to come into town and fix it." She knew her aunt meant well. She herself was all for hiring Amish and local when they needed something repaired, but it was early in the growing season. It could be days before Vern found his way into town.

Sylvie flashed her a knowing smile. "He'll come in sooner than you think. I've promised him a home-cooked meal and whoopie pies."

Millie's annoyance faded away at her aunt's self-satisfied look. She supposed she shouldn't worry so much. After all, her aunt had been running the inn for years before Millie took it upon herself to come help. Her aunt had it all under control. And what she didn't, God certainly did. "*Jah*, okay," Millie finally said.

"Good." Sylvie smiled with a quick nod. "Now go inside and sit down." She started to turn away, back toward the street and the sidewalk she would follow to walk Daisy the mare down to the Paradise Stables. But she turned back one last time. "And look through the recipe book," she said. "We need to come up with a new flavor whoopie pie for when Vern and Henry do come into town."

Millie managed not to stand outside with her mouth hanging open too long after her aunt had disappeared with the horse. She thought for a moment about going ahead and putting the buggy away but figured when her aunt got back from the stables, she would never hear the end of it. So instead, she made her way inside and into the kitchen.

Get down the recipe book for a new version of whoopie pies. She had never heard of such foolishness. Sure, it would cost more to have a professional plumber come in to check the leak in the Green Room lavatory, but wouldn't it be worth it in the long run?

Millie took down her aunt's whoopie pie recipe book and sat it on the table. Then she eased into the closest chair, but she didn't open the book as the truth hit her. This wasn't about whoopie pies or even saving money. This was about Sylvie thinking that Millie needed a man in her life. And it didn't seem to matter what Millie herself wanted.

"It was a good sermon," Vern said as he and Henry rode along home from church.

"*Jah*," Henry said. He supposed it was a good sermon, but he wasn't sure he would know a bad sermon if he ever heard one. It was, after all, the word of God, from one of God's own chosen servants. What could be bad about that? But it seemed that for the first few days after church, that's all anyone wanted to talk about: the sermon and whether or not it was "good."

Henry could almost feel his grandfather's gaze on him as they rode along, but he didn't turn to acknowledge it. He knew what was coming.

"Ain't no sense in moping about it, boy." His *dawdi*'s words were gruff and caring at the same time.

Henry didn't bother to ask what "it" he was referring to. He knew. "I'm not moping."

"I know what tomorrow is . . . or was, I guess. Not many Amish people get married this late in the growing season."

Henry bit back a sigh. "Anna Kate wanted a spring wedding." *Like an Englisher*. He pushed the thought away.

So what if tomorrow was the day that Anna Kate Ebersol had promised to marry him, then broken that promise and headed off to Belize? It didn't mean anything to him, that day. It was just a day. Nothing special, though there had been a time when he supposed there had been.

"What self-respecting Amish person gets married on a Monday anyway?" Vern shook his head, unaware that his words sliced like a knife at Henry's already damaged heart.

It was for Anna Kate. Everything was for Anna Kate. All he had wanted was to make her happy. So he had bent to her every crazy whim. Getting married on a Monday. Getting married in May. Well, those were the only two he could think of right at the moment, but he was sure there were more. There was always more where Anna Kate was concerned.

"What I really don't understand is why she went down to Mexico with the Mennonites," Vern continued.

That's you and me both, he wanted to shout. "Belize," he corrected instead. His fiancée had gone to Belize to live in a remote Mennonite community. Just after the new year began, she had tearfully told him that she felt God wanted something more from her. At first she wasn't sure what the call was, then she saw something in the newspaper about a Mennonite settlement in Central America and she had known immediately.

Those first tears were tears of joy and excitement, but they had quickly turned to tears of heartbreak and sorrow. She might have felt God calling her to go half the world away, but Henry had no such pull.

He prayed about it and prayed about it, then prayed about it some more, but if God wanted her to go to Belize, He surely meant for her to go alone.

There had been a time when Henry had held the smallest strand of hope that she would go back on her decision, especially when he told her that he couldn't leave Oklahoma. He couldn't leave all that they had known behind in order to join a conservative group of Plain people in another country. Even the thought of it didn't make sense. But the more he tried to understand, the more he understood that Anna Kate was as committed as he was destined to remain right where he had always been.

Except now he was in Missouri. But it was a right sight closer than Belize.

"It's just a day," he told Vern. Maybe if he kept repeating it to himself he would start believing it. Or at the very least accepting it. Anna Kate was gone and that was all there was to it. She had left two months ago, taking with her all the hopes and dreams he had of a family of his own.

"There are other fish in the sea," Dawdi said.

This time Henry couldn't stop himself. He turned to gape at his grandfather. Thankfully he managed to pull his mouth closed before he did so. At least he wasn't staring at him, mouth open like one of the fish he had just mentioned.

"What?" Dawdi innocently asked.

Henry straightened and turned to face front once again. They were almost home, and it was a tricky thing to pull into their drive from the highway road they were currently on. Most people went slow enough through the hills and valleys in their little area, but that didn't mean everyone did. It was dangerous to sit in the road, waiting to turn for too long. If someone topped the hill and didn't see them in time . . . Well, it wouldn't be good for the horse, the carriage, or whoever was inside.

"I've decided I'm not going to respond to that."

"Don't like fish, eh?" His grandfather chuckled.

"You never remarried," he pointed out. And Vern King had been widowed since before Henry could remember. Thirty years was a long time to go without a life mate, a companion to walk beside you. Or even having to worry about your own food and clothes every day.

"Never had to," Dawdi said. "Joy's always looked after me."

But that time had come to an end. Joy, Vern's youngest daughter, had been widowed herself for a time now. But she had pulled herself together and opened a bakery in the basement of her house to make ends meet. Of course it helped that she was one of the best bakers in Central Missouri, and now people came from miles around just to buy a loaf of her bread and grab a fresh-baked cookie for the ride home. Joy had been able to accomplish such feats with the help of family and friends and, more recently with the help of her oldest daughter, Leah. Though only twelve, Leah Lehman was as hard a worker as Henry had ever seen.

He checked over his shoulder at the hill behind him before slowing his buggy to make the turn. His heart sank as he saw a car coming from the other direction. If he had to sit there too long to wait for the car to pass, having no one behind him now could change in an instant.

Thankfully, the car passed and another one didn't top the hill. Henry turned them safely into their drive and urged the horse toward the house. That was one thing about Oklahoma: It was a great deal flatter than Missouri, and a person could see cars coming from almost any direction. Or perhaps the benefit was that English drivers could easily spot a buggy waiting to make a left turn.

It didn't matter. He was only staying through the fall. Then he was returning to Wells Landing with his grandfather, and they would all be happy and, hopefully, safe.

Henry pulled the buggy to a stop, and the two men climbed down and set to work, unhitching the horse, brushing him down, and storing the buggy until the next time they needed it. The gelding got water and an extra scoop of oats because it was Sunday, then they made their way into the house to find their own snack.

"We got a job this week," Dawdi said as he pulled a package of cheese and a jar of pickles from the fridge.

"A job?" Henry asked.

Dawdi set the items on the table, then reached back into the icebox to remove the ham Joy had brought over three days ago. His cousin was a great cook, but they had eaten ham every meal since he had arrived and it was starting to get old. Not the meat, the eating of the meat. What he wouldn't give for some bacon. Or even a nice roast. He should say something to Joy about it, but knowing her, she would cook a roast the size of their tabletop and they would be eating it until Revelation came to pass.

"Well, not a job-job, but a job."

Henry sighed. He was getting used to his grandfather's doublespeak. "What is it?" That was probably the best question. At least it was straight and to the point.

"Sylvie Yoder—she runs the B&B in town—she has a leaky sink in one of the rooms. I told her I would stop by to take a look at it sometime this week."

And this was his grandfather's other problem. The man couldn't say no. It was an admirable trait, but an annoying one as well. It seemed to Henry that just in the time he had been in Paradise Springs, his grandfather had been taken advantage of countless times. And it had only been a week!

"Dawdi," he said, gearing up to protest. He'd already had this conversation with Vern.

His grandfather held up a hand. "Hear me out, son. She's going to make us supper and whoopie pies. I think that's a fair trade for fixing a leaky sink. In fact, I think I might be coming out on top in this one."

"Maybe," he said, doling out the paper plates as Dawdi grabbed the mustard.

They said their silent prayer, then began to eat.

"Who was that with her?" The question was out of his mouth before he even thought about asking it.

Vern swallowed his bite of cracker and ham before answering. "Dark hair?" he asked, then he made a whistling noise as he arced his hand in front of himself, mimicking the belly of the woman in question. Vern was just old-fashioned enough not to say the word "pregnant" even when it was just the two of them.

"That's her," Henry said with a nod. He wasn't sure why she'd caught his attention. She was beautiful, no doubt, with ink-black hair and deep blue eyes, but it was more than that. Maybe it was the sadness around her eyes, a sadness he felt was mirrored in his own. It was something he had immediately recognized. Or maybe because she had such striking features: blue eyes, ivory skin, and hair as dark as a crow's feathers. Or perhaps it was because she was alone. Whatever it was, something about her drew him in and made him want to talk to her, see what secrets her peaceful expression hid from view.

Ridiculous, he thought. She was most probably married and had a passel of kids running around to go with the one she would have before the end of the year. Maybe even the summer. It seemed losing Anna Kate had made him sentimental.

"That's Millie," Dawdi said with a knowing smile. "She's Sylvie's niece," he continued. "And she's single," he continued with a waggle of his bushy eyebrows.

Henry shook his head, but opted not to say the words shooting through his mind. Her status didn't matter to him. No matter how pretty she was and how nice and single. He had made up his mind, he was never getting married. Of that much he was certain.

Chapter Three

From her spot in the kitchen, Millie heard the door to the Paradise B&B open and a familiar voice call out, "Sylvie, we're here."

Her aunt hastily wiped her hands on a dish towel, then tossed it over one shoulder as she ran quick fingers down her apron—the clean one she had just changed into, anticipating this moment—then over the top of her prayer covering. The moment was the weekly meeting of the Whoopie Pie Widows Club. She took a deep breath, then started for the door, only to stop, take the towel from her shoulder, and flip it toward Millie.

She reached out and snatched it from the air.

"Good reflexes," her aunt said with an appreciative smile.

Millie grinned in return. "You should see me with a baseball."

"I think your baseball days are over."

Millie gave an exaggerated pout that wasn't so put-on after all but didn't comment.

"Sylvie?" the voice called again.

"Be right there." She turned back to Millie. "You are coming in, right?"

She shook her head. "I hadn't planned on it."

Sylvie gave her a sly smile. "What else do you have to do?"

"I was supposed to man the front desk," she said, trying to stall from actually telling the truth.

"We have a bell. The whole house will know if someone needs to check in."

Millie gave a shrug. She didn't feel right going into the meeting. It was as if she didn't belong with the other widows. And besides, they were all at least a decade older than her. And—

"I think you want to read that romance novel I saw you with at the thrift store."

Millie sputtered, but still couldn't find the words. "I—you—I—"

Sylvie's grin deepened. "You didn't think I saw you."

What else could she do but fess up? She straightened her spine and gave a delicate sniff. "It's a Christian book. I thought it might be fun to read about other people."

"There are other people in the Bible," Sylvie pointed out unnecessarily. Of course there were other people in the Bible, and there were valuable and interesting stories. But that was beside the point. This was different. "Tell you what," Sylvie said. "You come to the meeting tonight and I'll forget that I ever saw that copy of *Redeeming Love*."

"That's blackmail!"

Sylvie shrugged. "Who are you going to tell? The bishop?"

She knew her aunt was just teasing her, but her point

was also valid. "And I suppose you're going to tell him if I don't?"

Her aunt shook her head and grabbed one of Millie's hands, tugging her toward the front sitting room. "Just come on. The socializing will do you good. You don't get out near enough."

Accepting defeat, Millie allowed her aunt to pull her into the other room.

The Whoopie Pie Widows Club . . . er, the Paradise Springs Widows Group met at a different house each week, but Millie had been living with Sylvie long enough to have seen them more than once in their collective form. They were a motley troupe, though she suspected that to the Englishers who stayed at the B&B, all Amish women looked the same.

"Millie!" Joy Lehman stood and came to greet her, arms outstretched as if to give her a hug that Millie knew from experience would never fully come to be. Instead, Joy would wrap her fingers around Millie's hands, pulling her a bit closer before moving away.

"Good to see you, Joy." Like she hadn't seen her just two days before at church.

Joy waved a hand, as if to erase Millie's words, then retrieved her plate and returned to her seat.

A chorus of other greetings went around as Millie smiled and nodded at everyone.

Jah, the gang was all there. The Whoopie Pie Widows Club. Even Katie Hostetler had come out, and she had managed to talk her daughter Imogene into attending as well. Katie was the oldest at seventy-ish. She had been around long enough that everyone pronounced her name like Ketty, the old way. She had a no-nonsense attitude toward everything. Millie supposed that came from having twelve siblings and ten children of her own.

She was sitting next to Betsy Stoll, sister-in-law of Jason, who ran the town's stables. She and her husband had opened the Paradise Apothecary shop just after they married. When he died, Betsy continued on. The two of them, Betsy and her loving husband, only managed to have one child, a boy, before James died. Now Betsy was blessed with three wonderful grandchildren and another on the way.

She was a petite thing, barely bigger than a minute, but she was as mighty as they came. Some folks said it was because she didn't have any sisters growing up, but Millie suspected it came from losing the love of her life. Tales around town told of the love Betsy and James held for each other. It was like something out of one of the books Millie liked to sneak and read when no one was looking.

Millie had loved her husband, but hearing about Betsy and James made her stomach ache in a weird way. Almost as if she had missed out on something.

She pulled herself out of that ridiculous thought and smiled at Hattie Schrock and Elsie Miller. The cousins owned Poppin' Paradise, just a few doors down from the B&B. The women lived together upstairs from the popcorn shop and were about as opposite as two people could be. Elsie never had any children, worried constantly, and spent more time in prayer than any person Millie had ever known. Hattie's favorite phrase seemed to be, "Hand it over to God." She had six children, all of whom were married, and she always had a smile on her face.

And of course, Lillian. Sweet Lillian Lambert, who never seemed to be able to make up her mind. She worked at the Paradise Variety Store with her father-in-law, the owner. Millie had been in several times when they were working together, and it was almost painful to watch. Lillian seemed unable to stand up to him on any matter, from what shoes she should wear to work all the way to what they would eat for lunch.

Sylvie often said that she wished Lillian would grow a backbone, but Millie didn't see that happening anytime soon. At least not where Karl Lambert was concerned.

"Come sit by me," Hattie said, patting the seat next to her.

Millie smiled her thanks and crossed the room to take that chair. Hattie might be twice her age if a day, but she was by far Millie's favorite Whoopie Pie member. Her aunt excluded of course.

"How are you feeling, dear?" Hattie asked as Millie settled into the chair next to her.

"I'm well," Millie replied. It was her standard answer whether she felt all right or not. After all, who really wanted to know that her feet ached constantly and she was having to go to the bathroom what seemed like every five minutes? And she still had three months to go!

"Good. Good." Hattie patted her hand and leaned a little closer. "Whatever you do, don't eat Lillian's whoopie pies."

Millie's eyes went wide. "Why?" she whispered in return.

"She bought them at Buster's Grocery Store."

Millie had to stifle a laugh and thankfully, Hattie didn't notice her amusement. She had expected the older woman to impart some sage womanly advice concerning the effects of strawberries on pregnancies, but had gotten quite a different warning instead.

"Who wants to eat store-bought whoopie pies?" Hattie asked with a small shudder. "Especially from an English grocery."

Millie managed to make a noise that passed as a suitable response.

Sylvie walked to the middle of the circle of ladies and clapped her hands over her head. "Okay, everyone, let's get started."

"You don't have a plate," Hattie said, just then noticing that Millie hadn't gotten something to eat. "Millie doesn't have a plate."

Sylvie nodded, but gave Millie a small frown. "We can wait till Millie gets some refreshments."

But Millie waved away the suggestion. Sweets had started to lose some of their appeal. She supposed that was a good thing really. After all, she seemed to be gaining weight at an alarming rate. Maybe cutting out a whoopie pie or two would help.

Sylvie gave another nod. "Okay, then, let's begin."

Joy picked that moment to stand and brush the crumbs from the front of her apron. "I guess I should have said something earlier. But I'm not going to be able to stay. I was just in town and thought I would drop by because I was already in the neighborhood."

Several members said commiserating things like, "We wish you could be here for longer" and "I'm just glad you came at all." Then, with a small goody bag to take with her, Joy waved and headed out the door.

Once it shut behind her, Sylvie faced the group again. "Shall we begin?"

"Who's taking notes?" Lillian asked.

"You should elect a secretary," Katie said, her words

dry and a bit exasperated. It wasn't the first time she had made the suggestion.

"I will." Elsie raised her hand.

Sylvie went to the sideboard and pulled a small notebook and a pencil from one of the drawers. She handed them to Elsie and went to stand in front of her seat.

"The first thing she should write is that Katie Hostetler said we needed to elect a secretary—again," Hattie said in a low voice.

Millie bit back a chuckle.

But she wasn't the only one who heard. A few snickers went up around the room, but thankfully, Katie herself was a little hard of hearing and missed the joke entirely.

"I was hoping that Joy would be able to stay," Sylvie started. "But because she isn't here, it's the perfect time to organize a fundraiser for her."

"What do you have in mind?" Hattie asked, then said out of the corner of her mouth, so only Millie could hear, "Because you know she already has a plan."

Millie hid her smile behind the back of her hand.

"I say we have a walk-around bake sale."

"What is that?" Elsie asked.

"We'll go around door-to-door selling whoopie pies to raise money for her and her family." Sylvie smiled, obviously pleased with herself.

"Is that your name for it?" someone asked. Maybe Katie.

"*Jah.* Cute, huh?"

"Love it," Elsie said. "How about Saturday?"

A chorus of agreement and nods went up around the group.

"Good, then, Friday we bake and Saturday we sell." Sylvie nodded, happy with the plan.

"Write that down," Katie said with a nod to Elsie.

"Sylvie," Hattie called. "Can Elsie and I come over here and bake? Our kitchen is just so small."

Even Millie, with as short a time that she had been in Paradise Valley, knew that last part was unnecessary. The two women might have a booming popcorn business, but their apartment above the shop was tiny, and the popcorn kitchen wasn't set up for baking things like whoopie pies. Every time they had a fundraiser that required cooking, they asked to come to the inn and to Sylvie's equipment.

"Of course," Sylvie said, just as Millie knew she would.

"We'll bring all the ingredients," Elsie chimed in, just as Millie knew she would.

"Write that down," Katie said, just as Millie knew . . . Sigh.

The group was filled with sweet ladies who'd lost their husbands and never planned on marrying again. Just like Millie. Other than their age, there wasn't much that separated them. But in times like this . . .

Well, Millie started to wonder if there was more.

She closed her eyes.

Lord, please settle my heart. I don't like these feelings of unfulfillment. Please give me peace to stop these wandering thoughts and content my unsettled heart. Amen.

"So what do you think?" Hattie asked, gently nudging Millie with one elbow.

Prayer complete, Millie opened her eyes. "About what?"

Hattie gave her a knowing smile. "Henry King. Don't tell me you didn't notice him at church on Sunday."

"Oh . . . *jah*," Millie said, just then remembering that Hattie hadn't been among the widows group members who were making certain that she knew Henry King had come to town. "He's leaving come the fall," she said, repeating Joy's words from Sunday afternoon. Hopefully, that would be enough to dissuade Hattie from continuing her ploy to make Millie see what good husband material he was.

Of all the would-be matchmakers in Paradise Springs, it was the widows who seemed determined to see her marry again. Maybe because she was so young.

These days she didn't feel it. She felt old. She hoped it was just pregnancy hormones getting her down. *Jah*, she missed Joshua, and there were times when she missed her family—her mother and father, all her brothers and sisters—but she felt if she didn't do it—come to Paradise Springs and make something for herself—she would never be more than Joshua's widow. She wanted more from her life than that.

And just like that, there went her restless heart again.

"He doesn't have to, though. Leave," Hattie clarified with a wink.

Somehow Millie managed to smile. "I guess we'll just have to see." And now it was time to make her exit.

She stood and stretched, making as big a play out of it as she dared. She didn't want her aunt to think she was overly tired, but she wanted her to believe the act enough that she would allow Millie to escape to her room upstairs. That book she'd found was still calling her name. "I think I'll turn in." She stifled a fake yawn with the back of one hand.

All heads swiveled in her direction; all eyes were centered on her.

"Are you okay?" Sylvie asked.

Millie nodded. "Just tired. I think I should go to bed early tonight."

"You haven't eaten one bite," Hattie protested.

"You should try my key lime whoopie pies," Elsie said. She motioned Millie toward the dessert table. "It's a new recipe."

"I'd love to," Millie said, hating the necessary lie. She didn't want to hurt the woman's feelings. But before she knew it, she was holding a plate with one of each kind ready and waiting for her. She recognized her aunt's mint chocolate chip recipe, as well as the offending strawberry pies from Buster's. There was also a plain vanilla and one she didn't recognize but looked like some sort of banana nut recipe.

She made her way up the stairs and into her room, knowing that she would have to return to the kitchen when everyone was gone to put the pies in a container. But for now she had made her escape.

Millie let herself into her room and closed the door behind her. She crossed to the bed and slipped out of her shoes as she set the paper plate containing the sweets on the nightstand. Then she retrieved the paperback from her dresser and settled down on the bed to read.

The story sounded intriguing. It was a historical tale that mimicked the story of Hosea in the Bible. She had always liked that story, even if it had a sad ending. Something about it spoke to her. Maybe because it was comforting to think of one man loving a woman as much as Hosea loved Gomer. Or maybe she was just being a romantic.

She opened the book and started reading, immediately enthralled with the story on the pages. Without even thinking, she reached out and took one of the pies from the plate, barely noticing that of all the flavors, she had chosen vanilla.

Such was her life. And so it would continue.

Chapter Four

"I thought you said we were going over to Honest John's," Henry said when his uncle pulled his buggy to a stop behind the Paradise B&B.

Honest John Beery was an Amish man who did a little bit of everything, Henry had learned over the last couple of days. Apparently, Honest John bartered and traded for anything he could sell or trade. He sharpened knives and every other sort of blade from scissors to plows. He also had the best junk shop Henry had ever seen, though he hadn't been inside yet. He had only waited in the buggy as his uncle ran his lawn mower blade in to the man when they were in town the day before.

Vern had told Henry that he was going in today to pick up the blade, and Henry had readily agreed to ride along on the chance that he might get to browse around all the wonderful items Honest John had piled up outside his little house.

It was a wonder that the English city officials of Paradise Springs didn't make him do something with the place: organize it better or clean it up a bit. But it seemed that they liked the stuff the old man collected about as much as the Amish did. That was the first thing he had heard upon arriving in Paradise Springs: If you need something, check with Honest John first.

"In a bit," his uncle said, jumping down from the buggy with more enthusiasm and energy than a man one quarter his age. He tied the horse's reins to the hitching post. "In a bit," he said again. "Sylvie wanted me to stop by to look at her faucet today."

"Sylvie?" Henry asked, getting down from the carriage, though a bit more slowly than his uncle. Obviously he wasn't in as big of a hurry, though he did worry that if anyone was looking, they might think him the senior citizen and Vern the young nephew who'd come to visit from out of state.

"Sylvie Yoder. You met her at church on Sunday. Well, I think you met her." He stopped and stroked his beard, mulling over the particulars of the after-church meal. "Maybe you didn't. Anyway, she has a sink that needs fixing and we're going to fix it. I told you about it."

Henry gave a shrug, remembering that his grandfather had said something about a leaky sink and supper. Worked for him, Henry thought as he waited for his grandfather to get his toolbox from the back of the carriage. He followed Dawdi to the back door.

The stoop was small, with only enough room for his *dawdi* to stand and knock. Henry made do, waiting in the yard for Sylvie to come to the back door and let them in.

The woman who answered had deep blue eyes and was very pregnant. Not Sylvie. Millie, her niece. The very woman he had asked his *dawdi* about just after the service. Who was reportedly single, though given her round state,

Henry wasn't sure how that could be. Perhaps Dawdi was mistaken.

"Hi, Millie," Vern said with his usual charm.

"You must be Vern." The young woman took a step back.

Vern turned to Henry and waved for him to follow, then he went inside the house with the woman.

It was a simple thing—go by a friend's house or business, lend a helping hand. It shouldn't have felt strange or off, but somehow it did.

The first thing Henry noticed as he stepped inside was the wonderful smell coming from the kitchen.

His stomach rumbled in response.

His grandfather must have heard it, for he leaned back and said, "Remember, supper and whoopie pies," before taking his hat off and greeting the woman of the house. "Sylvie."

Sylvie Yoder was about the same height as his grandfather and plump in that typical way of women over sixty. Perhaps too many years of working in town or a regular indulgence in a favorite treat. She was merely a little thick around the middle with thin arms and legs. What he could see of them anyway.

"There you are, Vern King," she said, her tone somewhat admonishing. "I wasn't sure you were going to make it."

"I promised I would be here, so here I am."

"You can hang your hat up there." She pointed to a line of pegs jutting out of the wall like a line of pickets in a fence.

He did as she bade him, and Henry followed suit, hanging up his hat and walking behind his uncle through the house. The structure was old but well-kept, a somewhat rambling Victorian style with three floors and charming touches that Henry was sure the English visitors loved— a little alcove fashioned exclusively for a telephone, a built-in china cabinet, and vaulted ceilings with fans turning lazily around in the sun that filtered in through the upper, uncovered windows.

"You have electricity?" Henry asked. He supposed that only made sense, seeing as how the B&B most probably catered exclusively to English patrons, but he had to ask to make certain.

"Of course." Sylvie smiled, revealing deep dimples on either side of her mouth. "We don't have central heat or air, but each of the rooms has its own window unit." She covered her mouth with a quick laugh. "Goodness, I sound like I'm about to rent y'all a room."

Henry smiled in return. "It looks like a mighty fine place to stay. And if the smells coming from the kitchen are any indication of what you can do with breakfast . . ."

Sylvie shot him a hooded look. "You are a charmer, aren't you, Henry King?"

Not sure how to answer, he merely kept smiling and waited for his grandfather to step in and say something. But when it looked like that wasn't going to happen, he cleared his throat. "Which room is it again?"

"The Green Room. Top of the stairs, all the way on the end."

"I'll show them," the younger woman said, reappearing from seemingly nowhere.

"*Danki*, Millie. I'll go check on supper." She looked to the clock on the wall just above the fireplace. "Or maybe we should call it dinner."

His grandfather was halfway to the staircase in the corner of the room when he stopped and turned around to face the innkeeper. "Are we too early?"

She gave him a dazzling smile. "Never, Vern King. I'd say you are right on time."

What was she talking about?

Millie continued on up the stairs, all the while pretending that her aunt wasn't acting as if she had some sort of strange fever or something. That's what Millie had always heard—a high fever could make a person act in a strange and bizarre manner. If that were truly the case, her aunt's fever had to be one-hundred-and-ten degrees.

But Millie wasn't about to ask what her problem was in front of the guests. Especially not when she had a fair idea what was going on.

"Right through there, gentlemen." She opened one side of the double doors that led into the most sought-after room in the inn.

As its name implied, it was indeed decorated in shades of green, with a few pinks and yellows thrown in for good measure. A vase holding fresh pink tulips, a picture of landscape art abstractly drawn to look like a blue sky over a field of yellow daffodils. Jade green rugs on golden oak floors, pale-green-painted walls with pristine white trim, and gauzy white curtains. The room had its own seating area, complete with an antique rolltop desk, an oatmeal-colored sofa and chairs, and a treadmill off in one corner. The couch made out into a bed for extra sleeping space and the area itself was big enough to hold a cot if need be. The bedroom itself had another green carpet, a white counterpane on the natural wood bed, and the pillows of pink and yellow to add relief. All in all, it made Millie think of a beautiful meadow, and she wanted the same feeling when she got ready to make the baby's nursery. Not that she was doing that anytime soon. She had heard of Englishers who decorated their baby's room right after finding out they were pregnant, but that just wasn't the Amish way. Though she was hoping to at least get a crib and a car seat before the time came to have the baby. Some things couldn't be put off till the last minute.

But before she decided on a nursery, she had to decide if she was staying at the B&B with her aunt or looking for her own place. Not that she wanted to move, but she really didn't want to take up more room from her aunt's business. Of course, Sylvie would say that it was no bother, but Millie didn't want to intrude.

"The bathroom is through here." Millie led the men with their toolbox over to the far door. The bathroom could be reached from the sitting area or through the bedroom itself. "I didn't know there was a problem in here," she said, throwing open the door. She wasn't sure what she was expecting to see, but it certainly wasn't a dishpan with about an inch of rusty-looking water in the bottom sitting underneath the exposed pipes of the sink.

Vern nodded his head, as if he knew just what to do. "We'll take it from here," he told her, and Millie took that as her opportunity to escape.

She made her way out of the room, stopping once she was in the hallway to suck in a deep breath. She didn't seem to be able to get enough air inside her sometimes. She figured it was because the baby was crowding everything.

If that was indeed the case, it would only get worse from here.

But today she almost felt as if that breathless feeling had something to do with those knowing brown eyes of Henry King.

Which was ridiculous.

Because he wasn't anything to her. And if he was, or could possibly be . . . well then, he wasn't her type. Not that she had a type. But if she did, Henry King would not be it. He was too big and burly. The kind of man who looked like he could crush walnuts in his hands and whose footsteps left deep tracks in the dirt. Like some giant in a long-ago fairy tale.

Which was really ridiculous.

But Millie couldn't help but think that there was some other reason for Vern and Henry to be at the inn today. Something to do with everything that Sylvie had said on Sunday. Not just about how handsome Henry was—more than that. Like the fact that her aunt kept dragging the subject of their conversation back to Henry King. As if she hadn't wanted Millie to forget who Henry was.

Which was really, really ridiculous.

Not that she was going to forget, but that it even mattered. Henry wasn't staying in Missouri after the growing season ended. And Millie had no plans to leave. That in itself should have put the brakes on any ideas that her aunt might have had about the two of them. But Millie knew one thing was absolutely certain about her aunt Sylvie. Once she set her mind to something, it took the power of God to get her off it.

And unfortunately, it was looking like Sylvie had decided that Millie needed to remarry, and her candidate of choice, Millie suspected, was none other than Henry King.

Now the question was, what was she going to do about it?

Vern stood back and scratched his head. "I don't understand," he said, looking at the U-pipe first one way and then the other. "It doesn't need tightening and I can't see any other place that a leak could be coming from."

"And you're sure this is where the water was dripping?" Henry asked.

His *dawdi* gestured toward the pipes. "Do you see anywhere else for the water to be coming from?"

Henry shook his head. "Maybe it was an overflow or something."

"Maybe," Vern said, but he didn't seem convinced.

"So what now?"

Vern scratched his head again, then shook it. "I guess we go down and tell them that there wasn't a problem after all."

Henry wasn't sure that was such a good idea. That seemed an awful lot like telling a woman she didn't know what she was talking about. And that was never a good plan. Not if a man wanted to eat. And judging by the smells coming from the kitchen as they had been coming into the house, Henry very much wanted to eat with the ladies of the B&B.

Together, he and his grandfather tromped back down the stairs to the bottom floor of the house. Briefly, Henry wondered if there were rooms on the third floor, but he wasn't able to ask as his grandfather spied Sylvie and headed in her direction.

"You got yourself a tricky pipe, there," he said.

"*Jah*?" She raised one brow coolly and waited for Vern to continue.

"The way I see it, the leak is a strange one. It must have been there at some time or another, but there's no sign of it now."

Sylvie turned her head to the side, as if studying the problem. Something rang a little strange about the gesture, but he didn't take the time to figure out what it was. Instead, he listened as his grandfather tried to make excuses for the unique situation.

First it was there because Sylvie said it was, and now that Vern and Henry had come to fix it, low and behold, it up and disappeared.

"That's all right," Sylvie said with a bright smile. She bounced back from the problem with no problem at all. Maybe because Vern was still somehow trying to take all the blame for not being able to locate said problem. "Come on in the kitchen here and we'll have us something to eat."

Vern shook his head. "Now, Sylvie, I don't feel right taking you up on that offer seeing as how I couldn't isolate and correct the leak."

Sylvie propped her hands on her hips and eyed him the way a schoolteacher looks at naughty little boys who come back in late from recess. "Vern King. You mean to tell me that I've been cooking this ham all morning long and you're not going to eat it now?"

He shook his head slowly, and Henry had to stop himself from laughing at his grandfather's comical expression. "No. That's not what I'm saying at all."

She continued to study him.

"Only that I feel a might bad about not being able to repair it, and if you have any more problems with it, I'll be out here day or night. Just as long as you give me a big ol' slice of ham."

Ham. Henry almost burst into laughter at that one. Wasn't it just two days ago when he and Vern were saying that they were both tired of eating ham?

Apparently they weren't any longer.

"Good, then." Sylvie nodded her head and gestured for them to make their way into the kitchen.

Ham or no ham, it was about the nicest meal Henry had seen since leaving Oklahoma. Joy did what she could to help Vern, but any meal she brought over was in plastic containers or foil pans and had to be heated up. Sometimes they timed it right and pulled the meal from the oven when it was perfectly the right temperature, and sometimes—more often than not—they got a little side-tracked with the horses or the cows, or any of the chickens and ducks that Vern had running around the place, and when they got around to pulling the meal from the oven, it was overly brown and unrecognizable.

And the niceness of the meal had absolutely nothing to do with the dark-haired woman sitting across from him.

Chapter Five

Or maybe it had everything to do with her.

Even though they had just met a few days before, Millie Bauman was at ease in his presence, as if they had known each other their entire lives. And somehow he felt the same.

Or perhaps he just missed the camaraderie of his large home in Oklahoma.

There were eight of them total, the King kids, though he had two sisters and a brother who had already married and started their own families. He was to be next, but . . . well, it hadn't worked out. But he was used to suppers consisting of ten or twelve people, depending on who stopped by and who was gone for the evening. At any rate, meals that consisted of just him and his grandfather were oftentimes a little too quiet for his taste. Sometimes even he could hear the ticking of the kitchen clock. It could be maddening.

So that was why he was enjoying this meal with Sylvie and Millie. Nothing else. Because he certainly wasn't in the market for anything more. He was done with romance. And he certainly didn't want a romance happening miles from home. Come the fall, he was heading back to Oklahoma, and that was that.

"I think we lost him," Sylvie said with a nod toward Henry.

Millie glanced over toward their dinner companion. True enough, he seemed deep in thought. But truth be known, she had seen that look on his face quite a few times even in the short while they had known each other.

What was the saying?

Still waters run deep.

She had never understood it until she met Henry King.

He was large and quiet and thoughtful. He didn't speak just to hear himself or to be assured that he wasn't left out of the conversation. He was content, it seemed, to allow whatever to go on around him, and though he was a part of it, he was still somehow separate.

Like now.

Lost in his own thoughts.

"What?" He snapped back from wherever it was he had been in his own head and looked around at the three of them.

"You were a million miles away," Sylvie said with a smile. "Homesick?"

He shook his head.

"You sure you're not missing a sweetheart back home?" she continued.

"Auntie!" Millie couldn't stop her exclamation of horror. If she had had any doubts about her aunt thinking that she and Henry would make a good match, they would have been annihilated in that instant. Kind of like one of those bug zappers people put on their front porches. Zing and gone.

"It isn't polite to ask such things," Millie admonished in a lower voice. If only she could call back the words. Her aunt meant well, even if she was meddling and nosy, and Millie wished she had waited until they were alone before expressing her chagrin. It was bad enough that her aunt was obviously trying to set her up with Henry; Millie herself had just made it worse by pointing it out to everyone.

"Just everyday conversation," Sylvie replied, not the least bit ruffled by the exchange.

"Henry was engaged," Vern added.

Henry's cheeks turned red. But Millie couldn't tell if it was from anger or embarrassment. Maybe a combination of both. "We don't need to talk about that," Henry finally said.

His words, like the rest of him, were big. They held a softer edge but brooked no argument.

For a moment, Millie thought that Vern might go against his grandson's wishes and explain the entire situation to them, but instead he shrugged and shoveled in another bite of green beans.

Millie pushed her plate back lest she give into the urge to dish out seconds. She and Sylvie didn't normally have such a big meal at lunch, and if she was going to get any work done this afternoon, she needed to stop eating before she had to sleep it all off.

"What are you doing this afternoon?" Sylvie asked, thankfully changing the conversation.

"We're heading over to Honest John's."

"I hear he has some new tomato hybrids. Been meaning

to get over there myself and check them out, but we've been pretty busy around here."

School was out and the Englishers had started to vacation. Millie couldn't say that Paradise Valley was a big draw for people who loved the Amish culture. Not like Lancaster County or even Sugarcreek in Ohio. Not that she knew firsthand, but she had read of accounts in *The Budget*. Still, Paradise Springs had a fair share of visitors. And with the Whoopie Pie Festival just a few weeks away, the traffic through their town was about to increase greatly.

"Why don't you head over there with us and you can take a look at them yourself?"

"Or you can take a look at the drip I have in the kitchen, and Millie and Henry can go get the plants."

"You've got another leak?" Vern asked.

"Not a leak, a drip," Sylvie corrected.

"Sounds good to me." He turned to Henry.

"I suppose."

What could Millie do but go along?

"But first . . . whoopie pies," Sylvie said. She started to get up, but Millie stopped her with a hand on her arm.

"I'll get them. I need to stand up and stretch anyway." And maybe some of the big dinner she just ate would settle and make room for one of her aunt's experimental whoopie pie flavors.

It was always a contest, even when there wasn't a festival, to come up with the most flavorful and exotic concoctions of whoopie pies. Though truth be known, Millie preferred vanilla. Always had. Not that she was telling her aunt that anytime soon. No, sir.

Millie made her way into the kitchen and returned a

few short moments later carrying the tray of whoopie pies that Sylvie had made. There were two trays, one for them and one for the guests at the B&B. Of course the one she brought in was the smaller of the two trays, but it was still piled high with the tasty cakes.

Vern rubbed his hands together in anticipation. "Is this going to be the one you enter into the Festival contest?"

Sylvie gave him a sly look. "You think I'm going to divulge all my secrets, Vern King?"

"So now I'm a spy for the opposition?"

The opposition being any baker in Paradise Valley, which of course included Paradise Springs *and* Paradise Hill.

"A girl can't be too careful."

Not when it came to the three-hundred-dollar cash prize and bragging rights for the year and beyond. Especially the bragging rights.

"Let me try one," Henry said, reaching for the tray. He took a big bite, then his eyes lit up.

It seemed that Sylvie outdid herself with this batch.

Millie set the platter on the table and picked a pie for herself. One bite and she knew that Sylvie might just have a winner on her hands.

"It's so good," Henry said, stuffing the rest into his mouth and reaching for another. Vern too was on his second. "What is it?"

Sylvie smiled secretively. "Piña colada. I take it you like them?"

The men nodded.

Millie had to admit they were good. Pineapple cake with coconut frosting inside and toasted coconut sprinkled over the top. Still, there was another flavor that Millie couldn't quite place.

"This is Millie's recipe," Sylvie said, directing her words toward Henry.

"Delicious," he said, giving an appreciative nod to Millie.

She sighed, albeit quietly, so as not to give her aunt's lie away. But it *was* a lie. Millie hadn't even pulled the cakes from the oven. This pie was Sylvie's from beginning to end. But for some reason her aunt wanted Vern and Henry—or maybe it was just Henry—to believe that she was the creative genius behind the tasty dessert.

"Do these have rum in them?" Vern asked, even as he reached for a third. He looked to Millie for the answer.

If she had baked them, she would know. But since she hadn't . . .

She cast her glance over to Sylvie, who shook her head. Millie wondered if even that was the truth.

"Of course not." She laughed. "I used the rum extract from Buster's."

"Well, they certainly are amazing," Henry said.

And that's when Millie knew why Sylvie had told her fib. A way to a man's heart was through his stomach, and Sylvie seemed determined that Millie should capture Henry's heart. But she had a feeling it had already been captured long ago and never returned.

"I'm sorry about this," Millie said as she climbed into the buggy next to Henry.

"About what?"

"My aunt pushing us together. I think . . ." She shook her head. "I don't know what to think."

"Pushing us together?" he repeated with a frown.

"*Jah.*"

His frown deepened. "Then your husband . . . ?"

"Joshua died six months ago."

His gaze immediately fell to her belly, but he said nothing. A lump rose in her throat as always when she thought about her baby never meeting his—or her—father. She knew it was something that God had willed. She had been raised to believe as such, but it still was hard to understand. Or accept. One day. She knew it would get easier, but until that time she took it as it came, tried her best not to talk about it and surely not cry in front of men she barely knew.

"So it's true," he said, his own voice a bit rusty. "I'm sorry."

"*Danki,*" she said with a small nod. What else was there to say? Somehow, she managed to swallow back her tears and add a trembling smile to her lips.

"You're in mourning," he said quietly, almost in a whisper. "Of course you're in mourning."

She nodded again, but she couldn't look at him. Not directly. If she saw one ounce of pity in those deep brown eyes, she wasn't sure she would be able to hold off the tears.

He started the horse into motion and off they went toward Honest John's.

The silence between them was awkward. They seemed to have hit it off when they were eating, but somehow, between the lies about the whoopie pies and the questions about their pasts, that easiness had turned into a thick, heavy silence.

Even if she wanted to break that silence, she didn't know what to say. Was there anything that could wipe out the last few minutes? Did it even matter?

It was obvious to her that Henry had given his heart to another. This fiancée she had heard about, the one he once had but who no longer seemed to be in his life. So even if Millie was in the market for a new love—and she wasn't— that love wouldn't be Henry King.

They rode through town, and thankfully, the noise of the wheels against the pavement, along with the clop of the horse hooves and the town noises themselves, eased the awkward silence that stretched between them.

By the time Henry pulled up in front of Honest John's, they were almost back to the way they had been before.

Honest John's was a sight to behold. The house itself was a little white structure with peeling paint and a rusted roof. The whole place could use a fresh coat, but there was so much stuff piled up all around the house, Millie wasn't sure anyone could get a ladder close enough to actually complete the chore. So Honest John's went unpainted. Rusted hulls of almost every type of appliance known to man peppered the front yard and continued on toward the back. He even had a couple of old cars in the mix, but Honest John said he only kept those as a shelter for the cats. And there were a lot of those running about. Millie supposed he needed the felines to keep down the mouse population. Wind chimes of various sizes and shapes hung from the porch and an old rocking chair sat off to one side. Everyone in town knew that the chair wasn't for sale.

That was John's, and no amount of money would make him part with it.

English and Amish alike came to his place when they needed something that no one else seemed to have. If it had been made, it had passed through Honest John's hands at one time or another. And he could find things too. Fixtures for older houses. Parts for older cars for the English. Parts for older buggies for the Amish. He dealt in a little of this and a little of that, and he supplemented it all by sharpening blades and selling tomato starts.

"How many plants do you think your aunt wants?" Henry asked.

Millie winced. "I probably should have asked that before we left." But she had been in too big a hurry to get the chore over and done with so she could go on with her day.

"*Jah.*" He nodded. "Personally, I think it's a little late to be starting tomatoes."

"If you plant them late and cover them during a frost, you can sometimes have fresh tomatoes at Thanksgiving."

He smiled, and she noticed once again that he was a really handsome man. It was a shame that someone had broken his heart. Millie was sure he would make someone a wonderful husband.

"Let's get six each," Henry suggested. "That'll bring in a good mess of tomatoes. If they want any more than that, they'll just have to come get them themselves."

"Sounds good to me."

He gave a quick nod. "I'll go find John. I may be a minute. I need to get the lawn mower blade while I'm here. The grass is getting out of control."

Millie laughed. "With all the rain we've been having, is it any wonder?"

Henry didn't answer, just smiled, showing that slightly crooked front tooth that seemed to make him even more handsome. Real.

Millie watched him go. It really was a shame. Henry King was a good man.

"Millie?" The familiar voice sounded behind her.

She turned to find Betsy Stoll.

"Hi, Betsy."

The tiny woman gave a quick nod of greeting. "I thought that was you. Out and about today?"

"*Jah*." Millie waved a hand in the general direction where Henry had disappeared. "We just came for some tomato plants."

"We?"

And that's when Millie realized her mistake. "Me and . . . Henry King," she reluctantly admitted.

She knew there was nothing between her and Henry and that there never would be. But Betsy didn't know that. And though the woman's heart was always in the right place, she had a tendency to tell stories while she worked. Since she owned the Paradise Apothecary and everyone in Paradise Springs went through at least once a week for something or other . . . well, it wasn't looking good.

By sundown she and Henry would be getting married in a secret ceremony in Paradise Hill or some such nonsense.

Maybe she could stave off the rumors before they even happened.

"Henry is picking up plants for his uncle. I'm getting some for the inn. We just rode over here together. But only because he was already at the B&B, fixing the leaky sink. Which wasn't even leaky."

Shut up, Millie! You're making it worse!

She gave Betsy what she hoped was an innocent yet encouraging smile. But she could already see the wheels turning in Betsy's mind. The shopkeeper was putting together two and two and coming up with seven, or maybe eight. Certainly not four, which was this outing—totally innocent, with no romance brewing between Millie and Henry. Four.

She could tell Betsy about Henry's ex-fiancée and how she left him, but she didn't know the particulars and it really wasn't her story to tell. So she pressed her lips together lest the urge become too strong to resist.

"Well, I guess we'll have one less widow at the group now."

Millie shook her head. "No, no, no," she said. "It's not like that. Henry and I are just friends." She might as well have taken up a billboard at the edge of town and announced their intentions to marry.

"*Jah.* I see." Betsy looked from Millie to where Henry was talking to Honest John. They seemed to be making some sort of bargain for the plants and the blade sharpening. But they were too far away for Millie to hear what they were saying.

Millie realized that she hadn't given Henry any money for the plants, but she was afraid that if she excused herself from Betsy and rushed over there now, it would only make things worse.

Then again, could they get any worse?

"I should go," Millie said. "I need to give Honest John my part of the money for the tomato starters."

Now, that wasn't so bad. At least it sounded like she

and Henry were two separate individuals, who had two separate bank accounts and financial plans. Sort of. Because they wouldn't blend such things until after the wedding.

She was grasping at straws.

"I hope you'll still come to the group meetings until the two of you . . ." Betsy trailed off, but her meaning was clear. *Until the two of you get married.*

Millie could only hope that no one standing around heard what she said. She glanced at the others. Most seemed to be English and would have no idea about the workings of the Amish community and who was marrying whom. Or not marrying whom, as the case would be.

As she moved away toward Honest John and Henry, she could feel Betsy watching her. Millie took in a deep breath as she approached the two men.

The transaction was complete. The men shook hands, money was exchanged, and Honest John moved away to box up the starters.

"At least think about it," Betsy called. "Continuing to attend the meetings, that is." She waved and turned away.

Henry frowned. "What was that all about?"

Millie shook her head. "It seems the two of us are about to get married."

Chapter Six

"What?" Of all the things he could have imagined Millie would say, that might possibly be the very last one on the list. No. It wouldn't even make the list. "Married?" His voice was close to a squeak.

But then, the thought settled around him. There were worse people he could think of marrying. In fact, if he had to choose, Millie would be on the possibilities list for sure. He might have only just met her, but she was a fine woman, that much was obvious. Not that he was planning to ever get married.

"How did we go from buying tomato starters to getting married?" He managed to keep his voice low. There were several people milling around at Honest John's, but it seemed that most of them were English. In the back of his mind he registered that it was probably one of those tours that took the English visitors around to all the Amish sights, but he was too caught up in Millie's startling revelation to give it more than passing attention.

"Betsy Stoll," she said. As if that explained anything.

"Come again?"

"Betsy Stoll saw us, and now we'll be planning to get married before the sun goes down."

He scratched his head, knocking his hat askew in the process. "Are we *planning* to get married before the sun goes down or are we planning to get *married* before the sun goes down?" He pinched the bridge of his nose to stop the sudden pangs of a headache.

She reached up and straightened his hat, then pulled away, as if the object was hot to her touch. "Sorry," she gasped.

He closed his eyes as he realized just how intimate the gesture was.

He opened them again, but nothing had changed. He could only hope that no one in her circle saw the gesture and interpreted it in the same manner he was sure Betsy Stoll had. "Maybe this Betsy person won't say anything?" It shouldn't have been a question.

"She runs Paradise Apothecary. I don't know if you have an herb shop in Wells Landing, but—"

"Everyone goes through there at least once a week."

"And Betsy likes to visit with people."

He propped his hands on his hips and straightened his back. "So what do we do?"

She didn't answer. Honest John took that moment to come up with the box of starters.

"I put the blade there on the side," he explained.

He was an interesting-looking man. And he reminded Henry of Bacon Dan back home. Bacon Dan sold eggs and just about everything else imaginable—even bacon, though it was his love of the breakfast meat that gave him the nickname. Like Bacon Dan, Honest John was stooped at the shoulders, walked with a limp, and somehow came across as spry. Henry just figured that was the Lord's light shining through them.

Henry nodded and took the box. Something inside him answered the man and said farewell and somehow managed to walk back to his buggy on legs that had gone strangely numb. He felt as if someone else was in control of his actions as he placed the box in the back of the buggy, then went around to help Millie climb in.

The action was automatic. He had always helped Anna Kate get into the carriage. He helped his mother when they were traveling together. Of course he would help Millie. She was pregnant.

He didn't know for certain, because they—Amish men and women—didn't talk about such things, but he supposed that having all that weight in just the front did something to a person's balance. And he would not have her falling out of his buggy. Not ever.

But he realized what it might look like to the casual—or not-so-casual—Amish observer. Like, say, Betsy Stoll who ran the apothecary.

And that was just what he didn't need.

Though his grandfather knew that Dale, Henry's father and Vern's son, wanted him to move to Wells Landing in the fall, he wasn't up for the idea. Dat always cited that Vern was not as young as he used to be and had started getting a bit forgetful. But mostly, Dat told Vern that he didn't have the help to farm like he'd had in the past and it was time to give it up. Regardless, his *dawdi* seemed perfectly happy staying right there in Paradise Valley. And if he thought that he could get Henry to stay and say . . . marry someone . . . like maybe Millie Bauman, then Vern himself wouldn't have to leave. And Dale would have no leverage to make him move.

Perfect. Just perfect.

He untied the horse from the hitching rail and climbed into the buggy beside Millie.

"It may get worse," he said with a sigh. He had taken up the reins and was still facing forward when he said the words. He couldn't look at her just yet.

"Worse?" she squeaked. "How can it get worse?"

He explained the situation about his father and his grandfather and the power struggle that was playing out between them. By the time he got to the part about the two of them getting married and how it would solve his grandfather's dilemma of not wanting to move, she had lowered her head into her hands.

Horror struck as her shoulders began to tremble, then moved into an all-out shake.

Heaven help him! She was crying. He didn't know what to do with a crying female. Anna Kate hardly ever cried. Only once she had, when they said goodbye, and she told him that she was sorry for hurting him. It had nearly ripped him apart. It hadn't been his fault, but he felt every tear. And this . . . this was at least partly his fault.

"Millie?" He reached out a hand and touched her shoulder. Then he drew back lest someone see. "Millie, please don't cry." Those were stupid words, but he said them anyway. He was at a total loss. This was going to be fine. "It'll all blow over in a day or—well, maybe a week or two." But it would probably take months. Maybe by the time he left to go back to Wells Landing the rumor would be dying out. Maybe.

She raised her head, wiped her eyes, and in that moment he realized she was laughing.

"This town," she said when she finally caught her breath. "Never in my life have I seen a town like this one." She raised the tail end of her apron and wiped her face.

"It is something else," he replied, not really knowing what to say. "So what do we do?"

"Ride it out, I guess. The more we try to explain, the more it'll sound like we're trying to hide our romance."

He felt a strange pang in his stomach at those last two words. *Our romance*. "So we just ignore whatever anyone says and live our lives?"

She nodded.

He thought about it for a moment. It was the most logical thing they could do. Rumors were like weeds, but even weeds could be choked out. "You're right," he said. "Eventually it'll have to die down."

She muttered something as he started the horse into motion. He wasn't certain, but he thought she said, "I wouldn't count on it."

More haunting than the thought of the rumor that was surely spreading all over Paradise Springs, even as he sat there that evening and stirred his supper around on his plate, was the look on Millie's face when he asked her about her husband.

He should have known. His grandfather had told him that she was single. Single and pregnant in the Amish world was rare and almost always meant widowed. So Henry felt a little stupid not having noticed that she was dressed in black. There seemed to be a lot of that going around these days—stupidity. Or maybe because he was so used to seeing women dressed in dark colors. Most of the women in Wells Landing wore dark blue or green, even a deep wine color, whereas the women in Paradise Springs seemed to like colors that were a little brighter. Sea blue and pretty lavender. Maybe that's why he hadn't noticed. Or maybe he hadn't noticed because he had been caught up in her beautiful face and serene expression.

But that look in the buggy hadn't been about serenity and peace. It was sadness, plain and simple. She had lost the man she loved and she was in mourning. And he felt like a heel for bringing all that sadness back to her.

For a moment there, he thought he had seen the sheen of tears in her eyes, but time passed and no tears had fallen. Another reason why he had felt doubly bad when he thought she had been sobbing over the rumors that were starting about them.

She had been laughing and seemed to have thought the whole thing to be entirely too funny. He wasn't sure he agreed with her on that one, but what were they supposed to do? Yet even as her laughter rang in his ears, the dim light of sadness in her eyes still plagued him.

"You gonna eat that food or just stir it around until it's mush?"

Henry pulled himself from his thoughts and looked at the mess he had made on his plate.

"I know I'm not as good a cook as Joy, but that came from a box. Hard to mess that up."

Tuna casserole. Not really his favorite, but not so bad that it warranted such treatment.

He scooped up a big bite and shoveled it into his mouth to show his enthusiasm for the meal.

"And that was a little too much too. What's ailing you, boy?"

Henry shook his head. He hadn't mentioned a word of what happened to his *dawdi* when they left the inn that afternoon. They had simply split the tomato plants and headed for home. Back at the farm, they had tilled the earth, placed some fertilizer, and given the starters a new home in the ground. Now supper. Henry had managed not to mention Millie's name once and yet she had been on his mind all afternoon and evening long.

"I think I'll go over to the B&B tomorrow." He said the words before he even thought about them. What they meant. How they sounded. Not even what it would mean for him and Millie if he made such a trip.

But then the sadness in her eyes . . .

"There's not anything wrong with that sink," his *dawdi* said in something of a huff.

"I'm not saying there is."

"Then why do you want to go back there?" Vern asked.

Henry stopped, trying to figure out how to phrase the words so they didn't fuel the rumors that were no doubt flying around Paradise Springs. How could he say that he wanted to make it up to her, that he had made her sad and miss her husband all the more? He wanted to see her and make sure that the sadness hadn't swallowed her whole. That she could fight all that off with the laughter that had spilled from her later that same afternoon.

But he must have waited too long to speak, for his grandfather jumped in again.

"Just because I left the barn door open this morning . . ."

And, thankfully, none of the animals cared enough to wander out. Still, it could have been disastrous. Henry supposed they had the good Lord to thank for that, for watching over them. And he suddenly understood why his *dat* was so worried. Henry wasn't, because he was right there with his grandfather, but if he had been miles away, off in another state, he would be concerned that Vern was losing his memory. But he wasn't. Just like he said, it was a simple mistake.

Yet Henry knew that his grandfather did indeed need to move to Oklahoma. He might not be overly forgetful, but the man couldn't cook. If he had to eat much more of this food, he might starve to death.

He needed to take something with him. It was a crazy thought, but he wanted something tangible to help her see how sorry he was that he had upset her.

Maybe he would run by Buster's to see if there were any flowers. Flowers would be a nice gesture. Sylvie kept fresh flowers all around the B&B. He had witnessed that firsthand the day before. So flowers would be a fine idea.

Or not. He knew bringing flowers to a lady was something of an English custom when going on a date, or for an apology. If he was spotted walking into the inn with a bouquet of flowers . . . well, the innocent gesture might trigger even more rumors, and that would never do.

Henry rode into town trying to come up with another plan. Taking her food or candy seemed sort of ridiculous, seeing as how her aunt was one of the best bakers in the area. So what did one person take to another as a way of apology?

He had no idea. He had never had the need to apologize

in such a manner. Or maybe it was that he had never *felt* the need.

He was almost to the B&B when a sign caught his attention.

Pardise Apothecary

He wasn't sure why, but the name rang in his memory. Maybe it was a sign.

Well, it was a sign. But maybe it was the other kind as well. Like God directing him where he needed to go.

Without a second thought, he pulled the buggy into the parking lot in front of the little white building. There were a couple of buggies out front and a couple of English cars. He tied up his horse and went inside.

Like most Amish-owned businesses, it was dim and cool inside. Natural light filtered in through the high windows that lined the walls of the store and through the front plate windows. The shelves were shorter than the ones in the English stores, hardly anything above eye level, for people a great deal smaller than he was, and he felt a little conspicuous as he walked through the aisles. His head and shoulders stuck up above the top shelf.

Or it could be that he just felt that way because he was looking for something for Millie.

It had to be the perfect something. But he had no idea what that might be.

The shelves were lined with bags of dried herbs, bottles of essential oils, and stacks of cloths and boxes of diffusers, and a whole bunch of other things the purpose of which he had no idea.

How was he supposed to find something for Millie in here?

He walked to the next aisle and started looking at

the goods. Half the names he didn't even know how to pronounce, much less what the products were used for.

He picked up one tiny brown bottle and stared at the label.

Oil of Chinese Star of Anise.

He had no clue.

"Hi." A woman's voice sounded behind him. "You must be Henry."

He spun around to nothing. Then he looked down to find the smallest woman he had ever seen. Okay, maybe not that small, but she was a tiny thing. She barely came up to his elbow, yet something about her gave the impression of steel-threaded tires.

"*Jah*," he said with a nod. "I'm Henry. How did you know?"

"Betsy Stoll," she said with a smile. "I saw you at Honest John's yesterday. With Millie Bauman."

The way she said Millie's name raised the hairs on the back of his neck.

Now he remembered. Betsy Stoll. Ran the apothecary. Would tell everyone that she had seen Henry and Millie together buying tomato plants and somehow that would translate into there was a wedding coming soon. That Betsy.

"*Jah*," he said. He gave an uncomfortable nod.

"Are you here looking for something in particular?" she asked.

He wasn't sure if she meant anything else by the question or was merely trying to be helpful. "No. I was just looking for . . ." He held up the bottle he held in one hand. "This," he finished. "I was just looking for this."

Even though he had no idea what it actually was used

for, and he hoped she didn't ask him what he intended its purpose to be.

He almost breathed a sigh of relief when she didn't. "I'll set it up at the counter for you if you still want to look around."

"No. *Danki*." It wasn't worth the risk. He had to get out of there before he said something that would turn into even more rumors about him and Millie.

"Good, then," she said. "This way and I'll ring this up for you."

He nodded and followed her over to the low counter, where a push-button cash register sat.

Henry shifted from one foot to the other as he waited for her to figure the tax on the small calculator next to the register, to punch in the price on the machine, then for the numbers to pop up in the window on the back.

She repeated the amount with a smile.

He couldn't decide if she was merely being friendly or if she was trying to keep him off guard, so he would say something incriminating about him and Millie.

Or maybe he needed to get a hobby. He had obviously been staying at the farm with only his grandfather for company too long without other human interaction.

"Here ya go." She handed him a small paper sack and his change. "I also put a piece of paper in there about all the uses of star anise."

Was she trying to get him to divulge that he had no idea what the oil was used for? "*Danki*," he said with a nod and headed for the door.

He didn't breathe right until he stepped out of the building. By the time he had gotten to his buggy, his breathing had almost returned to normal.

He untied his horse from the hitching rail and climbed into the buggy.

It was only a short trip from the apothecary to the inn. Thankfully. He didn't think his heart could take much more. What was it about these people that had him on such an edge?

No answer came as he pulled the buggy into the drive at the side of the house and around to the back of the building. A couple of cars were parked in the small space. He directed his horse over to the hitching rail and parked him there.

His hands were sweating as he hopped down, tied up the reins, and started for the back door of the inn.

He knocked and waited for someone to answer. Maybe he should have gone around the front and just walked in like the guests surely did. He had seen a bell there on the front table where the sign-in book was kept. Maybe he should—

The door opened and there she was. Millie Bauman.

"Henry," she said, blinking at him as if she didn't trust her vision and he wasn't there after all. "Hi. Come in. Come in." She stood back and waited for him to enter.

Henry stepped inside the house and handed Millie the small sack he carried. "I brought you something," he said.

She opened the sack and peered inside.

"It's oil of Chinese star anise," he said, hoping it sounded like he meant to bring the item. That he had thoughtfully picked it out and carefully determined how useful it would be for her to have.

She looked up from the bag and gave him a bright smile. "*Danki*," she said. "But what am I supposed to do with it?"

Chapter Seven

As Millie watched, he shifted from one foot to the other. "Uh hmmm . . . There's a page in there to tell you what it's used for."

Not exactly the answer she had expected. She had figured that since he had thought to bring her the oil, it had some sort of special meaning to him, or at least a special use. "You don't know?" She blinked at him.

His face turned a sweet shade of pink. Somewhere between bubble gum and cotton candy. "No," he finally admitted. "But I figured you would."

He brought you a gift, she admonished herself. *Be grateful, not suspicious*. "Okay . . . Let's see here." She took out the page and started to read. "'Chinese Star of Anise Oil is instantly recognizable by its warm, licorice-like smell. It is beneficial to women as they undergo the natural transformation of menopause—'" She stopped. Cleared her throat. "Uh-huh."

"I'm sure it has a great many other benefits." His color had turned from the sweet pink to the wicked purple of pickled beets.

She continued to read, but to herself this time. "Oh, see

here. Promotes healthy skin, supports the respiratory system, and boosts the immune system, as well as promotes healthy digestion." She needed to stop while she was ahead. She wasn't far ahead, but she would have to take what she could get. "Isn't that nice?" she asked no one in particular. She shoved the little brown bottle and the paper back into the sack. "*Danki*, Henry. Your thoughtfulness is very much appreciated."

He shook his head. "I wanted to bring you something special."

She smiled. "That certainly is special."

"No," he said. "No, it's not. I felt bad about yesterday. Asking about your husband."

"So you wanted to bring me a gift?"

He didn't have time to answer as a couple came down the stairs, laughing as they walked hand in hand.

She nodded at them and smiled, greeting them silently while not interrupting their momentum. Then she motioned for Henry to go into the sitting room. "Let's get out of the walkway."

He did as she bade, though she could see the stiffness in his legs and posture as he made his way over to the couch. He eased down onto the edge and waited for her to join him, one knee bouncing the entire time.

"I wanted to bring you something special." He closed his eyes. "I already said that."

"*Jah*." She smiled, wishing to ease whatever trouble seemed to be chasing him. "You didn't have to bring me anything."

"I don't know," he said. "I just—when you—I wanted to bring you something special."

"I believe you have mentioned that."

"At first I thought flowers. But I was afraid that if someone saw me coming in here with flowers, they might get the wrong idea."

She looked down at the paper sack she still held. "No one's going to misjudge that." She chuckled.

He shifted uncomfortably and she felt bad about making a joke at his expense. "About that . . ."

"What?" she asked. Maybe he wasn't acting strangely because of the gift. Maybe it was something else . . .

"I got it from the apothecary."

He didn't have to finish for her to understand his meaning. She closed her eyes. "Betsy."

He nodded. "I'm afraid so."

And Millie knew Betsy well enough to know that if anyone could misinterpret star of anise essential oil as a courting gift, Betsy Stoll was that person. If they hadn't already decided to get married, surely by this evening wedding plans were being made.

She sighed.

"What do we do?" he asked.

She shook her head. "There's nothing we can do. Ride it out, I guess."

"I wasn't thinking," he said. "I'm sorry."

"You had no way of knowing."

"I thought I heard a man out here." Her aunt came into the room, smiling and wiping her hands on a dish towel. She tossed it onto one shoulder. "Hi, Henry."

"Hi, Sylvie." He stood. "I guess I'll be going."

"What's your rush?" Sylvie asked. "You just got here."

"Auntie," Millie said. Honestly, she wasn't sure who was more meddling, Betsy or her own aunt.

"I know. I just baked up a new recipe of whoopie pies.

How about I bring you some and a tall glass of lemonade out onto the front porch? Y'all can sit out there and enjoy the weather. It's a might cooler today."

And it was. But the last thing Millie wanted to do was sit on the porch with Henry King while the world believed them to be a couple. Seriously? If they did that, could they look any more like a couple? Not hardly.

"Auntie," Millie said again. But she wasn't sure why she bothered. When her aunt got like this, the scolding utterance of her name was in no way a discouragement.

"That sounds like a fine idea." Henry stood as Millie shot warning looks his way. But he didn't seem to be paying attention to her. Or maybe he was simply ignoring her.

"I hardly think that's necessary," Millie protested.

"But it'll be fun. And just think how the Englishers will love the two of you out there, swinging back and forth. We'll be booked solid in no time."

"As tempting as that sounds, I have lots of work to do." She wasn't sure what, but it seemed that she always had a ton to do. Why should today be any different?

"Posh." Her aunt waved a hand as if to erase all Millie's excuses. "You deserve a break. Now go on out there and sit on the porch while I get your snack ready."

Millie turned helplessly to Henry, but he seemed to be enjoying himself.

He made a motion as to say he would follow behind her. What else could she do but turn on one heel and head for the front door?

Her aunt was right; the weather was a bit cooler than it had been the day before. Unlike the states farther north, Missouri didn't have much of a spring. It seemed to go from stinging cold straight to blistering hot. There were only a few nice days in between that told the tale of spring. Today was one of those special days.

Henry gestured for her to sit down on the swing. After she was settled into place as far to one side as she could go, Henry joined her on the narrow wooden planks. Funny, but it had never seemed so small before. Not that she had sat out here many times; there was always laundry to be done, beds to be made, and whoopie pies to bake.

As if she had heard Millie's thoughts, Sylvie suddenly appeared with a tray holding a pitcher of lemonade, two glasses—tall, as promised—and a plate piled high with almost-too-pretty-to-eat pink whoopie pies.

"Here we go," she said brightly. "Now y'all just sit out here and enjoy yourself."

Before either one of them could say anything, she was gone again.

Millie was still trying to figure out what to say when Henry started to chuckle. "Is she always like that?" he asked.

"No," Millie said on a sigh. "Sometimes she's worse."

"At least we'll eat good." He pulled the swing forward with his long legs and snatched a couple of whoopie pies from the plate. He handed one to her and studied the one he still held in his hand. "What flavor is this?"

She shook her head. "Not telling. That's half the fun, trying to figure out what it is."

He eyed her as if contemplating the benefits of that idea. "Okay. And what will you give me if I guess it right?"

She thought about it a moment. "A bottle of peppermint oil. It's also good for digestive issues."

"I'm not sure I deserved that."

She shrugged. "It was funny, though."

He was smiling and shaking his head. But he didn't respond, just took a big bite of the whoopie pie. He closed his eyes in apparent enjoyment. "It's a good thing I'm leaving come the fall," he said after he had swallowed that bite and another, devouring over half the cake in two seconds. "I'd be big as a house if I could have these whenever I wanted."

She took a bite of the pink cake. It was just as she expected. Strawberry lemonade with pineapple frosting, but she wasn't sure if he would get all the flavors.

"So good." He ate the rest of the cake in one bite, then reached for another.

Millie blocked him with one hand in front of the coveted desserts. "First, what's the flavor?"

He smacked his lips together, as if retasting the cake even though it was already gone. "Strawberry . . ." he said.

"Of course. It's pink. That much is obvious."

"It could have been cherry," he said. "Or raspberry."

"What else?" she asked.

He smacked his lips once more. "Pineapple." He turned to look at her. "Am I close?"

"Very, but that's not all."

He shook his head sadly, as if she were breaking his heart by keeping him from the tasty cakes. "I thought I had it, but I'm going to need another."

She pretended to think about it for a moment and finally moved her hand from in front of the plate. "One more. But if you don't guess then—"

"I'll run right over to the apothecary and get your oil."

"The oil was for you," she said. "Two bachelors living together, the one woman who cooks regularly for you is having to take care of an injured son. I thought you might need a digestive agent."

He laughed and reached for the whoopie pies. "You got that right. You would think that some of the good people of the community would take pity on us and invite us to supper." He batted his eyes at her.

"You're terrible," she said.

He just smiled and took a bite of the cake. "Lemon!" he exclaimed.

"Excuse me."

Until that moment Millie hadn't realized how enthralled she was in her conversation with Henry. It was as if the world had fallen away and there was only the two of them and a plate of whoopie pies. He was just so easy to be with. Every minute with him was so comfortable, so relaxed. And she didn't want it to end.

But she turned toward the voice to face an English couple. It appeared that they had been walking down the sidewalk, spied the inn, and stopped right in their tracks.

"*Jah* . . . I mean, yes?" she asked.

The man nodded toward the sign in the yard. "Do you have any rooms available?"

Millie stood and brushed the whoopie pie crumbs from her apron. "*Jah*, of course. Would you like to come in and see the room first?"

The couple looked at each other, then the woman shrugged. "No," the man said. "We were walking by and this place . . ."

"Well, it's charming," she finished for him.

"We have a room off the highway, one of the hotels, but this just looks so quaint."

Leave it to her aunt to have grown men—grown *English*

men—saying words like "quaint," with her picture of an Amish couple on the front porch enjoying the afternoon.

She bit back a sigh. She had been enjoying the afternoon, but now it was time to go back to work. "I'll need to check them in," she told Henry.

He stood.

"Doesn't your husband work here too?"

Millie felt the heat of embarrassment rise into her cheeks, and for a moment she wondered if she was as pink as the whoopie pies. "He's not my husband," she said.

Henry ducked his head. "Bye, Millie." And before she knew what had happened, he had hopped over the railing and disappeared around back.

"Not your—" The woman's gaze fell to Millie's rounded belly.

Maybe it was just her week for starting rumors. "He's just a friend," she said, hoping that explained everything, but knowing that it didn't. "My husband is gone . . ." She shook her head. She didn't need to finish. The couple was smart enough to take it from there.

"I'm so sorry," the woman said. "Please forgive me."

"No forgiveness necessary," Millie murmured. She smiled, though her lips felt tight as she started through the check-in process. It wasn't that she minded them asking about her husband. She just simply didn't know what to say. And she supposed it would be no better once she had the baby. People were naturally curious. Englishers seemed to be especially nosy about such things. Or it could be that because she was part of the Amish community, everyone there already knew her story, and every day there was a constant flux of new English faces in Paradise Springs.

"Thank you," the lady said once Millie gave her the

code for their rooms. Her smile was tight, and Millie pasted on a reassuring expression.

"And don't forget," she said. "Whoopie pies at three in the sitting room each day."

The man patted his stomach. "I can hardly wait."

"There goes my diet," the woman said, though her smile turned less stressed and more genuinely pleased.

"We'll go get our things from the hotel and be back by then for sure."

Millie gave them both a nod, and kept her smile in place as they left the inn. Then she turned and made her way into the kitchen.

"I told you." Her aunt grinned in a self-satisfied way as Millie collapsed into one of the chairs around the rustic table situated in the kitchen area.

Millie released her breath, not realizing until that moment that she had pent up the air. She laid her head down on her folded arms and tried to relax the tension growing in her shoulders.

"What was that all about?" her aunt asked.

She raised her head. "When did people stop asking about Andrew?"

Sylvie turned from the batch of whoopie pies she was mixing up and seemed to think about it a moment. "I'm not sure. It happened gradually, I suppose. Why do you ask?"

Millie gestured toward the front of the house. "The new couple I checked in . . . they thought Henry was my husband, and when I told them that he wasn't . . . well, then I had to explain and—" She broke off as the words left her.

"It gets easier," her aunt said quietly.

"It's not even that it's so difficult. I know," she said, "I know that somehow Joshua's death is part of God's plan, but I can't move forward if I feel like I'm talking about him every day. Even if it's to tell guests here at the B&B that he's gone."

"Maybe that's part of God's plan too," Sylvie quietly mused.

Millie resisted the urge to snort. "I doubt that."

"And you want to move on?"

"*Jah*," she whispered. She had a baby to think about, a new life, a new town, new opportunities. She had done everything in her power to make her life fresh and free of Joshua. But it seemed that even though she had done everything she could to start anew, Joshua was still in each direction she turned. Like the whisper of a prayer.

"Well, maybe Henry is the answer to that."

"Auntie," Millie said, her tone exasperated. "Henry is a nice man, but I'm not marrying again."

"It's been six months, Millie. You don't know what the future holds."

"Who does? But marriage is not in my plans."

"You shouldn't shut yourself off to the idea," her aunt admonished.

"Please," Millie said, growing exhausted from the conversation. "Don't try to—" Though she didn't even know what to call it. "Leave Henry out of it. He doesn't want to get married." He was as done with romance as she was.

"You both are far too young to make such a decision."

"And yet it's our decision to make."

"Give it time, Millie. Who knows how you'll feel in a couple of months, even a year."

"And why did you never remarry?" she asked.

Sylvie shrugged. "It just never came up. It wasn't like I planned it that way. God's will, *jah*?"

Millie sighed. There was no getting through to her aunt when she was like this. Who was she trying to kid? There was no getting through to her aunt most days. But she loved her still.

"New recipe?" she asked, deftly changing the subject.

Her aunt's brow was furrowed in concentration as she carefully scooped the cake batter onto the cookie sheet in neat little circles. Whereas many bakers used a special pan to form the cakes into perfect little circles, her aunt preferred the old way. She said it made them taste better. And who was Millie to argue with that?

Her aunt finished pouring the batter and carefully slid the cookie sheet into the warm oven. Then she set the timer and turned to face Millie once again. "*Jah*. And this one's going to knock everyone's socks off!"

Chapter Eight

"Delicious." Millie licked the remainder of the filling from her fingers.

"Good, *jah*?" Her aunt's blue eyes sparkled with excitement. "Is it a winner?"

Millie thought about it a moment. "It's not my favorite, but I think it could easily take the bake-off."

There were only a few more weeks before the Whoopie Pie Festival and Sylvie was determined to keep the title right there in Paradise Springs. The competition was fierce. All the women kept their recipes carefully concealed until the day of the baking contest.

"Red velvet with raspberry cheesecake filling is not your favorite?"

Millie smiled. "I'm a vanilla girl."

Her aunt propped her hands on her hips and eyed her as if she had grown a second head. "Vanilla isn't even the original pie."

"You don't know that for certain," Millie countered. "If the exact origin of the pies are unknown, surely no one knows what the first flavor was."

Her aunt harrumphed. "Classic, then."

"Maybe that's what you should do," Millie said. "Go back to the classics."

Her aunt frowned. "Chocolate with white filling?"

"Why not?" Millie shrugged.

"Maybe not just chocolate, but . . . I could add a little coffee to the mix. French vanilla bean." She paused, her expression thoughtful. "With cherries. *Jah*, black forest."

And just like that, her aunt was off again.

Millie watched her with a smile on her face and a sigh in her heart.

Sylvie bustled around the kitchen, muttering to herself about what cherries would be best to use. She was halfway through her recipe book when she stopped and eyed Millie. "What's wrong?"

Millie tried to pinpoint exactly what was on her mind. "I feel bad about today," she said.

"Now, I've already told you, you work hard and you deserve a break. You're going to wear yourself out before this baby even gets here if you don't slow down a bit. You—"

"It's not that," Millie confessed. "It's Henry."

"Henry's a grown man—" Sylvie stopped. "What about Henry?"

"Wipe that look off your face right now," Millie said. "It has nothing to do with anything other than he got caught up in my life for a minute. You know, with people thinking we were married. I feel like I was a bit rude to him after they said something. He just jumped off the porch and left."

"He didn't say bye?"

"Well, *jah*, but it was so abrupt, his leaving."

"And that makes you feel bad?" Sylvie asked.

"You didn't see his face."

Her aunt opened her mouth to say something but stopped. She seemed to think it over, then finally asked, "What are you going to do about it?"

"Nothing, I suppose." After all, what could be done?

Her aunt snapped her fingers. "I have an idea."

And that was what Millie was afraid of. Sometimes Sylvie's ideas weren't beneficial to Millie. "What?" she asked cautiously.

"You take this batch of whoopie pies out to the farm tomorrow. That way I can keep the recipe a secret. And I'll start to work on the new idea."

"I don't think—" She wasn't sure what she didn't think. Only that she needed to think it. "Henry's pretty good at guessing the flavors." He had gotten the strawberry lemonade with pineapple frosting ones without much encouragement at all.

"Just tell him to keep it under his hat. That way if the new idea doesn't work out, I have a back-up recipe."

"I don't think—" she started again, but once again words failed her. She didn't think she could take the time off to go out to his farm. But her aunt would tell her that she worked too hard and there was no reason for her to be there all day tomorrow. She didn't think she should be so presumptuous as to drive out to his farm and bring him a present. Her aunt would tell her that she was acting like a friend, a good Amish neighbor. If she said she didn't want Henry to get the wrong idea, Sylvie would come back with "There's nothing in a box of whoopie pies that would make a man think about anything other than eating those whoopie pies."

So really, what argument did she have?

"Fine," she replied with a sigh, "I'll take them out there tomorrow."

Millie got up the next morning, did her daily rituals—brushed her hair, brushed her teeth, got dressed, pinned on her prayer covering—then she started to work. She made her bed first, then headed down the stairs to help her aunt get breakfast ready for the guests. Today's fare included a tomato-and-spinach quiche with bacon on the side and buttered biscuits with honey and jelly. The honey was local, the bees kept by Rufus Metzger, the jelly made by Sylvie herself. There was, of course, fresh fruit, cantaloupe and honeydew—grown by Christian Beachy, who ran the produce co-op for the local businesses and families looking to eat more healthy foods.

Once everyone had been fed and had begun their day, Millie started up the stairs to make beds and pull towels and other laundry from the bathrooms and get her own day going. But Sylvie stopped her.

"Don't you think you should go out to the farm to see Henry?"

Millie finished smoothing the crisp yellow quilt over the bed in the children's area of the Sunshine Suite, then straightened and faced her aunt. "It's awfully early."

"You think he's going to be asleep at this time?"

Millie shook her head and started piling the throw pillows back into place. "No, but there's still a lot to do around here. We haven't even cleaned the kitchen yet."

Sylvie waved a hand, as if to dispel the thought. "I can get that done in a jiffy. You can rest as you ride out to the farm."

Millie stopped, propped her hands on her hips, and eyed her aunt. "All this resting you have me doing is going to leave you exhausted."

Her aunt laughed. "I just think if you are feeling bad about what happened yesterday, you shouldn't leave it for too long."

"I think it can hold off till after the kitchen has been tidied up. And what about your walk-around bake sale?"

Her aunt paused. It was obvious to Millie that she had forgotten that today was Friday. That Hattie and Elsie were supposed to come by and bake whoopie pies with Sylvie and Millie for the traveling bake sale they were holding the following day.

"You'll be back long before they get here."

The cousins were supposed to come after lunch, and seeing as how it was barely ten in the morning, there was plenty of time. But Millie didn't want to confess that. She would never get her aunt to change her mind about her going out to see Henry.

Then again, it might already be too late.

"But—"

How did she explain? Once all was said and done, Millie felt a little strange about going all the way out there just to apologize. It was as if that would make the whole thing a bigger deal than it should have been. And it wasn't a big deal. At least she hoped it wasn't. Last night it had felt big, but after a good night's sleep it didn't seem quite as important as it had.

Yet her aunt was having none of it.

Millie shouldn't have said anything to Sylvie.

"Now, Millie," Sylvie said as they made their way

down the stairs and into the kitchen. "We decided that you would go out there and take him the whoopie pies."

"But it's not like they asked for them or anything." Even to her own ears that sounded like the worst reasoning ever. "And how are you going to get them to buy any tomorrow if you take them some for free today?"

Her aunt chose to ignore that. "If you don't go out there and talk to him now, it won't be long before you'll be moping around the table, telling me how you hated how the afternoon ended."

"I do not mope."

Her aunt grinned, taking all the sting from her words. "Sure you don't." Then she handed Millie a plastic container full of yesterday's whoopie pies.

"But—"

"I've got this mess, and if I don't, surely it can wait until you get back."

"I won't stay long," Millie promised, tucking the container into the crook of one arm.

"Want me to get Daisy for you?"

Millie hadn't thought about that. One more chore to do, and one made by the very trip she was making.

She started to protest, but her aunt interrupted her. "I'll walk down and get her. You wait here."

Millie didn't have time to utter one syllable of protest before her aunt turned and made her way out the back door.

Millie started to sit down at the kitchen table to wait for her aunt to come back with the horse but stopped herself. In the meantime she could at least start the kitchen.

Her aunt would fuss when she got back, but that was

why Millie was here, to help out, and she couldn't help out if she wasn't allowed to do the simplest of tasks.

But Millie knew that wasn't the case. Her aunt didn't mind her helping out when there wasn't a romance at stake. And Millie and Henry would never become a couple if Millie was in the kitchen all day and Henry out at the farm helping his grandfather.

Millie had news for her aunt: There wasn't going to be a romance. And that was all there was to it.

Romance or not, half an hour later the kitchen was clean and Millie was on her way to the Kings' farm.

The day was more than beautiful, and she found herself raising her face to the sky, closing her eyes, and letting the sun warm her. She didn't stay that way for long. It was a bad way to try to drive a buggy. But she did enjoy the blue sky, the light breeze, and the deepening greens of everything growing at the edge of the road. Crops were sprouting, gardens were in full swing. The world was beautiful.

Sometimes she had to remind herself of that fact when things got bleak. Joshua might be gone, she might be destined to raise this baby alone, but the world was still a remarkable place.

Though, she thought as she pulled her buggy onto the hard-packed driveway that led to Vern King's residence, this corner of the world could use a coat of paint.

The house itself wasn't in disrepair, but it seemed to sag a little at the corners and the paint was starting to peel in several places. The yard was trimmed and neat, most probably because Vern had just recently had the blade for his mower sharpened. But all in all, the place seemed like it had become a little more than one person could handle. Or maybe it was more than one person of Vern's age could handle. Millie wasn't sure exactly how old he was, but if his white beard was any indication, he was at least sixty-five, maybe even a little older. Sixty-five . . . she did the math in her head. *Jah*, that sounded about right.

She pulled Daisy to a stop, hopped down from the buggy—well, as much as a woman who's six months along can hop anywhere—and hobbled the horse, bypassing the hitching post. She retrieved the container of whoopie pies from the back seat of the buggy and started toward the house. A sudden thought occurred to her. Vern was a farmer. She had passed a number of farms on her way out of town and most all the farmers were around their fields somewhere. That would mean that Vern and Henry would be in their fields as well. Logically speaking. Which meant she could leave the whoopie pies on the porch with a note, saying that she was sorry he had to leave the day before, and that would be that. She could head back into town and start baking for tomorrow's bake sale.

She stared around for something to write on, as if there would be pen and paper nearby. She was wondering if there might be anything in the buggy when the front door eased open.

"Millie?" Henry stood in the doorway, looking about as confused as she felt. "What are you doing here?"

She hesitated, then thrust the container of whoopie pies toward him. "Here."

His face creased into a small frown as he accepted the offering. "What is it?"

"Whoopie pies." She shifted, not quite getting her

bearings back after having him surprise her. "Sylvie has been working on a new recipe for the competition coming up and this is one of her efforts."

He held up the container and looked through the milky plastic at the treats inside. "What kind are they?"

"I can't tell you that. If I do, she'll have to lock you up in the cellar until after the Festival."

He chuckled. "Say no more."

"And no guessing," she said to him. "Even that could be dangerous."

"I presume the ladies take their whoopie pies very seriously."

She smiled. "You wouldn't believe."

He stood to one side. "Come in," he invited. "Let's have one together."

"I can't." She shook her head. "I should be getting back to the inn."

He shifted in place. "Not even one?" He waited. "On the porch," he offered when she didn't respond right away. "Nothing wrong with two friends sitting on the porch sharing whoopie pies."

Except that it seemed like they had been doing a lot of that these last couple of days, but if she gave in to the idea of sitting on the porch and talking with him again . . . well, if someone were to happen by—which was entirely possible—how would that look?

"Or we could go inside," she said softly, the words so quiet that she almost didn't hear them herself.

He stopped a moment, then stood back and nodded. "*Jah*. We could go inside."

She stepped into the house, gaining a little courage once she was off the front porch. "There's going to be enough talk about us," she started. "No sense in giving the mouths more to say."

He nodded. "*Jah*. Sure."

"I didn't mean to be forward, it's just—"

He nodded. "Say no more. You were just trying to stop the rumors."

She expelled the breath she had been holding. "Exactly."

Millie followed behind him through the house toward, she supposed, the kitchen. The inside of the home Henry now shared with his grandfather was much like the outside. Clean, for the most part neat, yet a little droopy, slightly neglected. She noticed a few of the pictures on the walls were crooked, as if accidentally knocked askew and never straightened again. The walls themselves had a few scratches and marred places from moving furniture and the like. But the marks had never been removed. The calendar hanging just inside the kitchen was still showing the days for April, and her thoughts of the place being too much for one person resurfaced. It was after all a house built for a family.

She tried to recall what happened to Vern's family. She did remember that he had a couple of sons who had died in an accident and of course Joy still lived in the community. Apparently, some of the children moved to Oklahoma; at least Henry's father had. If there were any more children scattered about or gone to their reward, she didn't know. And she supposed in a way it didn't matter. Vern was alone in Paradise Springs except for Joy, who could no longer help him in taking care of matters.

The house might be a little much for one person, but

the floors were swept and the dishes washed and draining on the sideboard.

A small oak table with matching chairs was situated in the center of the kitchen, creating a cozy, homey atmosphere. Or perhaps all that was Henry's handiwork.

She eased down into one of the chairs as Henry went about getting them saucers for their whoopie pies. "Why aren't you in the field with your grandfather?" she asked.

"It's a good thing I wasn't or I would have missed your visit."

Millie smiled and kept it to herself that she had been sort of hoping for that outcome all along. But now that she had Henry all to herself . . .

"Would you like some coffee?" he asked.

She wrinkled her nose. "It's too hot for coffee."

His shoulders visibly relaxed. "Good. I'm terrible at making it."

She was on her feet in a heartbeat. "Do you want me to make some?"

"Not if you're not having any. No sense in wasting half a pot."

"That's not what I asked." She moved toward the stove. "Where are the grounds?"

He reached into a cabinet above her head and brought down a cannister of coffee, and she set about making him half a pot of coffee.

"So really," she started as the water began to boil. "Why are you hanging around the house on a great spring day when there are fields to tend?"

"My grandfather never asked for help."

She nodded. She might not know Vern all that well, but she had sensed that about him the very first time she met him: his independence and a mile-wide stubborn streak. "And you came out here anyway?" she asked.

"My father wanted me to come, and you know . . . help him this year, and get him to move in the fall."

These were things that she already knew, and yet the idea of Henry not being close after September or October made her inexplicably sad. Which was absurd. Not only had they only just met, but Millie was going to be a little busy come the middle of August. With a newborn to care for as well as her job at the B&B, she wouldn't have any time to worry about the life and times of Henry King.

"But he figures since I'm here," Henry continued. "That he'll put me to use."

"*Jah*?" Millie asked.

"Painting the house."

Which explained all the white splatters on his clothes. "That's a big job."

"I don't mind, and once we leave in the fall, we'll get a better price for the house if it's newly painted."

There went that pang of I-don't-want-Henry-King-to-leave again, but Millie pushed it aside and concentrated on pouring the hot water over the coffee grounds.

Once the coffee was made and the delicious smell permeated the kitchen, she almost regretted not making enough for her to drink some too, but ever since she had been pregnant she got hot so easily, and pouring scalding liquid into her stomach would not help her keep cool.

"What can I get you to drink?" Henry asked as he took a sip of the dark brew. "That's good." His tone was filled with humor and appreciation.

"Just water for me." She sat back down at the table and waited for him to join her.

"I've got some milk," he said. "That would be good. And good for you."

She smiled. He really was a good friend. He was a man, and he wouldn't say as much, even if she did need the calcium in the milk. She was pregnant after all. "Milk does sound good," she said.

He poured her a glass of milk and joined her at the table. "What flavor did you say these were?"

"I didn't." She gave him a pointed look.

"Oh," he said, taking the lid off the container and serving them each a whoopie pie. "I forgot. Top secret."

"That's right. Though I can say that this is the backup recipe to the one she's working on right now . . . as we speak."

He took a large bite of the filled cake and closed his eyes. "These are really good," he said. "And if this is the backup . . ."

She shrugged. "She's always looking for the best one to enter in the Festival bake-off."

"It's a really big deal, huh?" he asked after devouring half the cake.

"More than you can imagine." The ladies did take their whoopie pies seriously. "Plus the Festival brings in a lot of visitors and that really helps the town. English and Amish alike."

"It sounds like a lot of fun," he replied.

"It is. It's fierce competition, but a lot of fun."

"We'll have to go," he said. "I mean if you want to. As friends," he clarified. "Just because your aunt will be busy with the bake-off and—"

She laid her hand on top of his where it rested near his plate. "You don't have to explain."

And he didn't. She knew that he felt the same as she did. And she was grateful to have someone so easy to talk to as a friend. That he was a man and didn't expect anything from her was an added bonus. Only because he knew how to fix leaky sinks that weren't really leaky and was grateful for the smallest things like half a pot of coffee and a container of experimental-recipe whoopie pies.

Though if they were going to continue their friendship, she would have to learn to ignore the little zing that shot through her every time she touched him.

Chapter Nine

Henry pulled his hand from under Millie's and made a great show out of serving himself another of the cakes. Or maybe it wasn't honestly that big of a show and just felt like it because his hand was still tingling from where her skin touched his.

"Your grandfather's still doing well, though?" she asked. "Healthwise?"

He nodded, glad to have her change the subject. Everything he had been thinking about saying had fled his mind the moment she touched him. "At first I was really worried about him. But the longer I'm here, the stronger I realize he is." But convincing his father would be another matter altogether. "Dat still worries, though," he continued.

"Of course he does." Millie delicately finished her whoopie pie and he doled her out another without asking if she wanted it.

He wanted her to eat it. Well, it wasn't the actual eating that was important. But he wanted her to remain right where she was for as long as possible. He missed being around people. With his *dawdi* out in the field all day and him at home painting . . . well, that didn't leave much interaction with others. Having Millie stop by was an unexpected and welcome treat. And that was all it was, he told himself. It could have been anyone, from Lolly Metzger, who just might be the oldest person in Paradise Springs, to Honest John Beery, and Henry would have welcomed the company.

Though if he was being truthful with himself, that it was Millie and not Lolly or Honest John was just an added bonus.

"And you don't think you should ignore what your grandfather is saying and just show up out there one day and give him help whether he wants it or not?" she asked, dragging Henry out of his own thoughts.

It took a moment for her words to kick in. He threw back his head and laughed. "Have you ever tried ignoring something my grandfather has said?" he asked.

She shook her head, but a smile played at her lips. It was true what they said, humor was a bit contagious.

"I don't recommend you try it." He chuckled a little more and got up to pour himself another cup of the delicious coffee. It shouldn't have been a hard thing—boil water, pour it over coffee grounds, let it sit, then strain it, but there certainly was an art to it. An art he had never taken time to learn.

He supposed it might be worth getting married just to have decent coffee for the rest of his life.

Those thoughts screeched to a halt. That was the dumbest thought he had ever thought. Or something like that. Whatever. It was dumb. Getting married was serious business and worth much more than a good cup of coffee. Much, much more. Though he supposed coffee would certainly be a good factor to consider.

Do you love the girl? Check.

Does she love you? Check.

Are you willing to spend the rest of your life with her? Check.

Can she make a good cup of coffee? Check.

See? Worth throwing into the mix for certain.

He poured Millie another glass of milk despite her protests and returned to the place opposite her. And with a woman like Millie, that certainty went double.

"I'm glad you came by today," he said a bit later.

She smiled, and the action went straight to his heart. If that were possible, but it wasn't. He only recognized the action as sincere. That was one thing that could definitely be said about Millie Bauman. She had a genuine smile.

She looked up at the kitchen clock over the sink and her pretty blue eyes went wide. "Is that clock right?" She was on her feet in a heartbeat.

Henry looked behind him at the battery-operated time-piece. It was already past two. Had they really been sitting there all afternoon, talking and sharing whoopie pies? "*Jah*," he said.

"I have to go," she said. "I'm supposed to be helping my aunt bake whoopie pies for tomorrow."

He stood as well, though more slowly. He didn't want the afternoon to end. "More whoopie pies?" he asked.

She shrugged her shoulders, even as she made her way back toward the door. She was out of the house before he was out of the kitchen. He hastened his steps and caught up with her on the porch.

"Hey," he said, catching her arm, then immediately releasing her. Touching her was akin to the electric charge following lightning. Potentially dangerous and very unsettling. "You don't have to rush off."

She gave him an apologetic smile. "I do. I was supposed to be back at the inn hours ago. I just don't understand how I—" Her words trailed off as a whistle sounded from the direction of the road. "Please let it be Vern," she muttered under her breath. "Please let it be Vern."

They both turned to look at the same time.

But it wasn't Vern riding by on this fine May day, it was Betsy Stoll.

Millie groaned. "What is she doing way out here?"

"There's a farm down the way that grows herbs. I would imagine she's been there." He was trying to be helpful, but it didn't seem to register with Millie.

She closed her eyes and turned away from the road until the sound of Betsy's horse's hooves against the pavement faded into the distance. "Is she gone?" she asked.

"*Jah*." He bit back a chuckle.

"It is not funny, Henry King!"

He laughed outright. "It certainly is. It's hilarious."

"We have half the town talking about us. I don't see what's so humorous about that."

His shoulders rose and fell in a quick shrug. "I don't know," he admitted. "It just is."

"We're not going to be able to do this," she said, stepping off the porch and hurrying down the steps.

"Careful," he warned as she tottered on the last one. "What aren't we going to be able to do?"

"This," she said again, waving one hand around between them, as if that explained it all. "Being friends, hanging out, eating whoopie pies." She said the last as if it were somehow one of the seven deadly sins.

"Now hold on a minute." Henry loped down the porch steps, spurred to action by her words and the struggle she faced in pulling herself up into the buggy.

He put his hands under her elbows and supported her until she managed to scoot inside the carriage. Then she swatted him away, like a mother would the grasp of a toddler to a cookie.

"We can't be friends because the church district is talking about us?" he asked. Who had ever heard of such a thing, not being friends because people would talk? Neither one of them was married. There was no reason they couldn't be friends. And he surely wasn't letting something like gossipy old women tell him otherwise.

"Millie." He couldn't let her leave like this. Somehow her friendship was already too important to him. He wanted to be friends with her. He wanted to spend time together, eating whoopie pies and not.

She stopped adjusting the reins and turned to look down at him where he stood next to her buggy. "I need to go, Henry."

"I know. But I don't want you to come up with a hasty plan because the women in this town like to talk."

"It's not hasty."

"Sure seems that way to me," he said dryly.

"Well, it's not." She sniffed.

There was no getting through to her today. The afternoon they had shared, as lovely and innocent as it was, had been ruined by Betsy Stoll. How many of their outings would the woman spoil before they managed to get it under control?

"Fine," he said, though he hoped when Millie looked back on this conversation she would hear that his tone conflicted with the word. And he knew she would look back on it. He just knew she would.

She sighed and snapped the reins, clicking her tongue against her teeth to get the mare moving.

The horse remained standing there.

She clicked her tongue again.

The horse snorted and shook her head, but otherwise made no move to leave the driveway.

Millie started to flick the reins once more, then stopped, closed her eyes, and took a deep breath. Her eyes were still closed when she asked in a soft voice, "Henry, will you please unhobble my horse?"

One whoopie pie, she thought as she directed Daisy back toward town. One whoopie pie. She would eat one whoopie pie with Henry and then head back to the inn. That had been three whoopie pies ago.

Three.

But she had completely lost track of the afternoon. Sitting and talking with Henry was such a joy. Honestly, she might have sat there all afternoon if she hadn't caught sight of the clock.

She resisted the urge to push the horse faster. Breaking Daisy's neck wouldn't help the situation at all. She was hours late returning to the inn.

Sylvie would be ecstatic, Millie thought. Her aunt would love that Millie had spent the better part of the day with the man. She might not even give her much trouble over her lapse, other than shooting her knowing looks about something that wasn't even a thing. Her and Henry.

There would never be a Millie and Henry outside of

friendship, but she really wanted that friendship. She enjoyed his smile, his conversation, and his company. She even enjoyed that he wanted and expected nothing from her. They could talk, eat whoopie pies, and spend time together and neither one looked for more from it. They were the perfect friends.

But no one else in town would see it that way. Especially not Betsy Stoll.

Of all the people who lived in Paradise Springs, why had Betsy been the one who picked that inopportune time to drive by? Almost anyone else would have been preferable to Betsy. Not that she was the biggest gossip in town. That title went to Malinda Beachy.

Malinda sometimes made the vegetable deliveries for her brother and his farming co-op to the people in Paradise Springs. And even though most of Christian's deliveries were to English people, it just so happened that one Amish he delivered to was Betsy Stoll. She didn't have her own garden because she spent most of her time growing her own herbs and making her own products to sell in her store. But when Malinda made the biweekly delivery to Betsy, the information would be exchanged. Millie Bauman was seen out visiting Henry King in the middle of the afternoon on a random Friday. If that didn't smell like a wedding, Betsy had no idea what one smelled like. Or whatever it was Betsy said in those times. It didn't matter what words she used, the facts as she saw them would remain the same—something was going on between Henry and Millie.

Once the tidbit got to Malinda, the whole of Paradise Springs would know it by the following church Sunday.

And Millie would never be able to convince anyone of anything different.

She sighed as she pulled Daisy into the driveway.

All in all, she'd had a wonderful afternoon. Yet she wondered if she should even admit that to herself. The way Paradise Springs seemed to know every little detail about a person, she wondered if her thoughts were really her own. Then again, if the town did know what was going on in her mind, they would also know that she never planned to marry again. With all this talk about her and Henry, that couldn't be the case.

She relaxed a bit and allowed the thoughts to seep in. She was glad Henry had come to visit with his grandfather, though she was really sad that he would be leaving soon.

And in that moment she was glad to be home, but dreaded the interrogation she would soon be facing.

Maybe if she took her time unhitching the horse and walking her back to the stable, by the time she got back the baking would be over and she would be off the h—

"There you are!" Her aunt stuck her head out the back door, cheeks flushed pink, presumably from all the baking. "Land sakes, I thought you had gotten lost."

"No." Millie shook her head and patted Daisy's neck. "I'll just walk her down to the stable . . ."

For a moment she thought her aunt might protest, but she finally nodded. "Hurry up," she said. "We want to hear all about your visit."

"And that's what I'm afraid of," she muttered under her breath. To her aunt, she smiled. "Be back soon."

Her aunt dipped her chin one last time and ducked back into the house.

Millie sighed. There was no getting out of this one. Just delaying it.

Chapter Ten

And so fifteen minutes later Millie found herself sitting at the long kitchen table while Elsie, Hattie, and Sylvie put the finishing touches on the last batch of whoopie pies.

"These are strawberry cream," Elsie said, indicating the pale pink cakes she was wrapping in cellophane. "Those are chocolate." She nodded toward the obviously chocolate cakes.

"But we also made lemon meringue, chocolate chip, and pumpkin."

Millie made a face. "It's too early for pumpkin."

"Bite your tongue," her aunt admonished. "Pumpkin is good year-round."

"Good *jah*, but much better when the weather turns cooler. Besides, where did you get the pumpkin?" she asked.

Elsie leaned a little closer, as if divulging a trade secret. "From a can."

Millie winced.

"I'm with you," Hattie said. "Canned pumpkin? What are we, savages?"

Her cousin shook her head. "I'm all for baking, but you two take it way too seriously."

"Not possible," her aunt tossed in. But Millie knew her tone. She did take her baking seriously, but that was the reason she held eight bake-off trophies. In a competition one had to be competitive, and to do that, you had to take it seriously. She knew that was her aunt's motto. Not that she would have cross-stitched it on a pillow or anything. Sylvie did her best to keep her competitive streak under control, but it came out from time to time. Like now . . .

"And it's organic pumpkin that I canned myself last year," Sylvie continued.

Millie nodded. "That's totally different." She did her best to make her tone convincing. It must have worked too, for the ladies quit bickering about the merits of canned pumpkin versus fresh and turned their attention to her.

"So how did it go?" Hattie asked, shooting her a questioning, almost hopeful look.

Millie stopped picking at the edge of one of the reject chocolate pies. "How did what go?" She allowed her gaze to trail around the room, meeting each of their gazes in turn.

Her aunt smiled and nodded encouragingly. "You know . . . with Henry."

When her aunt had said *we want to hear all about your visit*, she supposed she took it as *her aunt* wanted to hear all about her visit. Not everyone. Well, not Hattie and Elsie. It was bad enough that she and Henry had been caught by Betsy Stoll. Again.

Millie closed her eyes against their expectant faces. What could she say to get herself out of this? She didn't know, so she said the first thing that came to mind. "We're just friends."

The women exchanged identical looks of excitement and hope.

"No," Millie said, shaking her head. "Not like that. He's leaving in a couple of months."

They continued to watch her.

"He's a nice man," she started again. "But that doesn't mean anything more than he's a nice man." She wasn't positive, but it felt like she was only making things worse. She opened her mouth once more, then shut it again and sat down in one of the chairs around the table.

It was no use. They had already made up their minds— no doubt with her aunt's encouragement.

"He would make a fine husband," Sylvie started, and Millie allowed it. Anything she said now would only look more incriminating. Yet she knew as well as she knew her own name that between Betsy Stoll and these three, a wedding would be imminent. At least in the rumor mill.

She sat and half listened as they went over all Henry's husbandly virtues, mulled over the things about him that they didn't know, and talked about how perfect Millie and Henry would be as a couple.

Millie sighed and continued to pick at the broken whoopie pie. Perhaps after the bake sale she should run out to Henry's and warn him. They didn't have to just worry about Betsy Stoll; soon the whole district would think the same thing—that the two of them were getting married.

"Where'd that come from?"

Henry looked to the table where his grandfather was pointing. The plastic container half filled with whoopie pies sat in the line of his finger. "Millie Bauman brought it out. Seems Sylvie's been practicing for the Whoopie Pie Festival bake-off and she wanted us to try this new flavor."

Dawdi crossed the room to the sink and started washing his hands. "New flavor, huh?" he asked.

Henry nodded.

"What kind?"

"Apparently it's top secret and we're not even supposed to guess."

Vern stopped and stroked his beard. "Any good?"

"Delicious," Henry truthfully replied.

"And Millie brought them out, you say?"

"*Jah*. That's right."

His grandfather pulled out a chair and joined him at the table. "So we have dessert to go with our supper." Vern looked around at the food Henry had prepared. Leftover rotisserie chicken from town, French fries from the freezer, and a can of green beans. "Looks good," he finally said.

Henry knew he was only being polite and they both were grateful to have food, but what he wouldn't give for one of his *mamm*'s suppers right now. That was the worst part of being away from home. Even more so than missing his little sisters Annie and Jodie, who still lived at home.

They bowed their heads, said their prayers, then filled their plates.

"So Millie brought them out, huh?"

Henry stopped dishing green beans onto his plate and looked to his grandfather. "That's right." Hadn't he already told him that?

"Tell me," Vern started. "Don't you think it's strange that Sylvie had her niece bring those cakes all the way out here when she could have served them to her guests at the inn?"

The thought had never crossed Henry's mind. Of course Sylvie could have used the pies for her guests. "Maybe she didn't want to risk the recipe getting out."

His grandfather eyed him over the top of his wire-rimmed glasses, then shook his head and went back to his meal.

Henry wasn't sure, but he thought he heard him mutter, "There are none so blind."

He had thought about it long and hard through the night, and Vern King came up with what he considered to be the exact right answer. Sylvie Yoder was up to something. First there was the leaky sink that had no leak and the I-don't-care-you-still-must-stay-for-supper attitude that she had adopted. And then the *Why don't y'all go get the tomato starters?* Then she sent Millie out with a load of pies that she could have given to her guests. The more he thought about it, the more it became clear to him that she wasn't just up to something. She was trying to get Henry and her niece, Millie, to fall in love.

He couldn't say it was a bad idea. The two of them were close enough in age. Both had suffered a loss in their lives. Henry was a good man, would be a good provider, and Millie was soon to have a baby. He knew that modern Amish women felt they could go it alone once they were widowed. Well, some of them did. It surely hadn't been that way back in his day, but times were changing. Now it seemed like Paradise Springs had more than their fair share of unmarried widows of the female kind. But having a newborn . . . that was a little different from being widowed with teenagers almost ready to go out and join the world.

Of course, he wasn't going to say that to Millie. That might ruin everything. He had thought it through, and it seemed to him that if Millie and Henry fell in love and got married, Henry wouldn't be pushing Vern to move to Oklahoma. And that suited him just fine.

So once the morning rolled around and the two men ate their breakfast, Vern stood and stretched his legs. "I'm going to run into town," he said.

Henry took his breakfast dishes to the sink and started running the water. "Let me wash these up and I'll go with you."

"Nah." Vern waved a hand in what he hoped was a casual manner even though it felt a little over-the-top. "I'm just going to pick up some . . . Sevin Dust from the co-op." That sounded reasonable enough.

"I thought I saw some in the barn," Henry said. "There on the right in the first stall."

And bless it all, there was some stored there. *Think, Vern.*

"I need more than what I have there. You know how the ants get this time of year. And the fleas. Can't be too careful with all the bugs around the house."

Henry frowned. "Isn't that what the chickens and ducks are for?"

Now was the time for Vern to hush up and get on into town while the getting was still good. He muttered something incoherent and pushed his chair back up to the table.

"You sure you don't want me to go with you?" Henry asked, elbow-deep in sudsy water. "This won't take five minutes."

"Nah." Vern did that wave thing again, and once again

it felt a little forced. But Henry seemed not to notice. He turned back toward the sink and continued with his washing up. "I'll be back in no time," Vern added and hurried out the door before Henry could say anything else in protest.

With lightning speed, Vern hitched up his horse and started to climb into the carriage.

"You might want this," Henry said.

His grandson was standing on the porch holding up Vern's wallet.

"*Jah*," he said. "*Jah, jah*." He got back down and met Henry halfway between the buggy and the porch. "*Danki*."

"Are you sure—" Henry started.

"I'm sure," Vern grumbled, climbing back up into the buggy. "It's just a quick trip into town."

Henry nodded, but Vern could tell from the look in the young man's eyes that he thought something was up. With any luck, by the time Vern got back home, that suspicion would be gone.

He could hope anyway.

Vern could feel Henry's gaze on him as he clicked the reins to get the horse started. *Quick trip into town*, he told himself. He would swing by to see Sylvie, find out if his suspicions were true and she was trying to be a matchmaker between Millie and Henry, then he would head over to the co-op and pick up another bag of Sevin Dust— whether he needed it or not—then back home. Easy stuff.

But Sylvie wasn't at the B&B when he pulled into the drive. In fact no one was. There was a plate piled high with individually wrapped whoopie pies by the door, along with a Mason jar and a sign that said "One dollar a pie, proceeds to benefit Joy Lehman's son, Johnny B."

He smiled. Leave it to Sylvie to do whatever it took to help out someone in need. Johnny B was his great-grandson, so Vern took a couple of dollars out of his pocket and shoved them into the jar, though he didn't take any of the whoopie pies. And he made a promise to himself to look in on Joy and Johnny B tomorrow. She had been looking after him for quite a time. Now it was his turn.

He repeated the vow to himself three times over. He really needed to remember this, and that seemed to be the best way these days. Not that he was getting all that forgetful. Not like everyone said. He just missed a few things from time to time. Like this morning, when he forgot to get his wallet. *Jah*, he had forgotten something, but it was no big deal really. No harm done. So he wished that everyone would stop making such a big thing out of a little nothing.

Not everyone. But Dale for sure. Henry's father.

Vern started to turn the doorknob and let himself into the B&B when he saw another note. One on the door that told any new guests they should walk down to Poppin' Paradise to pick up a key if they needed in. The note was written in Sylvie's steady hand, and the curl on her *P*s made him smile.

He straightened and looked down the street toward the popcorn shop. He didn't need a key, but he supposed Hattie and Elsie would know where Sylvie had gone if they had her keys to let in guests.

So Vern adjusted his hat and left his horse tied at the inn as he made his way down Main.

Poppin' Paradise wasn't far from the B&B and, as

always, the smell was deliciously overwhelming as he walked into the place. The scents of freshly popped corn and caramelized sugar tickled his nose as the bell on the door rang to signal his arrival.

It was a bright store, with shiny white countertops and red stripes, like on the popcorn bags they had every year at the Whoopie Pie Festival. Round, tiered tables held bag upon bag of flavored popcorn. Everything from the traditional caramel and cheddar to taco and birthday cake—not together, mind you. Unless you requested it. Hattie and Elsie would make up anyone any combination that could be thought of. And he supposed in the years that they had been doing this, they had probably come up with every combination under the sun.

"Vern." Hattie smiled when she said his name, as if he was the only person in the world she wanted to see in that very moment. But that was Hattie—always upbeat, always with a smile on her face. "What brings you in today?"

Vern nodded at the English couple who had just paid and were walking past him to the door. "I'm looking for Sylvie."

He didn't think how those words sounded until Hattie and Elsie shared a look.

"I just need to ask her something," he continued, hoping that would explain everything, but instead he felt like he was making things worse. "Do either of you know where she is?" he asked. No sense trying to backtrack over words that had already been said. "The sign on the inn's door says to come over here to get a key."

"If you're a guest," Elsie added with a small frown. Elsie wasn't always a frowner, but she was definitely a bit more worrisome than her outgoing cousin. "And you aren't a guest."

Vern sighed. "Can you tell me where Sylvie is?"

Hattie gave a small shrug. "Walk-around bake sale," she said baldly. "She's out selling whoopie pies for your kin."

Which meant she could be anywhere in the area. Maybe even as far over as Paradise Hill. How was he going to find her now?

"If I was you," Elsie said, "I would stop at the variety store first. They always buy some, but they usually take some to sell as well."

Vern smiled and rapped his knuckles against the slick white counter. "That's a mighty good idea."

A heartbeat later he was back out in the beautiful May sunshine. He faced the street and looked both ways, trying to decide. Should he walk there or go back and get his buggy at the inn? His horse would be fine. The variety store wasn't far. And the walk might do him some good. He turned and started down Main, away from the B&B and the popcorn shop.

The best way to describe the Paradise Springs Variety Store was to say that they sold a little bit of this and a little bit of that and a whole lot of nothing in particular. There was candy, birdhouses, crockery, and spices. Stationery, dishrags, brooms, dolls of all sorts, and flyswatters of course. All in all they managed to host a thriving business. The place was owned by Karl Lambert, who had bought it off Ben King—no relation—years and years ago. Now his daughter-in-law Lillian worked there most days, and it was her Vern was looking for when he walked in the door.

Lillian was sweet, thin, and unassuming, even if she was a bit malleable. She was in the Whoopie Pie Widows

Club with Sylvie. And he supposed if anyone would know where Sylvie was headed and wouldn't spread rumors that he'd been asking about her, that person was Lillian.

She was standing behind the first cash register when he came through the glass doors, a large basket of whoopie pies at the end of the counter near the plastic sacks.

"Hi, Vern," she said with a smile.

"I take it Sylvie's already been here and left," he said without greeting.

Lillian looked a bit taken aback as she nodded.

Vern took a breath and started over. "Hi, Lillian." He gave her a smile. He hadn't meant to be rude; he just hadn't thought about all the niceties. He and Lillian knew each other from way back. They had been at school together, though she was a couple of years younger than he. Sometimes all the so-called common courtesies were nothing more than time wasters. Especially when he was on a mission. He had told Henry that he was just running into town real quick and would be back in a jiffy. He had already been gone twice the amount of time he had planned. And he still hadn't found Sylvie. Or picked up the not-necessary Sevin Dust from the co-op.

She waited for him to continue.

"I'm looking for Sylvie." He nodded toward the large basket of whoopie pies. "I take it she's already been by here."

Lillian nodded. "That's right."

"Did she say where she was going next?"

Lillian seemed to think about it a moment.

Behind him the door to the shop opened, but he didn't turn to see who had come in. He merely waited for Lillian to continue. "You might check the lumberyard. I think they were going there next. Why do you need to talk to Sylvie?" she asked.

"Just need to," he said. Then he waved farewell and turned to find Malinda Beachy standing just inside the variety store, looking like she had been handed the juiciest steak in Missouri. Or at least that was what Vern's expression would have been had someone handed him the juiciest steak in all Missouri. For Malinda, it was gossip. And he realized that he had given her way more to talk about than was true, though with Malinda, details were for amateurs.

"Hi, Malinda," Vern said, sidestepping around the woman and out the door.

There was nothing he could do about it now. It would be all over town that he was out looking for Sylvie. And only the good Lord himself knew what she would make of that as she told her story.

Nothing that could be done about it now. He started across the parking lot and continued on to the lumber store, but there it was the same. Sylvie had just left and was on her way to the hardware store. It took three more stores before he finally caught up with her at the Paradise Amish Buffet.

The wonderful smells of home cooking greeted him as he opened the door. And there she was, standing at the front counter with Millie at her side as she talked with Imogene Yoder, who worked there.

All three women nodded to him when he came in.

"Just sit where you like," Imogene said. "Callie will be by to get your drink order in a minute."

Vern shifted in place. "I'm not here to eat." Though it did smell good. Better than anything he'd had since his meal at the inn.

All three women waited for him to continue.

He was messing this up and spreading his own rumors with the way he was going about this. "I need to talk to Sylvie."

They continued to eye him.

"Alone," he finally said.

Imogene's eyes grew wide, and she turned back to Sylvie. "Just leave the basket there and we'll collect the money."

"*Danki*," Sylvie said as Millie hoisted the basket full of whoopie pies onto the end of the counter. There was a sign taped to it that explained to whoever was interested that the money from the whoopie pies would go to benefit Johnny B Lehman, who was hurt in a terrible accident.

Then Millie pulled the wagon containing all the whoopie pie setups to the door. "I'll just wait outside."

Sylvie nodded. "Stay in the shade," she advised.

Millie moved out the door and Imogene made her way back to the kitchen. Vern was left alone with Sylvie.

"I know what you're doing," he said.

She nodded. "Most folks do. I'm trying to raise money for Johnny B and Joy."

That wasn't exactly what he meant, but he realized how his words could be misunderstood, but first . . . "I really appreciate that. I know you ladies work hard, and Johnny B is a good kid." He had come over many times in the last couple of years to help Vern with something or another. But since his accident, he was in a wheelchair. The doctors said it might be possible for him to walk again, but it was going to take lots of time and therapy.

And because Johnny B couldn't come by to help, Dale

started worrying and sent Henry up to convince Vern to move to Oklahoma. Strange how things all tied in together.

"But I'm talking about something else," he said. "I'm talking about Henry and Millie."

She stopped rearranging the pies in the basket and turned to face him. "What about Henry and Millie?"

"Come on, Sylvie. The leaky sink. There was no leak and Millie brought those whoopie pies to Henry. It's sort of obvious."

"You're upset?" she asked.

He shook his head. "No! I want to help you."

Her brow wrinkled into a frown. "Why?"

"I have my reasons." He gave a shrug.

"And you want to help Millie and Henry fall in love?"

"So that is your plan."

She propped her hands on her hips and shot him a suspicious look. "Maybe it is, maybe it isn't."

"It is and I want to help. Name it and I'll do it."

Sylvie studied him for a moment. "I get it. If Millie and Henry fall in love, he'll stay here and help you on the farm. That's sort of sneaky, Vern King."

"And I suppose your reasons are better?"

"True love." She gave a firm nod. "Everyone deserves love."

"And everyone deserves to live where they want to live." And die where they want to die. But his son Dale didn't understand. Vern was born in Missouri and he planned to die there too. That wasn't a lot to ask from life.

"Okay," she finally said. "But you can't let them know what we're doing or it'll ruin everything. They have to believe that they are falling in love all on their own."

Vern smiled, the plan firming up nicely. "You got it."

Chapter Eleven

"Hi."

Henry nearly rubbed his eyes to make sure his sight was correct. Once again Millie Bauman was the last person he expected to see today.

"I have whoopie pies," she said.

He nodded. "Another secret recipe?" he asked.

"Leftovers from the bake sale. Sylvie thought the two of you might want them."

Two bachelors on their own? Of course they wanted them. But he could tell that there was something else going on.

"Come in," he said, standing to one side. "Have one with me."

She shook her head. "I have eaten way more sweets this week than one should." But she followed him inside. "The house looks nice," she said as she trailed behind him.

"*Danki*." He had finished the painting yesterday and was glad to have it done. Painting was miserable work and he'd rather spend twice as long in the hot sun plowing than he would painting. At least he wouldn't have to paint the entire inside of the house. His grandfather's room had been recently painted. When Henry asked him about it, Vern said that he had started there and realized that painting wasn't his favorite chore. Then the planting started and he moved on to the outside duties.

Henry got down a saucer and stepped to one side so Millie could fill the coffeepot with water and set it on to boil.

"What?" she asked as she started the fire under the pot. "You wanted coffee, right?"

He nodded.

"And by some miracle have you mastered the art of coffee making in the last two days?"

He shook his head.

"Well, then."

Henry just smiled at her.

"What?" she asked again as she slid into one of the kitchen chairs.

"Nothing," he lied. He might be able to deceive her with words, but he couldn't in expression. The smile she brought to him stayed firmly in place as he moved opposite her and sat down as well.

"What?"

He ducked his head with a chuckle. "Whoopie pies?" he asked. "Again?"

"I warned you."

"That you did." He reached into the cardboard box and pulled out one of the cakes. He didn't mind that her aunt seemed bent on getting them together. As long as they knew what was happening, they could sit back and enjoy the ride.

"That's lemon meringue."

He studied it this way and that. "Any good?"

She gave him a playful frown and stood to attend to the coffee water, which had started boiling. "It's a whoopie pie."

He laughed. "Right." He continued to chuckle as he unwrapped the treat and took a large bite. "Good," he said around the mouthful. "Real good."

"I told ya."

He watched her as she strained the coffee and returned to the table with a cup for each of them. "You're having a cup?"

She shrugged. "Smells too good to resist."

"But these," he said, holding up the whoopie pie. "Good, but not as good as the ones from the day before yesterday. What was that flavor again?"

"You like to take your life into your own hands, don't you?" She shot him a look over the rim of her coffee mug.

"Can't blame a guy for trying." He sipped his coffee and finished the rest of the whoopie pie. They had never been his favorite treats, but they were quickly becoming that. The ladies of Paradise Springs had taken the art of baking whoopie pies to a whole nother level. "Besides," he continued. "I wouldn't care so much if it wasn't such a big secret."

"I suppose not." She continued to gingerly sip her coffee.

"Are you really not going to have one?" He nodded toward the box on the table between them.

"You go ahead." She smiled at him in that way she had, and suddenly he was glad he had come to Missouri. He might be having a time trying to convince his grandfather to move to Oklahoma, but he was thankful that he had found such a friend in Millie Bauman.

She caught his gaze and the moment stretched between

them. And Henry decided in that moment he could spend forever just sitting with Millie Bauman. Talking, drinking coffee, eating whoopie pies. Whatever and anything.

"You okay?" Henry asked.

Millie shook herself out of her thoughts, realizing only then that she had been staring dreamily at Henry King.

What was wrong with her? First she allowed her aunt to convince her to bring whoopie pies all the way out to the Kings' farm because she didn't want them to draw ants into the inn. Whoever heard of such an excuse! *Jah*, sweets drew ants, but if a person kept them in sealed containers . . .

Then she'd been caught staring moony-eyed at Henry like a young girl with her first crush.

"Uh-huh," she said, getting her bearings back. Must be some weird hormonal thing to do with her being pregnant. She felt a little rattled every time she got close to Henry King. But then, she enjoyed spending time with him regardless. Maybe she should ask the midwife about it.

She drained her coffee and stood. "I guess I should be going."

Henry was on his feet in an instant. "You're leaving so soon?"

She could hear the disappointment in his voice, and honestly, she felt the same. It was Sunday and there wasn't much work that could be done, but she couldn't sit around the table and chat with Henry all afternoon. She just couldn't. "*Jah*. I should be getting back."

"I'll walk you out," Henry said.

Millie just smiled and made her way to the front of the house.

Henry opened the door for her, and together they stepped out into the crisp sunshine. The sky to one side was blue and clean, but on the other, dark clouds had started to form.

"Looks like rain to the west," Henry commented.

"Then I definitely should be getting back to the inn." She said the words but made no move toward her buggy. Instead, she allowed her gaze to wander around the yard. "It really does look nice out here." Not only had the house been painted, the yard had also been mowed and raked.

Henry nodded his thanks.

"You know what you need?"

"No, but I have a feeling you're going to tell me."

She laughed. "You need some flowers."

The flower beds closest to the house were empty, as well as the ones around the mailbox and just in front of the barn.

Henry looked around and gave a small nod. "I suppose that would look good."

"It would look fantastic." She looked over the yard again, around to all the spots where flowers would add a dash of color. "You could put petunias around the mailbox, impatiens next to the barn because they like shade. And if you put a row of marigolds next to your garden, it'll help with the bugs." She turned to face him and felt a little sheepish as she caught sight of his expression. He looked a little dumbfounded, the way most men did when confronted with chores that traditionally fall to the women of their community. "I know," she continued. "I'll bring some flowers out tomorrow and plant them."

"No!" Henry practically hollered the word at her; then, as if realizing he had raised his voice, he said it again, though quieter this time. "No. That's not necessary."

"Of course flowers aren't necessary. But they are beautiful, and if God made them, we should care for them in our yards."

"You don't need to do that," Henry protested.

"Of course I don't. But I want to."

"No." The one word was sharp, even if it wasn't as loud as his previous protest. "You cannot come out here and plant a bunch of flowers. I won't allow it."

Something in his tone made the hair on her neck stand up. He wouldn't allow it? She was only trying to do something kind for a friend. What was wrong with that? Finally she shook her head. "I don't understand."

He turned a shade lighter than Sylvie's supped-up raspberry delight whoopie pies and waved a hand in the general direction of her belly. "You don't need to be planting anything outside in the heat."

In her condition.

He didn't say the words; he was too much of a gentleman. Amish men and women didn't discuss such matters as babies and pregnancies, not when they weren't married. There was no way he would come right out and say what he meant, but that one flick of his hand said it all.

He didn't want her to overtax herself.

And normally the idea would have been considerate, but somehow it didn't set well with Millie. She wasn't an invalid. She was pregnant. It was good to get out in the sun and dig around in the dirt. She missed having the large garden she had grown with her mother. Sylvie grew some vegetables for the inn but got most of her fresh fruits and veggies from the Beachys.

"I'm not crippled," she said, surprised at the haughtiness in her tone. "I can attend to a few flower beds, but if you don't want my help, then I retract it." She stepped off the porch and walked stiffly over to her buggy. She should have told Sylvie no when she made up that silly reason for Millie to come out here today. She had seen through it easily enough, but she had also wanted to see Henry and spend a little time with her friend.

How'd that work out for you?

"Millie, no." He stepped off the porch and started toward her.

Her face burned hot as she pulled herself into the buggy, thankfully without his help. She knew he was right behind her, but he didn't try to assist her.

She snapped up the reins but couldn't meet his gaze.

"Millie."

She stopped but refused to look him in the eye.

"That's not what I meant."

"I know what you meant. But I'm healthy. And my baby's healthy."

He cleared his throat, obviously uncomfortable with all that was being said and all that was left unsaid. "But you shouldn't be out doing such chores."

"And who are you to make such a decision for me?"

"Millie . . ."

"Goodbye, Henry." Without another glance at him, she started the mare into motion and headed back toward the B&B.

Of all the male things to do and say.

She shook her head at it all, even as her face continued

to burn with anger and embarrassment. She might have
expected something like that from her father or even
Sylvie from time to time, but she thought Henry understood her.

Boy, was she wrong. Henry was just as bad as everyone
else in her life who felt like she was too fragile after losing
Joshua to grow a healthy baby.

After everyone's talk about trusting God, and the Lord
knowing what was best, they sure didn't listen to their own
words when it came to her.

She had been devastated when she got the word that
Joshua had fallen from the roof at a neighbor's house. He
had lingered for three days before succumbing to his injuries. There had been hospital bills and stress and tears
and prayers, but in the end, he was gone. And there was
nothing she could do about it. But the sick feeling his
death had left her with hadn't eased after the funeral. Or
even the week after that. And then one chance look at the
calendar and she knew what the real problem was.

Not that it was a problem. She was grateful, so very
grateful to have one last piece of her husband. She had
heard other people talk about her when they thought she
wasn't listening. She heard what a terrible tragedy it was
that she was so young, and now widowed, alone and pregnant. And it wasn't one or two people who felt that way. It
seemed as if the entire community of Adrian cast her for-
lorn looks during church and afterward, in the post office,
the grocery store, or wherever it was she happened to be.
It wasn't long before she couldn't take it anymore and she
moved to Paradise Springs to live with her aunt Sylvie.

Because to her, it wasn't a tragedy. God had granted
her this part of Joshua that she could keep. It was as if

He had known that He was going to take her husband and He wanted Millie to have a walking, talking reminder of the man she once loved.

Okay, so it was a totally romantic idea, but it had sustained her through these months after losing him. And she wasn't changing her mind easily. Perhaps that was why Henry's actions vexed her so.

She was a survivor. She had buried her husband after only being married a year, and she had done everything in her power to move forward. And he thought she couldn't manage to plant a few flowers.

Her face was still on fire when she pulled the horse to a stop in front of the inn.

Sylvie must have been watching and waiting for her return for she bustled out the front door before Millie had even managed to scramble down from the carriage.

"What's wrong?" she asked as Millie stalked toward the inn.

Millie just shook her head. "Can you take Daisy to the stables?"

"Of course, but—"

"I need to lie down," she said truthfully. "I have a headache." And a pain in the neck by the name of Henry King.

"Sure, but what happened?"

Millie didn't turn to answer her aunt, afraid that she might self-combust if she stayed there any longer. "I'm sorry, Sylvie," she said as she continued her march toward the front door. "But I do not want to talk about it."

Chapter Twelve

She liked to have never got away from Millie this morning.

For someone who didn't want to talk about her own feelings from the night before, her niece sure had asked a lot of questions concerning where Sylvie was going, why she was going there, and when she would be back. Sylvie supposed she was asking out of mere curiosity, but when a person—say an aunt—didn't want to tell another person—maybe a niece—where they were going, mere curiosity could seem like an all-out interrogation.

But after half a dozen or so dodged questions, Sylvie managed to make it down to the stable, get Daisy, and head out to the King farm. Something happened yesterday between Henry and Millie, and whatever it was, it wasn't good. Sylvie could only hope that Vern knew what it was and could help her correct it. It was as obvious as the horse pulling her carriage that something was wrong.

As she drove, the town gave way to farmland. She waved at the familiar faces as she passed—Benjamin Lambright was out with his cows, though she saw no sign of his brother, Leroy, who also worked the farm. Christian Beachy was out adding a fresh coat of paint to the vegetable stand in front of his house. His sister Malinda was nowhere to be seen, and for that small miracle, Sylvie said a quick prayer of thanks. If Malinda had seen her, she would have started speculating, and then asking questions, and who knew where that would lead.

But as Sylvie neared King land one thing became apparent to her: the farmers were all out in their fields. Vern was a farmer, so the chance of her finding him at home was slim. She'd best head by his fields and see if he was there first. Which would suit her just fine. She wouldn't want Henry getting suspicious.

It didn't take long to find Vern. As she had suspected, he was in one of his fields doing some sort of chore that farmers did, though she had no idea what it was. To her, it simply looked like he was toting dirt from one side of the field to the other.

She pulled her buggy off to the side and tied the mare to a fence post. The carriage was off the road far enough that anyone passing by wouldn't hit it, but it was close enough that she could keep an eye on it while she talked to Vern.

"Hallo, there, Sylvie Yoder." He waved as he called to her, balancing the shovel of whatever he held in one hand as he greeted her. He had stopped all that dirt toting and was waiting for her to pick her way around the field toward him.

She flapped one hand at him in return, concentrating instead on her feet. There was a narrow road that circled the field and would have made it easier to navigate except that it hadn't rained in a while. Last night's showers were only enough to settle the dust, as her grandmother used to say. The storm that had been brewing all yesterday afternoon had missed them entirely, staying south of Paradise Springs and stretching all the way into Arkansas. But the last time it had rained, it had rained hard, leaving deep gouges in the land. Each step she took kicked up a cloud of dust that had her watching where her next step was landing to avoid any craters left in the path. Finally she grew even with him, but he wasn't at the edge of the path. He was pert near the center of the whole field.

"What brings you out today?" he called across to her.

He was a good ways from her, but not so far that she could see his gaze roaming over her, no doubt searching for a new batch of whoopie pies.

"What happened last night, Vern King?" she called in response.

He dropped the business end of his shovel and the soil or whatever it held spilled on the toes of his dirt-caked muck boots. Once he had a hand free, he scratched a spot under the edge of his hat, tilting it to one side as he contemplated her question. "Don't know what you're talking about."

She propped her hands on her hips. Men were so dense sometimes. Especially when it came to affairs of the heart. The good Lord knew she had loved her Andrew, but that man wouldn't know romance if it came up and introduced itself with a handshake. Seemed Vern King was cut from the same cloth. "I'm talking about Millie and Henry."

He did that head scratching thing again, this time knocking his hat in the other direction. "I'm afraid I'm going to need a little more information."

Of course he did.

"Millie came out here yesterday with some whoopie pies and she was in a state when she got home."

"A cake?" Vern frowned. "I don't know anything about a cake."

Sylvie shook her head. "Not a cake. A *state*."

"Like Missouri?"

Sylvie sighed. Really it was more like a growl, but she did manage to keep it short. "Come here," she demanded.

He tilted his head to one side, as if those two words had completely escaped him, along with the rest of their conversation.

"Heavens," she grumbled and started across the field toward him.

He grinned as she approached, the action totally messing up her annoyance with him. In his smile she could see the boy he had once been, much like Henry, kind . . . godly. Not that Henry was a boy. Not a boy-boy, but definitely younger than the two of them.

"So why are you here?" he asked.

And the annoyance came straight back. Sylvie sucked in a calming breath and eyed Vern with awe. "Henry," she said. "Henry and Millie."

Vern nodded, as if he had suspected as much all along. "What about them?"

Honestly. How was a good Amish woman supposed to keep her Christian character when she had to deal with such nonsense?

"What happened between the two of them yesterday?"

"They were together yesterday?"

"Vern King, this will go much quicker if you stop answering my every question with one of your own."

"It will?"

She bit back a growl. "Millie came out here yesterday

with a load of whoopie pies, but she was not happy when she got back to the house. Now what happened?"

"Millie was here yesterday?"

She propped her hands on her hips. "That was a question."

He scratched his head, his hat even further askew than it had been before. She resisted the urge to straighten it. Her Andrew used to do the same thing, some time ago. Another lifetime. "I wasn't aware that Millie was here," he said. "So I don't know."

"You don't know about yesterday or you don't know about Millie?" Heaven help her, she was starting to sound like him!

"Both."

"So you didn't see her?"

"That's what I just said." Now he was starting to grumble, his tone matching hers in aggravation.

"Vern King, now you listen to me. Millie came out here yesterday with a load of whoopie pies—"

"Whoopie pies, you say?" His eyes grew wide and now held an eager light.

"Focus," Sylvie snapped. "She came out here and she was in a good mood. And when she came home she was not in a good mood any longer."

"So something happened."

Sylvie bit back a sigh. "That's right. Now I need you to figure out what."

"Figure out what?" Vern asked.

"Figure out what happened between Millie and Henry," she said as patiently as she could. She had thought it might be a good idea to bring Vern on as a partner. Especially if Millie was going to come out to the farm and leave in a huff without anyone knowing why. But only if he would listen to her.

"I don't know what happened between them."

Sylvie propped her hands on her hips once more and gave him what she had heard the teens call the "stink eye." "Then you had better find out," she said as sternly as she dared. "How else are we going to get the two of them to fall in love?"

On that note, she turned on her heel and made her way back toward the edge of the field and her waiting horse and buggy. Her departure was supposed to have been on the dramatic side, but she felt as if the effect was ruined as she slipped and slid on the loose soil heaped up on both sides of the sprouting plants. It was only when she reached her mare that the scent caught up with her.

Manure!

Ugh! She might be Amish and she might have been raised on a farm, but she had grown accustomed to city living. At least she had grown accustomed to Paradise Springs living. And not walking through manure.

She stopped next to her carriage and did her best to wipe the smelly gunk from her shoes. And her best shoes at that. Why she had felt it necessary to wear her church shoes out to visit Vern King was anybody's guess, but she had and now they were practically ruined. She dragged her foot through the fringe of grass at the edge of the turned earth, then did the same with the other one. They weren't clean, but at least she wouldn't track too much manure into the buggy with her. At least no more than necessary.

Task accomplished, she straightened her dress and turned back toward the field. Vern was still standing where she had left him. It didn't appear that he had moved so much as a breath. And if she wasn't mistaken, she thought she saw him smile; then he turned away and went back to work.

But she was mistaken, she decided later, once she had almost reached the edge of town. Why would he be smiling while watching her try to clean her shoes? The thought was unlikely at best, strange at worst, and all around ridiculous all the time. And she was still no further in knowing what had happened between Millie and Henry than she had been the night before.

She continued to mull over the problem as she pulled into the drive at the inn, unhitched the buggy, then walked Daisy down to the stable at the edge of town. She worried over it as she made her way back to the inn. So much so that she was surprised when she set foot inside and Millie greeted her straightaway.

"Where have you been?"

Maybe it wasn't a proper greeting, but Millie's face held a pinched look and her eyes seemed a bit worried.

"I—I—I didn't mean to be gone that long."

Millie pressed her lips together. "I was worried."

"I'm sorry." Sylvie really hadn't meant to be gone such a long time. "I guess I'm not used to having someone fret over me."

Millie's expression crumpled into one of forgiveness. "It's okay. I just worry when I don't know where you are."

Sylvie smiled at her niece, so grateful that she had come to live in Paradise Springs. "I'll be more mindful of that."

Millie sniffed the air. "What's that smell?"

Oops! Sylvie had forgotten all about her shoes. "Nothing." But the word was proven a lie as she looked toward her feet.

Millie followed her gaze. "Where have you been? Walking through a manure field?"

"Something like that," Sylvie muttered. She ignored her niece as the young woman frowned. The last thing Sylvie needed was Millie finding out about her attempts to get her and Henry together. She knew that Millie wouldn't cotton to the idea, but sometimes a person didn't know what was best for them and right now was one of those times for Millie Bauman. She thought she wanted to live her life alone. That she wanted to raise her child alone, but Sylvie had chosen that path, and sometimes it wasn't all that it was cracked up to be. Sure she didn't have anyone to answer to save God when the sun went down, but that also meant she didn't have anyone to talk to. Only since Millie had come to live with her.

Sylvie didn't always miss having another soul around, but there were times when it would have been relaxing to share her day, or when she had a story to tell or something funny happened. During those times, when there was no one there to listen, that's when it got lonely.

Sylvie wanted more than that for her niece. Better than a life alone.

Not that she knew firsthand or anything, but raising a child alone wasn't easy. She had heard enough talk over the years to know it as sure as if she had witnessed it herself. Raising kids in a one-parent home was no picnic, as they said.

Of course Millie would have a child, not child*ren*. But that was beside the point entirely.

"I'm just going to go . . . clean my shoes . . ."

Stop looking suspicious, she told herself as she backed out of the front room and into the kitchen. *Turn around. Walk slowly away. She doesn't suspect a thing.*

With a mixture of concern and bemusement, Millie watched her aunt move into the kitchen and, she supposed, on into the mudroom so she could clean her shoes. But with the way her aunt was behaving, she wasn't entirely sure that was her aunt's intention. She was up to something, of that Millie was certain. It was only speculation—intelligent speculation—that it had something to do with Henry King.

Or maybe . . . the idea was so tiny she could barely grab ahold of it before it slipped away. Or maybe her aunt was seeing someone. As in courting a man. Most second romances were kept a secret until the wedding was announced. She supposed it was only fair to do it that way. The first marriage had been treated as a big deal, and any attention given to a second marriage would take away from that given to the first marriages that were currently taking place. Or something like that.

So if her aunt was courting someone, she would certainly keep it to herself for a while. And that would explain why she was acting so suspiciously. No, that wasn't quite the right word. Strangely. That was better. Her aunt was acting strangely. Coming in with manure all over her best shoes. Why else would she be wearing her best shoes to go tramping around someplace where there was manure unless there was a man involved? And where there was manure there were cows. Or horses.

Jason Stoll. He ran the stable. Maybe he was the secret love in Sylvie's life. Or maybe not. He was a good twenty years younger than her aunt. Millie supposed to some, such a gap was not important. Had she unknowingly added to her aunt's infatuation by asking her to stable Daisy the day before? She hadn't meant to. She really had had a headache after her stressful encounter with Henry King. Perhaps that alone had started some sort of attraction between the two of them. Still, it was a rather large difference in ages.

And perhaps Millie was just trying to find romance where there was none.

Her aunt had been a widow for a long time now. So long that no one in the family believed she would ever get married again. To think that she was in love could just be wishful thinking on her part, wanting happiness for her aunt by way of the companionship of others.

Millie herself might be widowed, but soon she would have a child to share her life. Her aunt didn't even have that.

She sighed and rubbed a hand across her growing belly. Then she started up the stairs to remake the Blue Room. They had new guests checking in that afternoon.

"Where are they?" Vern asked as he came into the kitchen.

Henry looked up from the pot he was stirring and eyed his grandfather. "Where's what?"

His *dawdi* propped his hands on his hips and eyed him as if he were a six-year-old who had gotten caught with his hand in the cookie jar. "The whoopie pies Millie Bauman brought out here yesterday."

Oh. That.

Henry nodded toward the container sitting on top of the refrigerator. "Over there."

His grandfather hightailed it over and pulled the container down, immediately opening it and inhaling the sweet scent of the tasty little cakes.

Henry didn't want to smell them or taste them no matter how good they were. Because just the sweet scent made him think of Millie and the angry tilt of her chin as she turned her buggy toward the road and left yesterday afternoon.

Why were women so sensitive? He had only been looking out for her. The thought of a woman planting flowers in the garden wasn't out of the question, but Millie was . . . she was . . . well, she was pregnant.

He had trouble even thinking the word in his own mind. Pregnancy and the other duties of women were not something men talked about. They just didn't.

And she might be fine planting flowers and such. But how was he supposed to know?

No, that wasn't it. He didn't want her expending her energy on the farm when they wouldn't be here past the fall. Flowers were nice but not necessary. And necessary was what he had to concentrate on.

"What flavor are they?" Vern asked.

Henry shut off the burner and moved to get down some bowls. It was too hot for soup, but once again they had been resigned to eating from cans. Surely there had to be a better way. One that didn't involve him cooking. "She wouldn't say."

Vern picked one up and sniffed it. "Chocolate," he said appreciatively.

"They're red," Henry pointed out.

"Then red chocolate. or whatever it's called."

"Red velvet. But I wouldn't go any further than that in your guessing."

Vern took a big bite, savoring all the flavors before he spoke again. "Why's that?"

"Millie said Sylvie would lock us in the cellar if we started divulging secrets this close to the Festival." He poured the soup into the bowls and took the pan to the sink. He ran water in it and said, over his shoulder, "Quit eating that and get down the crackers."

His grandfather frowned. "I can do both. And there's raspberry in there for sure."

"'Do not put the Lord your God to the test,'" Henry quoted.

"Bah." Vern waved one hand even as he stuffed the rest of the whoopie pie into his mouth and reached for the crackers. "How do you suppose women get the cake all red when it tastes like chocolate?"

Henry placed their bowls on the table, then retrieved their spoons from the drawer before pulling out his seat. "No idea."

"Or maybe they take red cake and make it taste like chocolate."

"Is there a difference?"

Vern shrugged. "No idea."

Henry just smiled and bowed his head to pray.

"You want to tell me what happened between you and Millie Bauman yesterday?" Vern asked once the prayers had been offered and they had begun to eat.

As a matter of fact, no. No, he didn't want to recount what had happened between him and Millie. Mainly because he was still trying to sort it out in his head. What had he done so wrong?

"Wait a minute," he said, the truth just dawning on him. "How did you know there were whoopie pies? And how do you know that Millie was here?"

"Because Sylvie Yoder came out this morning hopping mad that something had happened between the two of you. So what was it?"

"It was nothing," Henry said. It was almost the truth. It was nothing that he could understand. That was for certain. "Everything was fine, and then she said she wanted to come out here and plant some flowers in the yard. I told her she shouldn't, and then she left in a huff." That was the most of it anyway.

"You told her . . . no wonder she was so upset. You're young, but I thought you would have learnt by now not to tell a woman she can't do something. You might as well tell her to go on ahead, because now she'll be more than determined just to prove you wrong."

"Not all women are like that." Anna Kate hadn't been. But then, she seemed to have lost her caring about what he thought a long time ago.

"Women with spirit are, and Millie Bauman is a woman with spirit."

Henry frowned, started to take a bite of his soup, then abandoned his spoon altogether. "How do you know that?" he asked. "How do you know that Millie has spirit?"

"Look into her eyes, son. You'll see it too. And a strong woman like that needs to have her way most times or there's no peace for those around her."

Henry wasn't sure what that had to do with him. He and Millie were just friends, but he supposed his *dawdi*'s advice could apply to friends as well. Millie did have spirit. He had seen it in her eyes, and in the proud slant of her shoulders. She was ready to take on life and whatever God had in store for her. She wasn't meek or lacking in strength. She had it in abundance. And if he was going to be her friend, that was something he would have to address.

"So what do I do?" he asked.

His grandfather shook out a handful of crackers before answering. "First thing is apologize. The second thing is get some flowers so she can go to planting."

Chapter Thirteen

There was only one thing he could do: Vern needed to get himself into town and tell Sylvie Yoder what he had found out. And in the meantime, he would have to trust that Henry would take his advice and make amends with Millie. He was serious about what he told the young man. A woman like Millie had spirit, and that was a good thing. You just had to be careful sometimes how you handled a woman like that. He had never met Anna Kate, the woman Henry had been engaged to, but he'd bet his entire crop that she couldn't hold a candle to Millie Bauman.

But when Vern got up the next morning, it was to a river of water in the house.

"What happened?" Henry asked, coming out of his room and wading through the mess. Well, wading was a strong word, but still, they were up to their ankles in water in the living room and the kitchen.

"Hot water tank must have busted," Vern said. "It's been trying to go out for a while now." He looked to the clock over the kitchen sink. "The co-op should be open."

Henry nodded. "Hopefully they'll have one in stock."

Vern shook his head at the mess. "This water should

start going down in a bit. I'll go shut off the valve. You find us something to eat and I'll meet you at the barn."

Half an hour later they were on their way to town. This was not exactly how Vern had imagined his morning would go. He had expected to come up with some cocka-mamie story that would take him into town . . . alone . . . and then he would run by the inn and talk to Sylvie. The plan had hinged on him being by himself. He supposed he could run by after they went to the co-op, but with Henry looking over his shoulder . . . how was he supposed to talk to Sylvie about his grandson and Millie without him overhearing?

First things first, his father always said.

The co-op was busy as always in the planting season, but thankfully they had a compatible hot water heater in stock and they promised to deliver it by the afternoon. Vern would have preferred to take it with him, but seeing as how Zebadiah Miller, who ran the co-op was laid back in every aspect of his life save his deliveries, Vern would have to wait until the English driver could bring it out to him.

"We, uh . . . could go by the B&B, *jah*?" Henry asked as they got back into their buggy. That was another thing: Vern had been in such a hurry to get to town that he had hitched up the carriage instead of the wagon.

Vern straightened a bit in his seat. "You want to go by the inn?"

Henry nodded.

"Sylvie Yoder's inn?" he asked, just to be sure.

"*Jah*. You think we can do that?"

Vern stroked his beard. He was stalling just to see how his grandson would react. It wasn't the nicest thing for him to do, but he couldn't help himself from teasing the young man just a little. "The B&B, huh?"

Henry turned a bit pink. Well, all except the tops of his ears. Those turned bright pink. "I thought I might go apologize to Millie."

Vern grinned.

Henry shook his head. "It's not like that. She and I are friends, and I value that friendship. I didn't mean to hurt her feelings, or whatever it was I did. So you're right. I should apologize. And since we're here and going to drive right past on the way home . . ."

"Right," Vern said slowly, still stroking his beard. Henry's ears looked like they were about to erupt into flames. That would be a sight and maybe worth pushing the man a little more, but in the end he decided to cut his grandson some slack. "All right, then," he cheerfully added. "We can go by the inn."

Henry relaxed in his seat, though he still looked as stiff as a board. That just went to show how tense he was before Vern agreed to stop at the inn on the way home.

But when Vern opened the front door to the B&B chaos reigned. Millie and Sylvie were there, along with a young woman and a little boy who was crying, screaming, and cradling his twisted arm to his chest.

"I think that's broken," Henry said, close behind Vern.

He nodded without taking his eyes from the boy. It did indeed look broken. And a bad break.

"I don't know what to do," the young mother wailed in a tone to rival her injured son's. At least Vern figured the boy was her son. The woman looked close to tears. Sylvie looked as spry and alert as ever. She didn't seem to miss a thing, that Sylvie.

"Hospital," she was saying.

"I don't know," the mother wailed.

Millie tried to comfort the woman, but she held herself stiff as she tried to decide the next course of action.

"I don't know where the hospital is," she said. "I wish Fred were here. He would know what to do. But no. He just had to go golfing. If he were here . . ."

But, Vern supposed, Fred wasn't there.

"I'm so sorry," Sylvie was saying. "We have insurance for these sorts of things. But he needs to go to the emergency clinic right away."

The woman seemed frozen with grief or fear, or maybe just indecision. She was a lovely woman, but Vern could see that she didn't have the spirit that Millie and Sylvie had. Only one thing to do.

He took a step forward. "Do you have a car?" he asked.

The woman stopped and looked at him as if she had just then noticed that someone else was in the room with them. "Yes."

"Get the keys. I know where the emergency clinic is. I'll ride along with you and the boy." He waited a moment, then urged, "Go on, now."

Thankfully, the boy stopped wailing and was whining a bit, tears still leaking down his face. Perhaps it was the introduction of two men onto the scene, but it seemed as if he wanted to act more like a man than a boy.

"What happened?" Henry asked as the woman made her way up the stairs.

"Chester here was sliding down the banister and managed to fall off halfway down," Sylvie said.

Henry looked up to a spot that could have been about halfway up or down the banister. His gaze followed the trail to the floor, and he whistled under his breath. "That's some fall."

"It hurts," the boy, Chester, informed them with a sniff and another stream of tears. He used his good arm to wipe his nose.

"You need help up?" Vern asked.

Chester eyed him carefully. "You have a funny beard."

Vern touched the wiry strands that hung to the top button on his shirt. "You think?" he asked.

The boy nodded solemnly. "It's different."

"How so?" Vern asked.

"My dad has a beard. It doesn't look like yours."

Vern put a finger under his nose where a mustache would be. "Because there's nothing here?"

The boy nodded. "That's weird."

Vern nodded, thankful that the boy had at least stopped crying, and with his mother upstairs searching for the keys to her car so they could run him to the doctor, the large foyer of the inn had returned to normal. Well, almost. "Weird to you maybe. But everyone I know has a beard just like mine."

The boy's eyes widened. "Everyone?" he asked in awe.

Vern gave a serious nod. "Everyone."

"He doesn't have one," he said, nodding toward Henry.

"That's right," Vern said. "Because he's not married."

"You have to be married to have a beard?" he asked.

"Of course."

The boy shook his head. "I'm growing a beard just as soon as my hair comes in." He stroked his smooth chin with his good hand and Vern tried not to laugh. He wouldn't want the boy to think he was laughing at him, but the young man had a ways to go before there would be any hair on his chin.

"That sounds like a fine idea," he said.

"Need some help up?" Henry asked.

The boy seemed to think about it a moment, then gave a small nod. "I guess so." He said the words as if he were somehow compromising his manhood by giving in to assistance.

As Henry set the boy on his feet, his mother came down the stairs, a set of keys in one hand.

"Are you going to be able to drive?" Henry asked her.

"Of course," the woman said, but her voice quavered.

"I don't have a license," Vern started, "but I do know how to drive if need be."

The woman's eyes widened. "Aren't you Amish?"

He wasn't sure what bothered her the most—the idea of him driving or the idea of him driving without a license. Either way, he knew he could get them there safely if need be.

Vern nodded. "*Jah*, but when I ran around I got a car and . . ." He let his words trail off. He didn't want to finish. It had been a long time ago, but he had had a time in that car. Still, he wouldn't want Sylvie thinking he was some sort of wild man back in the day. Sometimes when a person let loose a little too much during their *rumspringa*, it was hard to get back on the right path. It might have been the case for some, but not for him. Once that time was over, he had returned to his faith and walked the line he continued today. He just didn't want Sylvie thinking any differently.

Not that he understood exactly why he didn't want her

to think ill of him. And he didn't have time to ponder it now. He had a little boy to get to the hospital.

He motioned for the two of them to follow him. "Let's go."

He just came in and took over the situation.

Sylvie breathed a quick sigh of relief as the door shut behind Vern, along with the mother and the son.

Her hands were still shaking and her legs felt as if they might give way any moment.

Her heart had nearly stopped when she saw the boy fall. She had heard people say that some accidents seem to happen in slow motion. This was one of the few times she had seen it for herself. It seemed as if his fall took minutes upon minutes instead of the quick seconds from banister to floor. She had cried out, tried to go to him, but if he fell in slow motion, then she moved like a snail in slow motion. She had been powerless to stop his fall.

But it was over now, for the most part, and she could return her breathing to normal and pray that he hadn't broken anything more than his arm. But what a bad break.

"Do you need to call the insurance people?" Millie asked.

Sylvie stirred herself out of her thoughts and centered them on her niece. "What?"

"The insurance people. Should we call them now or wait until we have more word about the boy's injuries?"

"I suppose now. We can always call them back with updates, but I'm sure we'll have to file a claim. I just never have before."

Sylvie had gotten the policy to satisfy the loan agreement for the house, but in all honesty, she had no idea how insurance worked. She only knew that she had to have it in order to run a B&B.

"I'll call," Millie said, starting for the office at the back on the house. It was no more than a closet where Sylvie kept all the important papers and the checkbook she used to pay the inn's expenses. "Where's the number?"

"That Rolodex thingy on the desk," she answered, still a little numb. What would she do without Millie here to help? What would she have done if Vern hadn't been there to help? He'd just stepped right up and taken charge. She had frozen in place, which wasn't like her at all. Maybe she was just getting old. Back in her younger days she would have been in action in a split second. But these days, with all the new technology and rules about liability and such . . . well, there were times when she felt completely in over her head.

Lord, thank you for sending Vern King to me today. I don't know what I would have done without him. And thank you for bringing Millie here. She is such a blessing to me. Amen.

Jah, they were both blessings, both so helpful. The only difference was after autumn Millie would remain in Paradise Springs, but if Henry King had his way, Vern would be packed up and on his way to Oklahoma. And she had to say, she would be disappointed and perhaps a little sad to see him go. The whole community would miss him, she was sure.

Millie returned a moment later. "I had to leave a message," she said, "but I'm sure they'll call back soon."

Sylvie nodded.

"Auntie," Millie started in that concerned tone of hers. Most Amish didn't use such titles for their kin, but in recent weeks Millie had picked up the habit, most likely from their English visitors and guests. "Why don't you go lie down?"

Sylvie pulled herself together just then, realizing she had been mooning over Vern King. Thankfully that action had been misinterpreted for another—at least one not so embarrassing—shock over the little boy breaking his arm. "I'm fine," she insisted. She pulled on her dress and apron, as if that proved her wellness. "Y'all go on in the parlor and have a snack while you wait for Vern. He may be a while." She shooed them into the parlor and bustled her way back to the kitchen. Tomorrow night was the widows' club meeting and everyone was gathering at the inn once again. She needed some new whoopie pies. Something so tasty it would knock everyone's socks off. Well, if they were wearing socks.

She hummed a little under her breath as she started gathering ingredients. She was saving the dark chocolate idea, keeping that one under her hat, as they said. But the one for tomorrow night's meeting needed to show just how creative and talented she could be.

Carrot cake, she decided. Carrot cake with toasted coconut and vanilla bean filling. Perfect.

She bustled around the kitchen gathering ingredients and bowls and such. To the refrigerator for carrots and coconut and back for sugar, salt, flour, and baking powder.

It really was fortunate that Vern and Henry came along when they had. She and Millie would have managed, she was certain, but it was mighty helpful that he had stepped in when he had. And offering to drive!

She measured the flour into the bowl and started cracking the eggs. She had done a few crazy things on her *rum-*

springa, but she hadn't bought a car and she certainly hadn't learned to drive. His stepping in and offering to drive if need be had calmed the mother greatly, it seemed. And that was something Sylvie herself wouldn't have been able to do.

Jah, Vern was an important member of their community. She just wondered why she had never thought about it before now. If someone had asked her a month ago if she was upset that Vern might be moving to Oklahoma, she would have probably said no. Or maybe even that she never knew it was a possibility. But now her answer would be a resounding yes! She would hate to see him go. Just another reason why she needed to get Millie and Henry together. It would solve a multitude of problems.

She picked up the container of salt. Had she added some already? She felt like she had, but she couldn't quite remember. Perhaps she had. Or maybe she hadn't. If she added some again, what harm would there be? There wasn't enough salt in the recipe that a double dose would do any harm at all. And with all the salted this and that recipes that were out there, it might just come out tastier than she could imagine.

With a contented smile on her face and thoughts of Vern King still circling around in her head, she grabbed up the measuring spoon and added a bit more.

"I apologize," Millie said the minute they stepped into the parlor. Honestly, if she didn't love her aunt so much she might strangle her.

"No need." Henry smiled, and Millie found it harder and harder to keep her anger with him. She had never been one to hold a grudge, but after a good night's sleep and looking at the situation from his point of view, she'd realized that he was only trying to be mindful of her health without actually saying it was something of a concern. And how many men worried about such things if they weren't married or related to the woman? Not many she knew. But that was what made Henry King different. That was what made her want to remain friends with him until he left. And maybe even wish that he wasn't leaving at all so they could stay close for longer than the month leading up to fall.

She smiled gratefully at him. "Would you like a whoopie pie?" she asked. Pointing to the tray that sat in the middle of the sideboard.

In the afternoons, her aunt laid out refreshments for anyone staying in the B&B. And this time of year, whoopie pies were always the star attraction as she prepared a new recipe for the upcoming Festival.

Henry snatched up a whoopie pie in the way only a bachelor can, then smiled as he took a bite. "Mmm . . ." he murmured around the cake. "Lemon."

"Don't let her hear you say that." Millie shook her head, but smiled to take the seriousness from her words.

Henry shifted his weight from one foot to the other and carefully studied the cake. Well, what remained of the cake. "That's what I don't understand. If you make a lemon whoopie pie, shouldn't it taste like a lemon whoopie pie? And shouldn't everyone be able to taste that it's a lemon whoopie pie?"

"*Jah.*" Millie nodded. "But Sylvie doesn't want you to let anyone else know that the whoopie pies you're eating have a lemon taste." She stopped. Shook her head again. "It's complicated."

"Always is where women are concerned."

She was about to ask him what he meant by that when he spoke again.

"Listen," he said, examining the cakes on the sideboard as if his very life depended on it. "You can plant flowers . . . if you really want it. But I'll buy them. Deal?" He turned toward her then. The light in his eyes was apologetic and sincere.

"Deal."

Why did her heart feel light at the prospect of planting flowers in Henry's yard? It wasn't like he had agreed to stay any longer than he had planned.

"Does this mean you're still leaving come the fall?" she asked, despite herself. She hadn't meant to let the question loose. "Is that still the plan?"

"*Jah*." He turned back and started loading his plate once again. "What other plan would there be?"

"I dunno." She shrugged, acting like it was no big deal when she wished she could call back her words. "You could stay here. In Paradise Valley."

He started to protest, then grabbed another whoopie pie and a napkin instead. He shook his head but didn't reply.

She could see that he was thinking about it. And she wondered where his thoughts had gone. "Tell me," she said. "What do you have keeping you in Oklahoma?"

Chapter Fourteen

Henry's breath hitched in his chest, but he somehow managed to answer with the truest word he could. "Nothing."

Truth was, he had more than nothing in Oklahoma, but nothing that was keeping him there. He would miss his family, his brothers and sisters, his nieces and nephews, but he could go visit. It wasn't that far.

He took his plate over and sat close to the window. He wanted to give the guests a measure of privacy, but he also wanted to have a quiet corner, just him and Millie.

"I was engaged, you know." He said the words as she settled into the chair opposite him.

"*Jah*," she said. His grandfather had told that tale when they had come to fix the leaky sink that didn't really have a leak. But Vern had said no more than that. Just that Henry had been engaged.

"Her name was Anna Kate. I mean, her name is still Anna; she's just not my fiancée anymore." He cleared his throat.

Millie waited patiently for him to continue, but he couldn't until he knew she wanted him to. "What happened?" she asked.

At the look of sadness that took over her expression, he immediately regretted his decision. After what happened to her husband . . .

"She moved," he hurriedly clarified. "She heard about the Mennonites in Belize and what their community is like. Then she got it into her head that was what God wanted for her. So . . . she moved."

"To Belize?" Once again Millie's eyes were roughly the size of the plate he was currently eating off. When he had started loading it with whoopie pies he hadn't thought it large enough, but once he saw it in relation to her surprise, he noticed just how big it was. "That far away? I mean, isn't that in South America?"

"Central America," he gently corrected. "But *jah*, it's a ways off."

"And you didn't want to go?" she asked. Then she shifted uncomfortably in her seat. "I'm sorry. It's really none of my business."

"It's okay." He gave her what he hoped was a forgiving smile. It might do him some good to talk about her. He hadn't said three words about Anna Kate since he had told his family of her new plans and their breakup. Maybe it was time to get some of it out in the open. He took a deep breath and began.

"Tell me again why you're having the meeting here tonight when you just hosted it last week," Millie demanded as she and Sylvie set out the chairs for this week's meeting of the widows group.

"Imogene Yoder called and said her boys are sick. She's worried about leaving them with Katie."

"So neither Imogene nor Katie are coming?"

"Katie's coming. Imogene is not."

Millie nodded. "What does that have to do with having it here at the inn?"

Her aunt waved one hand, as if it were no matter of importance. "She was supposed to host the meeting tonight."

Millie almost asked, *Who? Katie or Imogene?* before she stopped herself. Did it really matter? No. It did not. Her aunt was hosting the meeting again and that was the whole point. Knowing the details about how it came about wouldn't change the fact that, once again, Millie would be invited and hard pressed to turn them down, seeing as how it was being held in the house that served as both work and home.

"So now it's here," she said instead.

Her aunt straightened, smiled happily. "*Jah.*" She said the word with a note of "naturally" in her voice. Where else would they have it?

Millie didn't even bother to try and opt out; she knew any protests she could come up with would be waved aside like a pesky fly. Part of her supposed she should be happy to be included, and she was blessed to have an aunt and friends who cared about her, but the other part of her wanted to simply go upstairs and sleep.

She had heard about pregnant women who fell into depression after they had their babies, but she supposed it might be possible to be depressed before she had hers. What with everything she had gone through. She had vowed to trust God and not get down, but there were days. . . . Today was one of those. Well, it was enough that she wondered if she was truly tired or simply sad. It had been raining all morning. Normally the weather didn't bother her, but perhaps it did today. After all, that was the only change she had made. Or maybe it was one of those days, as they said.

But she figured it would be better for her to be among a bunch of chattering hens than upstairs alone in her room. On the off chance that she really was experiencing some sort of prenatal sadness. So she settled down in one of the chairs off to the side with a plate of vanilla whoopie pies and a glass of milk.

"Have you heard about that woman over in Paradise Hill?" Lillian Lambert addressed the group as a whole. Because Lillian worked in the general store, she got the best gossip and sometimes heard it days before anyone else.

"Which one?" Sylvie asked, as if there were so many questionable women in Paradise Hill that she needed a name.

"Astrid Kauffman," Lillian said with a satisfied nod.

Millie half listened to the chatter.

"Isn't she the writer?" someone asked. Millie thought it was Betsy Stoll, but she wasn't certain. "The romance writer . . ."

Some of the other women muttered their disapproval, while Millie took a big bite of her whoopie pie. But it wasn't vanilla. It was pineapple. She couldn't stop the face she made. Not that it tasted bad. It just didn't taste like vanilla. And she hadn't been expecting that.

"You know what I mean." Lillian must have seen her grimace and misinterpreted Millie's expression. Millie was grateful for that, seeing as how Lillian was the one who'd brought the whoopie pie in question. And there really wasn't anything wrong with it other than Millie had been expecting vanilla. She tried to swallow as Lillian nodded enthusiastically. "You know exactly."

Millie couldn't speak. She had a mouth full of cake and no idea what Lillian was talking about. Yet she gave a small nod, hoping that would get her out of the conversation as quickly as possible.

"Well, now she's calling herself a matchmaker." Lillian sat back with a self-satisfied smile on her face. This was the biggest news to come out of Paradise Hill since they had found out that Astrid Kauffman was writing romance novels on the side and publishing them under the name Rachel Kauffman. Rachel was her middle name and her publisher insisted she use that because it sounded more undeniably Amish than Astrid. Or at least that's what Millie had been told at one of the other meetings she had been wrangled into attending.

"A matchmaker?" Imogene shook her head. She had made it to the meeting, but Katie hadn't. So if Katie wasn't opposed to staying with Imogene's twin boys, Millie could only wonder if Imogene had canceled the gathering at her house because she didn't want to take the time to clean it. Or maybe the time simply wasn't there. Word around town was that her boys had reached "that age." Which for them seemed to be ten. Millie was quickly learning that it was different for all children. And if they had indeed reached "that age," her house could very well be a disaster, seeing as how she didn't have her husband there to back her up against the pair of them.

Millie liked Imogene. She honestly did, but Imogene was almost as docile as Lillian Lambright. Lillian at least seemed to blossom at the widows' meetings. Every time Millie saw her in the variety store, she was noticeably quiet, not raising a protest at whatever her father-in-law demanded. Good thing he was a decent man. Hard, but decent.

"I don't know about that." Betsy frowned.

"You don't know if it's true or you're against match-making?" Imogene asked.

Both," Betsy replied. "But mainly matchmaking goes against God's will, now doesn't it?"

"Does it?" Imogene asked.

"Of course it does," Sylvie replied. Her aunt nodded firmly, as if that was the last word that needed to be said on the subject. "If a matchmaker is trying to get two people together, then God's will would be interfered with."

"Not if it's God's will that the matchmaker matches the two people," Imogene said, but her voice turned up on the end and made it sound more like a question.

"That's ridiculous," Betsy firmly replied. "I don't believe that at all."

But something in her expression made Millie believe that Imogene wished that was the way it was. Imogene Yoder, believer in romance and fairy tales. For Millie, both had been ruined the day her husband fell to his death. She wished she could get back that happiness that had been hers before, that untouchable bubble of God's protection that had been shattered when she was made a widow.

More power to Imogene for keeping that faith, Millie thought. She carefully covered the pineapple whoopie pie with only one bite missing with a napkin to hide it from view. Though she had been raised to clean her plate and not waste food, one bite of the pineapple cake had the baby kicking up a storm. It didn't seem to matter whether she liked it or not, the baby surely didn't.

"No," Sylvie agreed. "Love and attraction. All that should be left up to God and the singings."

Millie wasn't sure what the singings had to do with anything other than that's where most of the couples met and began to date, but other than that . . .

However, her aunt's words brought on a whole other conversation about the singings the women had attended over the years, meeting their husbands, and falling in love. They might not believe in matchmaking, but they did believe in love.

"That's what I'm saying." Her aunt nodded in agreement with herself. "That's the best way to fall in love. Not by having someone manipulate a man or situation so that you meet, or fall in love, or spend time together. Whatever it is."

Murmurs of agreement went up all around the room.

And that was when Millie realized: All her aunt's efforts to get Millie and Henry together were the exact opposite of what Sylvie was professing to the group. And as soon as they cleared out, she'd be talking to her auntie about it. For certain.

Chapter Fifteen

But that time never came. After the gossip session over the matchmaker in Paradise Hill, the women started to eat, and for that Millie was grateful. Their chatter was starting to give her a headache. Or maybe it was the fact that she was clenching her jaw together to keep from confronting her aunt about her dual opinions on matchmaking.

But as the ladies began to munch on the sweets provided, most were dropped back onto their plates with a look Millie was certain she had worn when she bit into the pineapple whoopie pie expecting plain ol' vanilla.

"What—?" Lillian exclaimed, unable to finish the thought.

She didn't have to. Imogene did it for her. "What happened to these pies, Sylvie?"

Sylvie, who hadn't taken one of the pies for herself, reached onto Betsy's plate and snatched the discarded cake from it while Betsy herself not so discreetly spat the bite she had in her mouth into a napkin.

Everyone had stopped eating to watch. Or maybe because they had all taken one of Sylvie's whoopie pies instead of another flavor. This close to the Festival, any little edge was a blessing. A necessary one.

Sylvie took a big bite and immediately exclaimed, "There's nothing wrong with these—" But apparently there was. Sylvie, in an even less discreet move than Betsy, opened her mouth and allowed the bite of not-even-chewed whoopie pie to fall back onto her plate.

"I don't understand," she said, reaching for her coffee. She took a large swig, then another, no doubt to clear the taste from her mouth.

Lillian looked at the offending cake on her plate. "It tastes like you added salt instead of sugar."

Imogene grinned slyly at Sylvie. "Are you forgetting how to bake, Sylvie Yoder?"

"Not at all." Her aunt sat up a little straighter in her seat and smoothed her hands over the bodice of her dress. "I was just making sure you were all paying attention. Don't be thinking that you'll have an edge on me at the Festival. This will not be my entry this year."

Yet Millie couldn't help but wonder what her aunt had on her mind that she'd messed up a recipe she could put together in her sleep.

Millie didn't have time to talk to her aunt about her contradicting views on matchmaking—not okay if someone else was doing it, but perfectly okay to subject her niece to it if she saw fit—but after the salt versus sugar fiasco and the cleanup from the meeting, Sylvie looked so browbeaten that Millie didn't have the heart to confront her.

The following morning when she woke up, her aunt was in a flurry about getting to the hospital. Chester, the little boy who had fallen from the banister, was having surgery to set the broken bone in his arm and Sylvie wanted to be there for the parents.

Neither one of them blamed Sylvie for the accident. Both the parents as well as Sylvie had warned Chester not to slide down the banister, but he had disobeyed and ended up hurt. Still, Millie knew that her aunt wanted to be there to support them. She had naturally comped their room and filed a claim with the insurance provider to absorb any out-of-pocket costs the family might have, but there was nothing like a hospital vigil to show you cared.

So Sylvie had bustled off to the hospital as soon as Millie made it downstairs. For the most part breakfast was done. All Millie had to do was set the table and bring everything out of the warming ovens.

She had wanted to head out to the farm and talk to Henry—after she talked to her aunt of course—but it seemed that both would have to wait.

It was some time after noon before Sylvie came back in.

"Everything's fine?" Millie asked.

"Just perfect." Her aunt smiled. "That little Chester is a trooper. But I think they are going home tomorrow. I told them they could come back and stay another weekend for free."

Of course she did. That was simply her aunt's generous nature.

Millie had spent the morning doing her normal chores, mulling over exactly what she would say to her aunt about her cockamamie matchmaking schemes once Sylvie returned to the inn, but she never found the best way to broach the subject. The truth of the matter was she loved her aunt very much. And she wouldn't do anything to hurt

Sylvie's feelings. Confronting her about Henry and the matchmaking Sylvie had been executing could hurt her feelings. And Millie couldn't have that. Sylvie had taken her in, given her a job, a place to live, and a new direction. If that meant she would have to put up with a few matchmaking attempts between her and a man she considered her friend, so be it. It would be fine. Nothing would come of it. And if she and Henry knew about the plan beforehand, they could simply laugh at it when they were alone and go about their business the rest of the time.

Telling her aunt that she had no intention of getting remarried ever wouldn't serve a higher purpose, so that was something she would keep to herself. She would live, enjoy the time she had to be Henry's friend, and count the days until the baby was born and life would continue on.

"I don't know what happened last night," Sylvie said after they had eaten and made some refreshments for the afternoon—double-checking the salt and sugar containers just to be certain—"but I think it was sabotage."

Millie bit back a chuckle. "Are you sure you just weren't confused? I mean, you've had a lot on your mind lately. What with the Festival coming up and Chester's arm . . ." She trailed off, hoping that her aunt would continue with the things that had been occupying her thoughts lately.

But her aunt wasn't biting. "Nope. It had to be a deliberate attempt to ruin my recipes before the Festival. I think we're going to have to start locking the door all the time now."

"Or maybe we should just lock up the sugar," Millie quipped. But she stopped when she realized her aunt was serious. "You can't keep the doors locked all the time. How are the guests going to get in?"

"We'll get keys made." Her aunt nodded decisively.

"You're going to give the guests keys? What's to stop someone in town from bribing a key from one of them?"

Her aunt hadn't thought of that, Millie could tell. "Then we'll hide a key out front. In the flower planter."

Millie shook her head, at the thought of her aunt's plan as well as to show her aunt the idea wouldn't work. "If the guests know where it is, everyone in town will know."

Sylvie sighed. "I suppose you're right. I guess locking up the sugar is the best option."

"It is not," Millie protested. "It's ridiculous."

"Maybe." Her aunt stopped, thoughtful. "Maybe I'll just put a lock on the kitchen door. Keep the back door locked and that will protect all the ingredients."

"Sylvie." Millie hoped the sound of her name would serve as a warning, but her aunt wasn't listening. Not really.

"It's okay," Sylvie said with a small smile. "We can go back to normal after the Festival."

When it came to Sylvie Yoder, Millie wasn't certain what constituted "normal." Honestly, Millie's life hadn't been her kind of normal since she moved into the Paradise B&B. But it had been interesting.

Still, she decided to head out for a breath of fresh air as soon as she had her aunt halfway convinced that locking up the kitchen wasn't the answer. Of course she was still looking for an answer as Millie trudged off to the stable and brought back Daisy for a buggy trip out to the King farm.

Millie was sure that Henry would get a kick out of the story of what happened last night at the widows' meeting.

Both the salt in the whoopie pies and the matchmaking Astrid Kauffman over in Paradise Hill.

No one knew when the rivalry between the two towns actually started. At least no one Millie had asked. And she had asked several people, from the bishop on down to Lolly Metzger. It seemed that the two towns had been destined to be rivals from the start. From what Millie had learned, the town of New Paradise was formed by an Amish family—the Millers—who came out to Missouri from Paradise, Pennsylvania. Everything was fine for a while; then, when the father died, the two oldest boys— twins Moses and David—argued over who would be in charge of things. Neither one wanted to leave it up to God, so they split the settlement into two different towns. Moses named his part Paradise Springs. To top his brother, David named his town Paradise Hill. And the competition was still going on to this day. To smooth out the rough edges, the locals—mostly Englishers—had taken to calling the whole area Paradise Valley. Because while there were no hill or springs, there was a valley. Just like Englishers to look for the logic in naming places.

Millie was halfway to the farm when she saw a familiar buggy headed her way. She smiled and waved, loving the flash of his teeth as he smiled in return. They were still too far away from each other for her to be able to see his expression, but that flash of white told her that he was smiling. That he was happy to see her too. And for that she was grateful. She was grateful to have found such a good friend in Henry King. It was selfish of her, but she wished she could find a way to convince him to stay past his autumn deadline.

When they got close enough, he waved her to the side

of the road onto a farm lane of packed dirt on both sides with a line of lush green grass down the middle. Millie hadn't been paying close attention to whose farm they were on, just that they needed to pull off to the side.

"Hi," she said, wishing her voice wasn't quite so breathless as she spoke. Maybe he hadn't noticed.

But she had. And she had also noticed that he was a little breathless too as he returned her greeting. "Hi. Where are you headed?"

"To see you."

He seemed surprised and pleased at her answer. "*Jah*? I was on my way to the inn."

"You don't say."

He nodded. "I bought some flowers today. I thought I would come let you know."

It would have been a much shorter trip to walk out to the phone shanty and give her a call at the inn, but he had hitched up his buggy and started into town to tell her in person. The thought warmed her from the inside.

"And you want me to plant them?" She couldn't resist teasing him. "Maybe I've lost interest."

He gave her a mock-hurt look. "Have you?"

She pretended to think about it. "Maybe I need to see them first."

His face split into an infectious smile. "Follow me."

He turned his buggy around and she followed him back out onto the road.

It was a short trip to his house from where they had met on the road. Sure as he had promised, there were pots and pots of flowers sitting to one side of the yard. Snow white impatiens, bright pink petunias, vibrant yellow marigolds.

He had even bought several colors of pentas and a few dusty millers thrown in for a little variety.

"That's quite a load," she said, taking in all the pots scattered around.

He shrugged. "I wasn't sure what to buy, so I got a little of a lot of things. That's what the woman said was good. Then I could—I mean, you can plant combinations to show off their colors the best. Or something like that."

Millie smiled. "That sounds like Geraldine."

Henry's forehead crinkled into a frown. "She introduced herself to me, the woman who helped me, but I don't remember her saying her name was Geraldine."

"Geraldine Lapp. That's who works the flowers at Paradise Lawn and Garden."

A flush of pink was working its way up the column of his neck and into his smoothly shaven cheeks.

"You did go to Paradise Lawn and Garden," she said.

"What would happen if I said no?"

Millie stared at all the plants dotted around. Most were clustered together, but a few had been moved, as if Henry had been trying to decide the best placement for the many different colors and types that he had purchased. "You mean to tell me that you bought these from Fiona Lapp?"

He gave her a sheepish smile that was a second cousin to an apologetic grimace. "I take it they're not kin."

"If they were, neither side would admit it." She shook her head, allowing her gaze to stray over all the plants once more. "This is bad."

He threw up his hands in exasperation. "How was I supposed to know? The other nursery is closer."

She had to give him that one. Because New Paradise had been pretty much split down the middle, there were things in Paradise Hill that would be closer to a farm like Vern King's, which sat on the Hill's end of the Springs.

"Okay, here's what we do. We keep this between the two of us, *jah*? If anyone asks, just don't tell them where you got the flowers. I'm pretty sure Geraldine and Fiona have about the same plants available. So once we get them in the ground, no one will be the wiser."

"How—"

"Just as long as you don't tell them," she admonished.

"Keep quiet," he said. "Got it."

"And for the love of Pete, if you need anything else, longer trip or not, make sure you go to Paradise Springs. We cannot have an all-out feud on our hands."

Henry almost asked what the relationship between Paradise Springs and Paradise Hill was if not an all-out feud, but he refrained. "Springs," he repeated. "Got it."

Millie quietly looked around at the flowers. "Paradise Hill flowers in a yard in Paradise Springs."

"What a disaster," Henry said dryly. "Why can't everyone just get along?"

"Some things just are," she said. "Like the Hatfields and the McCoys."

"Who?" he asked. He had never heard those names before and they sure didn't sound Amish.

She shook her head. "It doesn't matter. Just refrain from telling anyone where you got them. I'll come back out in a day or two and put them in the ground. Surely no one can see the containers from the road."

That was when he noticed them. All the plastic pots the

plants were in had been stamped with bright pink letters, HILL GARDEN SUPPLY. Not exactly subtle.

"So what brings you out today?" he asked, hoping to change the subject.

"Huh?" She tore her focus from the flowers and centered it on him once again. Those blue eyes so steadily trained on him was a bit of a jolt to his system. Or maybe he was just a little out of sorts, seeing as how he was about to start the Amish version of World War III.

"You were on your way out here when I was on my way into town. I told you where I was going. What brings you out here?"

"Oh." She visibly shook herself out of her thoughts, and he wondered where she had gone when she had turned inside herself. "I came out to . . ." She stopped as if she had forgotten why she had made the trip. Or maybe it was wishful daydreaming on his part to think that maybe she had made up an excuse to come out to see him. The thought was nice at least, and it played well in his head. But after October he would be leaving Paradise Springs and would most likely never see Millie Bauman again. "Last night at the widows' meeting—" She stopped again, shuffling over her words until she found what she wanted. "Well, it really became apparent that Sylvie is trying to set us up."

Hadn't they already determined that? Did that mean that Millie had come out to see him because she wanted to see him and not to tell him anything of great importance? There he went again.

"I think my grandfather may be in on it too," he said. The idea had been playing around in his head. Something his grandfather said the other day about Millie being a good cook and taking after her aunt. Why else would he mention such a thing unless he wanted Henry to see Millie in a light of spousal intent. "But you're right. If we make a big deal out of it, things will only get worse. They'll try harder and who knows what will happen from there."

"So you agree we should continue to play along?" Millie asked.

Henry hid his joyous smile and nodded. "I do." And if by playing along he would get to spend all the time he wanted with one Millie Bauman, then so be it. So be it indeed.

Chapter Sixteen

Friday morning Millie got up, refreshed and ready to go out and see Henry again. Just as friends. That's all they were. Friends. But she did so appreciate his company. And she was looking forward to planting flowers and making his yard look nice. He had worked so hard painting the house. And even if he might not be living in Paradise Springs come the fall, the flowers should help the property sell. Well, that was what the English said. She had heard it time and again at the inn.

Not all the farms in the area kept their yards up. Some of the older residents didn't have the energy to perform such tasks, and their children were too busy. There weren't many geriatric citizens in Paradise Valley who lived alone, but there were a few. Perhaps she should go around to see if she could help spruce up their yards and make the community look a little nicer. Not that it didn't look nice. Paradise Springs was one of the prettiest places Millie had ever lived. Or perhaps she should ask the widows club to help with such a chore. It sure beat sitting around all evening talking about the neighbors and whoopie pie recipes, and the neighbors' whoopie pie recipes. More productive anyway.

She sighed as she pulled Daisy out onto the street and headed for the other side of town. She had a feeling that was the point of the meetings. Not necessarily to help the community, but to give the ladies an outlet and an excuse to eat too many desserts. Nothing wrong with that either, she supposed. She wasn't one to judge.

The trip out to the King farm was as nice as it always was. The thought of seeing Henry again made her smile as she drove along. Now she was just being silly.

But when she got to the house, her smile froze on her face, silly or not. All the flowers that had been sitting around in the yard had been planted. Pretty much in all the places she had imagined they would go. Someone had come out and planted the flowers though she had promised to do so. Did Henry not want her planting? She thought they were past that.

She pulled Daisy to a stop in front of the house and hopped down just as Henry came out onto the porch.

"Hello, Millie."

"What happened?" she demanded. Her tone was a little too sharp, but she had been looking forward to this and now it was . . . already done.

He looked confused for a moment, then nodded. "Oh, the flowers. Well, I was afraid that everyone would know I had bought them in Paradise Hill, so I planted them and got rid of the evidence."

"The evidence?" The evidence was right there in the ground, taking root as they spoke.

"The pots they came in. Those bright pink logos could

be seen from the road, and Malinda Beachy seems to drive by every day—sometimes twice—so I didn't think it worth the risk. You know, in case I decide to stay here."

That did it. Her heart gave a quick jump in her chest as her irritation evaporated like dew in an Indian summer. "You're thinking about staying here?"

He shoved his hands in his pockets and shrugged. "I dunno. Maybe. Just keeping the options open, *jah*? If I'm run out of town for buying flowers in Paradise Hill, I won't have the choice at all, now will I?"

Be still, my traitorous heart.

She had read that in one of those romance novels she enjoyed when no one was around. The woman always thought that when she was falling in love with the male character in the book. But it didn't apply here. Not at all. So she didn't know why it had popped into her head. First, this wasn't a book, and second, she wasn't falling in love with Henry King. But her heart was acting up. Maybe she needed an antacid . . .

"I suppose not." Traitorous heart or indigestion, she would like to see Henry stay in town. He was the best friend she'd had since Joshua died and she would be sad to see him go.

But if the flowers were planted, there was no reason for her to remain at the farm. Not really. Yet she supposed if Henry asked her to stay, she would. What would be the harm in sharing a midmorning snack with a friend?

Well, nothing. If she had packed one. But she hadn't, and she had seen the King men's refrigerator and its lack of food.

She supposed she should be going. She was trying

to find the words to tell him she needed to leave when he interrupted her thoughts with a bashful grin and a twinkling look.

"Maybe we could go fishing instead," he said.

"Fishing?"

"You know." He imitated casting a line and reeling it in. "Fishing."

"I know what fishing is," she countered. But a part of her whispered that fishing was a much less strenuous activity than planting flowers. And perhaps he had done this on purpose.

"I know what you're thinking," he said.

"You do?" She wasn't even sure herself what her thoughts were telling her other than she didn't like it.

"This has nothing to do with . . ." He waved a hand in her general direction but didn't say the words. Her condition. "I just thought it might be more fun to enjoy a bit of fishing instead of sweating it out in the yard, planting flowers that won't see another year."

"You really want to go fishing?"

He nodded. "The outside of the house is painted and I'll be starting on the inside next week. That is, if Vern still won't let me help him in the fields."

Millie grinned. "I see a paintbrush and a drop cloth in your future."

"I'm afraid you're right about that. But the present . . . do you see a fishing pole and a picnic?"

And a handsome man to go along with it?

"I suppose," she said with a small grin of excitement.

And that was exactly how Millie Bauman found herself

fishing with Henry King on a fine and sunny Friday morning.

Fishing had never been high on her list of favorite activities. But being with Henry made it fun.

"Are you going to eat what you catch?" she asked him.

He tossed his hook back into the water and gently reeled it in. "If I get anything." They had been on the banks of the wide creek for almost an hour and he'd only gotten one nibble on his line. But the hook didn't set and the fish swam away. Henry had said it was a big one, but Millie had missed actually seeing it, so she would have to take his word for it.

"Uh-huh," she murmured, leaning back against the tree next to the bank and allowing the day to wash over her.

"You don't think I can catch anything, do you?"

"I didn't say that," she countered. But she grinned at him in a way that said she didn't, even when she wasn't at all certain about his talents and skills as a fisherman. It was too good an opportunity to tease him to just let it slip by.

"All right," he said, casting out his line once again. "Let's make a deal. How about you have to clean and cook every fish I catch?"

Her face wrinkled into a disgusted frown. "I don't think so. Gross."

"So you don't know how to clean a fish."

"That has no bearing on the fact that it's a messy, smelly endeavor that I want no part of."

"So you do think I'll catch something."

She smiled at him. "Let's just say it's not a chance I'm willing to take."

"Fine." The line came in and back out again. "I'll clean them, but you have to fry them up with all the fixin's." He stopped for effect, she was certain. "Including hush puppies."

"I can get behind that," she said. "But if that's the case, I'll want you to catch more than a couple so we can have enough for everyone."

"Everyone?" he asked.

"Me, you, Sylvie, and your *dawdi*."

He nodded with a smile. "Everyone," he agreed.

In the end, Henry caught five fish total, but he promised that with the ones he already had in the freezer there would be plenty for them all.

Now they just had to find a time to get together for a friendly fish fry. Millie promised to talk to Sylvie about it when she got home.

Together, they had gathered up all their picnic and fishing supplies and returned to the house.

Vern was just coming in as they were returning. He gave them a questioning look that almost made Millie laugh. Maybe it would have if she hadn't been having these random thoughts about Henry. What a good and honest man he was. How handsome he was with the sunlight glinting off the ginger strands of his hair.

She needed to get ahold of herself. There was nothing between her and Henry and there never would be. Nothing save friendship.

These thoughts and more swirled around in her head, distracting her from the things and people around her. Good thing Daisy knew the way home. The mare was nearly smart enough to take herself back to the inn, then onto the stable for a fresh stack of hay and a brush down. If only she could unhitch herself . . . then Millie would be set. But alas, the horse couldn't do that. So Millie pulled into the drive at the B&B. She unhitched the horse, then walked her down to Stoll's.

She was back again in no time, but the thoughts were still plaguing her. "Plague" was such a negative word. But then, so was "worry." And the thoughts were worrying her, taking up all her mind and not letting go until she realized . . . something . . . but what?

"How was planting flowers?" her aunt asked as she stepped through the back door. At least Sylvie hadn't taken to locking it on the off chance that someone tried to sabotage her whoopie pie ingredients again. Though Millie had a feeling that the mistake had been all on Sylvie's part. She had been distracted lately. As distracted as Millie herself was feeling right at the moment.

"We didn't plant flowers," she admitted. "We went on a picnic."

Sylvie stopped kneading the loaf of bread she was making and wiped her hands on her apron. "A picnic, huh? That sounds like a date."

Millie rolled her eyes. Only her aunt would think such a thing when she had already said time and again that she and Henry were only friends. "Fishing actually. We took a picnic basket in case we got hungry. Very romantic."

"Don't get sassy," Sylvie admonished. "My Andrew and I used to go fishing all the time." Sylvie looked away at nothing, that far-off gaze more telling than her words.

"Well, this wasn't like that," she said. "But he did catch

some fish and you and I are going to cook them for him and Vern. Sound good?"

"Perfect," Sylvie said with a smile. "What else happened?"

"Wouldn't you like to know?" Millie grabbed a muffin from the kitchen worktable and made her way to her room.

She didn't mean to feed her aunt's imagination concerning her and Henry, but she couldn't tell her aunt all of what she and Henry had talked about.

Well, maybe she could; she just didn't want to.

Henry was a sweet man. But if she told her aunt that, Sylvie would take the information and run. Even if it was the truth, Millie couldn't say it to Sylvie. And he was. He cared for his family, his grandfather, and he had been concerned about her. He deserved better than a fiancée who would just walk away.

Millie slipped off her shoes and eased down onto her bed. She was tired. Why did lounging about all day on a pond bank make a person tired? She should feel refreshed.

Her mind did, but her body wanted rest. She set half the muffin on her nightstand and stretched out on the mattress. She sighed as her muscles relaxed. Maybe Henry was right, and she shouldn't be out planting flowers in people's gardens on a whim. Maybe she needed a bit more rest these days . . .

Not that she wanted to admit it. Her mother always said she had a proud, stubborn streak and that it would get her into trouble one day. Millie had never believed her until now. Not the trouble part, but the proud, stubborn streak part. She was determined to make this go on her own. And she was afraid that she was about to find out just what a challenge that could be.

She only had a couple more months before she would have the baby. Truth be told, she was a little frightened by the whole thing. Not what to expect. She knew all the physical aspects of giving birth. It was painful for a time, but labor didn't last forever. It was afterward that concerned her. When she had a new person to care for and look after. Would she be able to make her son or daughter into a good and godly child who would grow up to be a good and godly adult? That was what worried her. Sylvie had promised to help her in all ways, but Millie still missed her husband. More than that, she wasn't supposed to be doing this alone. At least that had never been a part of her plans. Yet God had something different in store for her. Did that mean God thought she could handle it all on her own? She had no idea.

Suddenly Henry's face appeared in her thoughts once again. He would make a perfect husband. She sat up, startled into her realization. He would make a perfect husband, but not for her. He had already admitted that he never thought that he would get married. That was the main reason she had agreed to play along with her aunt's matchmaking—nothing could come of it. But here she was, daydreaming about him. Not giving a second thought to all the realities. She was close to falling in love with the man and she had to do something to stop it.

Chapter Seventeen

That was how Millie found herself on the way to Henry and Vern's first thing the next morning. First thing after breakfast and the cleanup rather. But that was okay. Even though she was as skittish as a newborn colt, she needed to give him time to get up and around, and for Vern to get out of the house before she went out there. Having to explain her visit to Henry was going to be hard enough. Having to tell Vern as well might prove to be next to impossible.

She gave a distracted wave to Malinda Beachy as she passed the woman on the road. Knowing Malinda, she would tell the next person she saw that Millie Bauman appeared to be heading back out to visit with Henry once again.

Not that Malinda had spread rumors about her before, but there was nothing like the present, and Millie supposed that a budding romance would be the best sort of gossip that someone like Malinda could uncover.

Or perhaps she was being a tad paranoid.

She was nervous. Plain and simple. She didn't want to have this conversation with Henry, but she had to. Furthermore, she didn't want to terminate their friendship, but she could see no way around it. He had been hurt in the worst way, betrayed. That would take some time to get over. She didn't need to be falling in love with a man who didn't have enough of his heart left unbroken to love her in return.

She didn't want to be in love at all. She had made up her mind. She was going to raise this baby by herself, live out God's plan right there in Paradise Springs, and that was that. There had been no plans for falling in love. And certainly none to fall in love with a man who wasn't capable of loving her back.

Henry came out onto the porch as soon as she pulled to a stop in front of the house. He was drying his hands on a dish towel, his expression one of pleased surprise. "Millie! Good morning."

She wouldn't let his smile affect her, she told herself as she hopped down from the buggy and took the horse's reins into one hand. She wouldn't be there long enough to tie her to the hitching post.

"Henry King," she said, trying to inject a bit of firmness into her voice. She didn't want him to think that he could change her mind. Because the truth was, he could easily get her to rescind what she was about to say. With little effort at all on his part, and she needed to make him see that it wasn't a possibility at all, right from the start.

He frowned at her, his forehead crinkled into perplexed lines. "What's wrong, Millie?"

She shook her head. Maybe she had come on a little strong, but she needed to be strong to get through this. "I've changed my mind."

The frown deepened and the perplexed lines grew more perplexed. "About?"

"We can't do this." She flopped a hand in front of her, as if that explained everything. "It's not fair."

He shifted and waited for her to continue. Or perhaps he was waiting for her to start making sense.

"We can't pretend to allow your grandfather and my aunt to matchmake between us. What if the community starts to see us as a couple? And everyone starts to invite us places thinking we're a couple? See how wrong that is?"

He crossed his arms and his expression grew shuttered. "No. I don't see anything. What's happened to make you decide this?"

"It doesn't matter," she lied, because nothing had happened. At least nothing she was willing to share with him. She wasn't about to tell him that if she kept this up, pretending to let them throw them together while they built a friendship, soon she would be head over heels in love with him. She couldn't say that. Nuh-uh.

"It does if it's going to cost me your friendship."

She shook her head. "It's not fair," she said again. It was the best defense she had. But she could tell from the stern set of his jaw that he was not willing to accept her answer. And yet what choice did he have?

"Goodbye, Henry." She swung back into the buggy. Well, as much as a woman who's almost seven months pregnant can swing herself anywhere.

She had one foot still dangling out of the carriage when she felt his hands on her waist, steadying her, their warmth comforting and disarming all at the same time. "Turn me loose," she screeched, embarrassed at her own tone. But she had to. She had to do something. She was feeling a little desperate and a whole lot off-balance.

He didn't listen to her, which was probably for the

best, though she wouldn't quite admit it even to herself. True, she had been emotionally off-balance, but she had been physically off-balance as well, leaning to one side as she tried to shift her growing girth into the small buggy opening. Without his help she could have crashed to the ground, baby and all. And though she didn't believe that she would have been hurt in the fall, it was better not to fall at all, *jah*?

She ignored the comforting feeling his hands gave her and managed to wriggle into the buggy. Whoever decided that those openings needed to be that small should have to crawl through it with a ten-pound sack of potatoes tied to their chest. That would fix that little problem. With a huff and a frustrated exhale of air, she flopped down into the seat and gathered the reins.

"Millie?"

His voice came from right beside her, soft, caring, so very Henry that she was almost afraid to turn and look at him. So she decided not to.

"*Jah?*" she asked, her attention centered straight ahead on the spot between Daisy's flickering ears.

"Look at me."

She shook her head, not willing to trust her voice to say the word "no."

"Millie . . ."

"Goodbye, Henry." She flicked the reins and clicked her tongue against her teeth to start the mare. She would not look back, she told herself as the horse ambled toward the road. She would not look back.

And she didn't.

She didn't need to. She knew what he looked like standing there, staring after her, wondering where everything had gone so wrong.

* * *

Just where had everything gone so wrong? Henry
wondered as he watched Millie's carriage roll toward the
road. He could go after her, but what would he say? All
the things that he had already said to her. All the things
she hadn't listened to the first time. No, he wouldn't
repeat them again. Not now. Maybe later. Maybe in a day
or two she would be ready to listen to what he had to say.
But for now, her mind was made up. That much was certain. She wouldn't even look at him!

Henry let out a frustrated growl, grabbed the dish towel
from his shoulder, and stomped up the porch steps and
into the house. Women! Who needed them? He let the
door slam shut behind him with a loud, satisfying whack.

It was just . . . he had thought Millie was different. He
thought what they had was different. They were friends.
How many people got to say that? That they had a good
friend who seemed to understand them better than anyone
else in the world? Most people found that with a spouse.
But they had lost theirs—hers to death, his to the call of
Belize. To find that again was rare. He knew it as sure as
he knew his name. So what had gotten into her that she
had decided it wasn't fair that they would be friends and
their kinfolk could matchmake all they wanted?

It had seemed like a fine plan to him. It had seemed
like a fine plan to her even yesterday. So what had happened?

Henry tramped into the kitchen, unable to sit still. The
dishes were clean and put away. He had finished that right
before Millie pulled up. And thank the good Lord for that.
If he had to handle fragile plates and cups with the way
he was feeling at the present time, they would be eating

off the floor. There wouldn't be an unbroken dish in the house come sundown. He prowled around the table looking for crumbs and mulling over every word she'd said. All ten of them. She might have said a few more than that. But the only ones he could remember were *it's not fair* and *goodbye*. Neither phrase was sitting well with him.

He stopped, exhaled his breath, reminding himself of the ornery bull his brother kept. That was what the beast sounded like. And he like it. Like a beast. Anger, he told himself. But he didn't remember ever being this angry or frustrated in his entire life. Not even when Anna Kate said she was going to Belize, that he could come or they could break off their engagement, but nothing was changing her mind about the trip.

His feet couldn't remain still, not when his thoughts were churning like the sky during a tornado. He began to prowl again. Out of the kitchen and into the living room, around the coffee table and back out through the kitchen. In. Out. He stopped at the bookcase just before the hallway that led toward the two downstairs bedrooms the house boasted. Books. Why had they captured his attention?

Not that there were many books there. A family Bible, a copy of a Bible study guide, and of course the standard copy of *Martyr's Mirror*. But there were a couple there that he supposed must have belonged to his *mammi*, though she had been gone for almost as long as Henry could remember. There was a book on roses, one on organic gardening, and a couple of cookbooks. Even one called *Prize Winning Breads*. He pulled it from the shelf, not sure why it had captured his attention above all else, but grateful for the small distraction.

He flipped through the pages, noting the different kinds of bread offered—fruit breads, sweet breads, cheesy breads, corn breads. Then he found it. A two-dollar bill tucked between the pages. He pulled the bill out and looked at both sides. He had forgotten. His grandmother used to give him and his brothers two-dollar bills when they came up from Oklahoma to visit. It wasn't often, but often enough that Henry remembered. And this bill, stuck here between these pages, seemed like a sign from his grandmother, long dead but not forgotten.

He smiled, settled the bill back between the pages. It had been a sign. A sign to calm down? A sign to trust God? Believe? Or perhaps a sign that he needed to keep going? How was one supposed to know how to interpret signs?

Without shelving the book, he walked into the kitchen and set the book, still open to the place where he had found the bill, on the kitchen table. Bread. Bread sounded good. He and Vern had been eating crackers for weeks, ever since Johnny B fell. Not that Henry was complaining. Johnny B might not ever walk again, and Joy definitely had her hands full being a widow with four children and now one of them potentially crippled for life. Henry couldn't be complaining about having to eat crackers instead of bread.

But he could make some. The thought was almost soothing. Maybe it would have been had he not been so out of whack after Millie's' unexpected visit.

Jah. That's what he would do. He would bake some bread. Whatever bread was there on the pages where his grandmother had tucked the special two-dollar bill, no doubt part of her collection to give to her grandsons when they came to visit next.

And in baking the bread she had marked, it would be like she was there with him.

That was a comforting thought.

Or perhaps he was slowly losing his mind over Millie and this second betrayal.

Or maybe it was just bread.

Vern stopped at the back porch and knocked the dust from his boots. It was something Helga had made him do each day when he was out in the fields and he had never broken the habit. Ah, well. He supposed it was even more important now that he was the one sweeping and mopping.

He smiled a little at himself. Henry was doing most of the cleaning these days, but Vern wouldn't push it with his grandson. He knew that Dale had sent the boy here to make sure he came to Oklahoma in the fall, a move Vern had no intention of making. But there was no sense in aggravating Henry over Dale's wishes. So he continued to knock his boots against the porch rails before going inside.

It was lunchtime and Henry was supposed to be painting. He wanted to get the inside of the house painted, stating that it would sell better if it was freshened up. Vern supposed it would, had he been of a mind to sell the house. But seeing as how he wasn't planning on moving any time soon—at least not until the Lord called him home—Henry's interior painting was for Vern and Vern alone. Not that it didn't need a sprucing up. It did, badly. In fact, Vern couldn't remember the last time the entire inside of the house had been painted. But that had been all Helga. She'd told him when she wanted something done and he had done it. Wasn't that how marriage was supposed to work? Well, it had been many years since she had been there to tell him that the walls needed paint, so it had been many years since they had gotten any.

Vern opened the door and stepped inside expecting to smell the sharp odor of fresh paint, but all he smelled was . . . yeast?

He made his way through the mudroom and into the kitchen, where he stopped dead in his tracks. "Have we been robbed?" he asked, looking to his grandson.

"Ha ha," Henry said wryly.

But Vern wasn't joking, Something had definitely happened. And whatever that something was, it surely wasn't good. Not with the mess that was before him. Vern wasn't sure what had the most flour covering it—Henry, the floor, or the countertops.

"What happened in here?" Surely something big. A struggle, a break-in. Maybe bears or racoons. He'd have to check the doors and the windows and the other various ways vermin could enter the house and wreak such havoc.

"I'm baking bread."

Vern stopped. "What?" He must have heard wrong. But when he looked at his grandson, he noticed that Henry, under all that flour, was wearing one of Helga's old aprons, the kind she kept there in the kitchen for when she was dressed and didn't want to get anything on her good apron. A cooking apron, she had called it. He hadn't thought of that in years. And the memory brought a small smile to his face.

"It's not a joke," Henry said. "We can't rely on these women to take care of such things for us and I'm tired of eating crackers."

"I see," Vern said, even though he didn't. He honestly didn't have any idea what Henry was talking about, but he didn't think now was a good time to point that out. Henry seemed a bit . . . frantic. And there didn't seem to be a spot in the kitchen that wasn't dusted with at least one layer of flour. At least now he knew where the smell of yeast had come from.

He cleared his throat. "You do this often, son?"

Henry shook his head. "This is the first time."

And if what Helga said about baking bread was true, that the more practice a baker had, the better the bread would turn out, Vern figured they'd still be eating crackers with their supper that evening. But that wasn't something he was willing to say to Henry yet either. All in good time.

He grabbed an apple out of the bowl on the table and eased back out the way he had come in.

But he had been wrong. Henry's bread did turn out. In fact, it was downright tasty. Just crispy enough on the outside to make it perfect for sopping up any juices left in their bowls, and just tender enough on the inside that the butter soaked in just right.

"You just might turn out to be a fair to middlin' baker there, son," he teased that evening.

Henry grunted.

Vern couldn't tell if the noise was in agreement or if it was just a noise, so he waited for Henry to continue. When he didn't, Vern sighed, put down his spoon, and eyed his grandson across the table. "What's got you so tied up in knots?" he finally asked.

Henry dropped his spoon with a clatter that made Vern jump in his seat. That noise alone probably took five years off his life. Five years he really didn't have to spare.

"Millie." Henry growled her name, then he pushed back from the table, his chair falling behind him with a sharp bang.

This time Vern was ready. "Millie?" he asked.

"She came out here today," Henry started, and Vern didn't mean to, but he allowed his gaze to look around the kitchen. Henry had gotten up most of the mess from his afternoon of bread baking, but Vern couldn't say that the space was clean. And if Millie came out, surely there was a container somewhere full of delicious whoopie pies hidden among the clutter. When he realized what he had done, he quickly switched his attention back to his grandson. Henry was obviously hurting, and Vern needed to be sensitive to that fact. Even if there were whoopie pies involved.

"And that's a bad thing?"

Henry closed his eyes and shook his head. "Not that she came out here, I suppose. But when she pulled up, she told me that we couldn't be friends any longer."

Vern frowned. Something was definitely wrong. But he would need to know more if he was going to be able to determine what really happened between the pair. Surely it wasn't as cut and dried as Henry was implying.

"She came inside, though," Vern said.

"She barely got out of her buggy. Stood right out there in the yard and said it wasn't fair for us to pretend to be thrown together by you and Sylvie, and we couldn't be friends."

Uh-oh. If she said that . . . "What do you mean, thrown together by me and Sylvie?" Better play dumb on this one until he knew for certain what was really going on.

Henry shook his head and gave him a grin, or maybe it

was a grimace. Or maybe his supper was upsetting his stomach. Hard to tell really. "It's okay. You don't have to pretend. Millie and I figured out what you and Sylvie were up to days ago."

"What we're up to?" One last attempt at pretending to not know what he was talking about.

"Millie and I know that you and Sylvie were trying your hand at matchmaking between the two of us. We thought we'd play along. After all, we enjoy each other's company and seem to get along fine. But then she came out here today and said that she had changed her mind. Not only does she not want to play along, she doesn't want to be friends either. And for the breath of me, I can't figure out what happened. Yesterday everything was fine."

Vern gave an understanding nod. It had been many years—decades even—since he had gone through pregnancies with Helga, but he knew that growing a baby could wreck a woman's thoughts. Sometimes they were fine and others . . . not so much. "It's just the . . ." He thought about how to say it. Babies and the affairs of women were not something men talked about. So he could find no words. As Henry waited for him to continue, Vern held up one hand in front of him and arched it over and down, mimicking the size and shape of Millie's belly. That should do it.

"And then what?" Henry asked. "She's going to be—" He stopped, performed the same arch Vern had executed. "—for a while to come now. Are you saying we won't be able to be friends until after . . . ?" He trailed off, no doubt out of proper words and hand gestures.

"Nah." Vern waved a hand, as if erasing the thought.

"Give her a day or two," he said. "She'll be back to herself in no time." Which might or might not be the truth. But one thing it would do: It would stall Henry from doing anything else and give Vern time to run into town and find out from Sylvie what was going on. Heaven above, he hadn't made this many trips into Paradise Springs without a list in his hand since he had been running around. And then he'd had a car.

For a moment Vern thought Henry might contradict him, or at the very least say something more on the matter; then he straightened his chair and stalked toward the kitchen door. "I'm going to bed." Then he disappeared on the other side of the doorway.

Vern sat and listened as Henry clomped up the stairs and into the main bedroom at the top. Vern had given up sleeping up there a few years ago. No sense climbing a steep staircase if there was no need. So he had moved his things to the bedroom at the end of the hall and called it good.

He heard the water run, then the squeak of the mattress springs, and realized his grandson was serious. He really was going to bed, and with the sun still well above the horizon.

No matter. Vern popped the last of the bread into his mouth, then took their dishes to the sink as he chewed. He'd have to go into town on Monday, he thought. Unless he could find a way to talk to Sylvie after church the next day. He needed to find out what was happening. If anything else had happened, or if perhaps Millie had said something about whatever mysterious event even took place between her niece and his grandson.

But for now the dishes needed to be done and the kitchen needed to be straightened and things put back where they went. But in all his cleaning, he didn't find the longed-for container of whoopie pies. And that was when it really hit him. This was more serious than he had even realized before.

Chapter Eighteen

But Vern's trip into town on Monday produced no results. He hadn't been able to talk to her on Sunday after church because the two women weren't at the service. He had asked around and discovered that they had gone over to Adrian to Millie's home church for the service. And he had known that it had been an impulse trip. Otherwise they would have said something at some time during the weeks leading up to the change.

So a trip to town on Monday had been required, but Vern knew no more now than he had before. At least now Sylvie knew to be watching for something. She might not know now, but women were chatty things. Sooner or later Millie would surely tell her aunt what had gone wrong, and then he and Sylvie would know how to get the pair back to being friends. He hoped anyway.

After all, there was only so much bread a man could eat.

Now those were words he'd never thought would be a part of his vocabulary, but there they were.

Three days had passed since Millie had come out to the farm—without whoopie pies—and told Henry that they couldn't be friends. That was three days—well, two, discounting Sunday as a nonwork day—that Henry could have been painting the inside of the house. Vern might not be interested in moving, but he was extremely interested in having his home updated. But what had his grandson been doing? Baking bread. Lots and lots of bread. Banana bread, yeast rolls, potato bread, zucchini bread—who even knew there was such a thing?—and onion cheese bread. All of it incredibly tasty with their canned soup and chili, or even their coffee in the morning.

That was when Vern wished that Henry had run across a supper cookbook instead of the one containing bread recipes.

Not that he wasn't grateful for the food he had. He was. But a nice chicken casserole or a pot of Helga's special *yumasetti* would really have hit the spot with some of those yeasty dinner rolls.

"I have a confession to make," Vern said over their quiet supper on Tuesday evening. He wasn't sure why he was bringing this up now, but once he said the words, he couldn't call them back.

Henry looked up from his bowl, waiting for him to continue. The boy hadn't said more than two words since Saturday when he'd stomped around the house because Millie said they couldn't be friends.

"I played along with Sylvie because I thought if you and Millie fell in love, you would want to stay here." He took a drink of water and waited for Henry to protest.

"*Jah*?" he said instead.

"*Jah*, you know. You would move up here and be able to help me, and your *dat* wouldn't be able to say anything about it."

"Dat is planning on you returning with me in the fall."

Vern let out a breath that sounded a little like a snort. "Dale can't always get his way." That boy always walked around as if the world was owed to him. Vern never could figure out where such an attitude came from when Dale had been raised to be a kind and humble Amish man.

Henry shook his head. "Tell him that."

"I'm telling you. I have no intention of leaving Missouri. Not in the fall or the spring or anytime. I was born in Missouri and I plan on dying here as well."

"Poetic," Henry commented and turned back to his supper. He really had a chip on his shoulder these days. "I'm getting the house ready to sell."

"You've been doing nothing save baking bread for nigh on a week now."

Henry stopped. That was one statement he couldn't argue with, and Vern wondered if the bread baking would cease the following day so Henry could start painting once again. No matter. Bread or paint. He wasn't moving. "*Jah*, I suppose."

Vern gave a quick dip of his chin, then wiped his bowl clean with his last little hunk of bread. "I just want to make sure we understand each other," he said.

Henry nodded. "*Jah*," he replied. "Of course we do."

As one week slipped into the next, Sylvie became increasingly worried about Millie. She had never seen her niece so . . . moody. And every time she thought about asking her what the problem might be, she dismissed it herself as the side effects of her pregnancy. But still Sylvie worried.

It seemed that Millie was sleeping more, eating less,

and barely leaving the house. Of course it didn't help that there was a nonchurch Sunday in the mix, but even then . . .

And Millie hadn't changed her mind about not being friends with Henry. Sylvie wasn't sure exactly what all that entailed—or maybe what it didn't entail—but one thing was certain. Millie hadn't been the same since her last trip out to the farm.

She needed to do something, Sylvie decided. But what?

She had tried several times, including an attempt the night before, to get Millie to talk about whatever was bothering her, but Sylvie couldn't get a straight answer. At least not one that made sense.

Millie only had a couple of months, maybe even a little less, and the baby would be here. Sylvie supposed that might have something to do with her mood. Motherhood was a big step, single parenthood an even greater one. She must be missing her husband, Sylvie decided.

It only made sense. Millie was thinking about Joshua, wishing he would be there to see his baby born. God's will could be hard to understand and sometimes even harder to accept, but mooning over something that could never be wasn't good for anyone. Sylvie's *mammi*, Millie's great-grandmother, used to say that worry during pregnancy would cause birthmarks. Now, Sylvie wasn't so sure that was even possible, but there was no sense in taking chances, now was there? And so she decided one more time to try to talk to her niece.

Sylvie gathered up a steaming cup of tea sweetened exactly right and a vanilla whoopie pie, one of the batch she had made especially for Millie. The girl claimed vanilla to be her favorite, and Sylvie was anxious to get

Millie to eat a little more. Nope, she wasn't above bribing her with sweets.

"Millie?" She knocked on the door to Millie's room. It was Tuesday, and the widows' group meeting that night was at Lillian Lambright's house. Lillian had willingly volunteered. So willingly that it seemed a little desperate, like she didn't want to be alone in her own house. Of course she wasn't alone, but everyone knew that her last daughter, Esther, would be marrying Mark Esh soon enough. They hadn't officially stated their intentions, but it was understood that it was part of their plans. Sylvie supposed that Lillian was looking around her house and seeing how it would be when it was empty.

Mark and Esther liked to go for drives and walks and anything else that might get them out of the house and into nature. Mark had no formal training, but everyone knew that had he not been Amish, he would have gone to school to become a veterinarian. As it was, he raised horses and was the first one anyone called before calling the actual English vet. Mark would work for a sack of potatoes and was always willing to help, simply for the love of the animals. If a situation was beyond his expertise, the animal's owner would call the real doctor, but only after Mark had deemed it necessary.

Not that any of that mattered right then. Sylvie just needed to concentrate on getting Millie up and out of the house. Which was a bigger chore than it sounded, because she was having to talk Millie into going to the widows' meeting that evening. Still, out of the house was better than moping, *jah*?

Sylvie knocked again and listened for any signs that Millie was awake and stirring behind the door.

Suddenly it was opened and Millie was standing there, looking sadder today than she had the day before.

"I brought you some tea." Sylvie held up the tray on which she had placed the tea and the whoopie pie. Now that she looked at the offering, she wished she had picked a flower or two to add to the arrangement. It would have made it look cheerier by far. But it was too late for that now.

Millie smiled, though the motion didn't reach her eyes. Those blue orbs looked as sad as ever.

"Can I come in?" Sylvie asked.

Millie stood to one side so she could enter.

Sylvie gave her niece a smile and stepped inside. She tried not to stare at the mess around her. She had never seen Millie's room look so . . . cluttered. Shoes on the floor, dresses and aprons slung over the chair that sat in the corner of the room. But she told herself not to be alarmed. This was just another way of Millie expressing how bad she was hurting.

"I made vanilla pies," she said in her most tempting voice. "Just for you." She set the tray down on the end of the bed and turned to face her.

"*Danki*, Auntie," Millie said, though her voice seemed rusty and choked.

"Millie," Sylvie started. "Do you want to talk about it?" She made her tone as caring as possible, sympathetic and open. She hoped that her vague question would at least help Millie tell her what was weighing on her. It was obvious something had gotten her down.

"Is it Joshua?" she finally asked. Millie hadn't answered her previous question and Sylvie thought it best to probe a little more.

Millie frowned. "Joshua?" She said his name as if she had never heard it before.

"Your Joshua," Sylvie clarified. "You've been so down in the dumps lately; I was worried that you were missing Joshua. The baby's coming soon and it would be hard to say you didn't wish he could be here for the birth." She stopped. "Not here," she continued, pointing to the floor. "But downstairs at least." *Alive*, she silently added.

"You think I'm missing Joshua?"

"You aren't?" Sylvie asked, her tone a bit more shocked than she wished.

"Well, *jah*, I suppose. But I've made peace with the fact that he's gone. Being pregnant and widowed, that's just all part of God's plan for me."

Sylvie smiled at her niece's plucky attitude. She was a strong one, her Millie. But if Joshua wasn't the problem, then what?

"Henry," Millie burst out, as if Sylvie had asked the question aloud. Or maybe she had. No matter now.

"Henry?" Sylvie asked. "Henry King?"

"Yes." Tears started to slide down her face as she sank onto the bed next to the tray Sylvie had brought in. The cup clattered against its saucer, tea spilling over the sides and onto the small plate holding the whoopie pie. Millie seemed not to notice as she picked up the little cake and started to eat it. "I mean, he's a good man, but I can't risk everything not knowing how he feels. You know what I'm saying?" she asked around the second bite of whoopie pie.

Sylvie nodded, though she wasn't entirely sure she was hearing her niece correctly. It almost sounded like

Millie was falling in love with Henry. And if that were the
case . . . that would be good. Better than good. Fantastic.

Well, fantastic if she could get the two of them talking
once again.

"But he has his own broken heart," Millie continued,
shoving the last bite of whoopie pie into her mouth. "Are
there any more of those?" she asked, her sad eyes now
blazing with an emotion Sylvie was a little afraid to name.

"There are downstairs," Sylvie said. "Would you like
to go down?"

But Millie was already off the bed and marching to the
door with an urgency only found in pregnant women
needing to pee. Except she was needing to eat, clear her
head, work things out. And maybe to pee, Sylvie thought
as she saw Millie slip into the bathroom at the bottom of
the stairs.

"Be right out," Millie called as she shut the door behind
her. Oh, the joys of a baby sitting on your bladder, Sylvie
thought with a smile. It was a good problem to have.

Sylvie could only hope that this pit stop didn't take
away Millie's momentum. They were finally getting to the
bottom of her problems. And if Sylvie was right . . .

The toilet flushed, the water ran, then Millie was back
again and once more striding toward the kitchen.

As promised, the whoopie pies were sitting on the table
in a plastic container, ready to go to the meeting that
evening.

Millie popped open the lid of the container and took out
another pie. She set the lid back on top but didn't bother
to seal it back down. Instead she took a big bite and paced
around the table. Muttering about friendships and

broken hearts. Sylvie listened without interruption. She even took a vanilla whoopie pie—a boring flavor even when she was the one making them—from the container and nibbled on it while Millie wandered about.

She wanted to ask questions, but she didn't want to throw her niece off her tirade. She just listened and hoped that Millie eventually said something that made sense and explained her behavior of the last two weeks. She muttered on about friendship and broken hearts, much as she had upstairs.

"And we know that you and Vern were trying to build a romance between us," she said, turning on her aunt with sudden clarity.

"What?" Sylvie put on her most innocent look, but Millie was having none of it.

"Don't even try to pretend. It was obvious from the start. 'Sit out here on the porch and eat these whoopie pies so I'll get more guests,'" she said mockingly in a voice eerily like Sylvie's own.

"But I did get more guests from that." She didn't mean to sound so defensive. Especially not when what she was saying was true. She *had* gotten more guests.

But what Millie was saying was also true. It had been a convenient excuse to have the two of them spend time together.

"And then the trip to Honest John's. And the broken sink."

"But—" Sylvie started, but was quickly cut off.

"It was never broken. Admit it."

"It was never broken," Sylvie managed to say. Though she didn't want to. Why admit her defeat? All she had wanted was for her niece to be happy. That wasn't so much for an aunt to wish for.

"And then all that about matchmaking over in Paradise Hill. You're lucky I didn't call you out right then and there," she continued.

"I—" Sylvie started once again, even though she had no idea what was supposed to come next. Everything Millie was saying was true and there really was no defense against the truth except the truth itself.

"Against God's will, my backside."

"I just want you to be happy," Sylvie finally managed.

That seemed to take some of the air out of Millie. "You think I'm unhappy?"

"Look at you. You've hardly eaten a thing." Except half the whoopie pies she had baked for tonight's meeting. "You've been moping around for weeks, depressed, sad, angry."

"I wasn't any of those things before you started meddling in my life," Millie said.

Another truth Sylvie didn't have an argument against.

"I didn't mean to meddle," Sylvie said, her voice smaller than she had ever heard it. And she had heard it plenty.

"But you did. And now everyone's unhappy."

Sylvie wouldn't go that far. Not everyone was unhappy. Just Millie.

But that was enough. She had to do something. All she had wanted was for her niece to be happy and she had gone and blown that to pieces.

Millie's pacing and ranting continued clear up until the time for Sylvie to leave for the meeting. But she didn't ask the young woman to attend. She had a feeling Millie needed a break from her just then.

But in the end, it wasn't what Millie *said* that was so important, but rather what she *didn't say*. One thing she made so perfectly clear she could have written it out on the kitchen chalkboard.

Millie Bauman was in love with Henry King.

Chapter Nineteen

The minute Sylvie laid eyes on Vern, she knew what her niece had been talking about. Millie might have been missing Henry, but Sylvie had been missing Vern. Even if she had only now realized it. It had been two weeks since she had seen him and he was a sight for sore eyes.

But it was a bit shocking to realize that you missed someone you hadn't even known you cared about until that moment. And she hadn't . . . realized that she cared for Vern. And she did. But this visit wasn't about her and Vern. It was about Millie and Henry.

Vern waved as he loped down the porch steps toward her buggy. Then she started when she realized that she was sitting staring when she ought to be climbing down and greeting him in return.

"Long time, eh?" he said as he grew near her.

"*Jah*." And it had been. A long two weeks, with her trying to figure out what was wrong with Millie and what she could do about it. But now that she knew . . .

"What brings you out—?"

"I think Millie is in love with Henry," she blurted out.

Not exactly the way she had thought to bring up the subject, but what's done was done.

A large grin split his weathered yet still handsome face. "That's good, because I think he might be in love with her as well."

"She's moping around the house. Only seems to get out of bed when she has to."

"He's moping around, baking bread all day long. If this keeps up, I'm going to have to start growing wheat."

"Baking bread?" She wasn't sure she'd heard that right. A man—an Amish man—baking bread? Why, that was almost unheard of. She knew some English men liked to cook, and that some even went as far as baking, and she had heard of a few Amish men in more progressive communities who had taken to trying their hand at kitchen chores, but she had never known any man who actually had. She wasn't sure how she felt about it, to be honest.

"He's not half bad," Vern continued. "His corn bread ain't as good as Helga's—nor yours," he continued with a grin in her direction. "But it ain't half bad."

"Vern."

"*Jah*?"

"Focus."

He nodded.

"If they're in love, what happened?" she asked, more to herself than to him.

"More than that," he added. "What are we going to do about it?"

Like she had the time to be coming up with plans. That weekend was the Whoopie Pie Festival. She had ingredients to gather, pies to make, a blue ribbon prize to win. But this was Millie they were talking about. Millie who had suffered so much. Millie who deserved so much better than she asked for.

But Sylvie's mind could hold only so many thoughts at once. "I can't concentrate on this right now," she said. She only had three days until the competition, and with as much boasting as she had done in the past year, she had to take the prize home or she would be suffering for the next twelve months until she had the chance to prove herself once again. Not that not winning was even an option. "You think about it. I'll give it some thought. We'll meet back up next Monday to discuss it. *Jah*?"

"*Jah*." He gave a quick nod.

She turned to get back into her buggy and head to the inn before Millie realized she had been gone too long for a quick trip to the grocery store.

"Say, Sylvie . . ."

She hoisted herself into the seat, grabbed the reins, and turned her attention to him. He really was a handsome man. Kind too. A little ornery. But show her one Amish man of his age who wasn't. It sort of came with the territory, as if they had lived enough life that they deserved to have a mischievous streak. "*Jah*?"

"You wouldn't happen to have any of those whoopie pie rejects with you, would ya?"

"Vern King," she primly started. "Are you insinuating that some of my efforts are below standard?"

His eager expression turned into one of horror. "Of course not. It's just that Millie had been bringing out the ones you were experimenting on and I thought maybe . . ."

She shot him an indulgent smile and held up the container that had been resting on the bench seat next to her.

"I might have a few. Though I was planning to take them to the roadside stand."

There was a community stand that everyone used to hawk their wares on the honor system. This time of year, when Sylvie was baking more than even her guests could eat in an attempt to nail down her final recipe, she would individually wrap the cakes and take them to the stand. Helped pay for the ingredients and kept even more extra pounds from hitting her hips. Of course when everyone found out that she was doing this, the competition immediately started buying up her pies in an effort to get prior knowledge of her plans. Well, they had that first year. The only year she had lost in the last decade. Now they accused her of planting false recipes at the stand to throw them off. Maybe. Maybe not. But they were acting no better. But, she had decided, it seemed all was fair when it came to love and whoopie pies. And this was both.

He smacked his lips together. "How about a trade?"

"A trade?"

"Some of Henry's bread for that container you got there."

She nodded. That sounded fair enough. She waited in the buggy as he jogged into the house and returned with a crusty loaf of bread wrapped in a towel. She handed him the container.

"Good trade," he said appreciatively.

She harrumphed. It was a good trade, but she was a shrewd enough businesswoman not to let him know that she knew it. Somehow she felt it was in her best interest to act as if he got the better of the deal. "That's all well and good, Vern King," she said. "But remember, we need a plan. And the sooner the better."

* * *

And though she said she wouldn't be able to concentrate on coming up with a plan until after the Festival, she couldn't help thinking about it as she wrote out her grocery list for the bake-off. And she thought about it some more as she gathered up all her pans and organized everything for Friday. Like all the other competitors, she would bake on Friday, knowing that the judges could stop by at any time for a spot check. The check was to keep things fair. The rules committee had thought to have all the contestants take pictures of themselves baking to prove completion, but a couple of years later they decided it was too easy to fake pictures when they caught one of the bakers trying to pass off store-bought cakes as their own. It had happened so long ago that no one remembered whether it had been an Amish woman or an English one, though both sides now claimed it was the other. At any rate, the judges would randomly select four or five contestants to visit to ensure that they had indeed baked the whoopie pies in their own kitchen. And that was fine with Sylvie. She knew enough not to leave any of her secret ingredients out where just anyone—judges included—could see them. A person couldn't be too careful where blue ribbons were concerned.

So Sylvie prepared and contemplated and wondered again and again how she and Vern could get Henry and Millie together in the same room long enough for them to realize they missed the other and were really in love. And who really knew how long that was?

She didn't have an answer Friday morning when she began to bake. Nor did she have one Friday afternoon when the judging staff stopped by. Nor Friday evening, when the committee picked up her entry, giving her the corresponding number to wear at the next day's Festival and taking her cakes away for judging.

By Saturday, the constant thinking about Millie and Henry mixed with the excitement over the day's arrival had given her a headache.

"Are you ready?" Millie asked, popping her head into Sylvie's bedroom.

"In a minute." She rubbed the spot between her eyes and wished she had a headache reliever.

"You okay?" Concern filled Millie's voice.

"I'm fine." She gave her niece a wan smile.

"That didn't look fine." Millie eased into the room. "Is there anything I can do?"

Sylvie shook her head. "No. It's nothing this afternoon's announcement can't cure." Well, that and a plan on how to get Millie and Henry together once again. But she couldn't add that last part. Millie had become suspicious enough these last few days. Her niece had noticed how preoccupied Sylvie had been and started asking questions. Sylvie had managed to put her off a bit, telling her that she was excited about the competition—not a complete lie, but not the whole truth either.

"How do I look?" she asked, stepping back so Millie could see her from head to toe.

"Fantastic."

Sylvie smoothed her hands down her best dress. Everyone said the blue complemented her eyes and complexion. And she told herself that she had worn it only because she was determined to look good when she accepted her blue

ribbon, not because it was her best color and she would
be seeing Vern later. Not in the least.

"Are you ready?" Millie asked.

Sylvie held out one arm. "Let's do this."

The Festival was barely farther than their front door.
As soon as they stepped out of the B&B, they were surrounded by a crowd on its way downtown, which was a
fancy way of saying down a little ways on Main Street.

The city sectioned off the five blocks of Main from the
post office down to the park. Each side of the street was
lined with booths. One side held games like a bean bag
toss and basketball shooting along with balloon twisting
and face painting. The other had rows of tables set up
where local vendors could sell their goods and services.

Unlike at other state fairs Millie had been to, the
products were all homemade or homegrown and not of
the commercial variety, which only added to the Festival's
charm.

At the park—which also served as the town square—
booths had been set up with everything from one where
men could buy kisses to a dunk tank where the English
high school principal waited for his students to hit the
target and send him into the water.

"I didn't even know there were this many people in
Paradise Springs," Millie said in awe as they walked
through the area.

"Some are from out of town."

She didn't say as much, but she knew that some had to
be from neighboring Paradise Hill. They came over for the
Springs' whoopie pies, but then, the Springs' residents

went over for the Fall Festival they held at the Hill each year. Not that either side would admit it.

Sylvie loved both festivals, though she didn't dare enter a competition at the other town's festival. That sounded too much like trying to start a war between the two towns.

"What time is the announcement of the winners?" Millie asked. She knew, but she felt like she needed to occupy her aunt's thoughts today. Sylvie was abnormally jittery, even for such a special day.

Briefly she wondered if something more was going on, but she pushed the thought aside. Her aunt had been all about the whoopie pies for the last couple of weeks. What other thoughts could have occupied her mind when the tasty little cakes and their coveted blue ribbon were all she could talk about?

"Two," her aunt replied.

It was barely ten. They had served breakfast at the B&B and hustled everyone out into the fresh morning air. Like hurrying anyone was really necessary. Even their English guests were ready to get to the Festival.

"That gives us a lot of time to look around," Millie said.

"Are you going to be all right?" Sylvie asked with a worried glance at Millie's belly. She had hit that point where she looked as if she might fall forward if a large wind gusted through. And she had been tired a lot lately, but she had gotten up this morning with a renewed vow to have a wonderful day and not let her feelings for Henry get in the way of the infectious joy the Festival brought to the town.

She gave her aunt a large though genuine smile. "I'm going to be just fine."

She would be the first to admit that she had been a little

melancholy lately, but she had been shocked—no, more
than shocked—to realize she was on the edge of falling
in love. And not with just any man, but a man who didn't
have a heart to give in return. A man who had no plans of
being in town past the harvest.

It took a while to realize that she was mistaken. Her
falling in love wasn't possible. Joshua had only been gone
six months, leaving her pregnant and dealing with emotions she had never experienced before. In short, she was
confused. She had only imagined that she was falling for
Henry.

Not that he wasn't a man she could fall for. Any woman
worth her salt would gladly fall for a man like Henry
King. His Anna Kate being the exception. And the only
reason Millie lumped her in with worthy women was Anna
Kate's willingness to help others. That had to count for
something, even if she was clueless when it came to love.

So after weeks of avoiding him, Millie was ready to
face him. She would have to eventually anyway. She was
fairly certain that she would have to see him at church the
next day. She didn't think it would be possible to convince
her aunt to return to Adrian a second time without a better
explanation than *just to visit*. Millie had pulled herself
together, gotten out her second-best dress—the first
reserved for church the following day—and headed off
to the Festival determined to have a wonderful time all
the while not worrying about Henry King.

"If you're sure. I don't want you to tire yourself out."
Sylvie's forehead puckered into a worrisome frown. "You
can take a break after lunch if you like. Go back to the inn
and rest. I'll send for you before the judging."

Millie shook her head. "I'll be fine. And if I need to rest, you'll be the first to know. Now . . ." She gazed out at the tables, booths, games, and other fun activities spread out before her. "What shall we do first?"

First ended up being face painting. Sylvie had a puppy face complete with black nose and pink tongue painted on her face, while Millie was torn between the rabbit and the butterfly. She felt almost a little silly, considering that most of the patrons of the booth were young, like, young-young. Eight and under sort of young, but there were a few others who decided to join in. But when Rufus Metzger, the local beekeeper, pushed his mother's wheelchair to the booth so she could have her face painted . . . well, what excuse did Millie have then? Lolly Metzger was ninety if a day, a stay-at-home busybody who barely left her house but somehow knew all the happenings in their tiny community. Lolly left the booth with the bunny face Millie had been contemplating, her wrinkled face transformed into round cheeks and prominent teeth through the magic of paint.

Millie laughed with pure joy at Lolly's painted face and twinkling eyes. She might not get around much these days, but Lolly Metzger still had a lot of spirit. And that's what Millie needed as well. She plopped down on the stool to be next and went with the butterfly instead.

"What now?" Sylvie asked after they had paid the artist and moved to the side so the next one in line could have their turn.

"Popcorn," Millie said with a decisive nod.

"We just had breakfast a couple of hours ago," Sylvie protested.

Millie shot her a look. *Like it matters.*

Sylvie gave a quick nod. "Popcorn. Got it."

They bought the popcorn from the Paradise Pops booth and munched merrily on it as they browsed around. They bought a new flavor of barbeque sauce from Hannibal's Smoke House, a load of dish scrubbers from a woman who had practically anything a person could want made from yarn, and a bottle of wine from the local vineyard.

"For after," Sylvie promised with a quick smile and a nod toward Millie's belly.

She returned her aunt's smile, glad she had roused herself out of her blues to come out and enjoy the day.

"And now . . ." Sylvie trilled with a dramatic air, "minigolf."

Millie blinked at her, waiting for the rest. Surely there was a punch line in all this. But her aunt just stared back. "Wait . . . you're serious?"

"Of course." Sylvie grinned. "Let's go."

And Millie's suspicions were immediately raised. She followed behind her aunt wondering just what she had up her sleeve. So far her aunt had asked her about every turn. *What next? What next? What next?* had been her mantra of the morning. Now it was nearing lunch and she wanted to minigolf? Without so much as a suggestion? Something was up.

But until she could be certain, she allowed her aunt to lead the way toward the edge of the park, where the minigolf course was located.

Paradise Putt-Putt was situated on the far side of the park, away from the bulk of the Festival, and received any overflow from the festivities. It was open year-round unless there happened to be snow on the ground and drew in crowds from both sides of the valley as well as statewide tournaments. Millie had been surprised to learn there even was such a thing as minigolf competitions, but it seemed there was a trophy up for grabs in almost every sport the English were in charge of.

But as they neared the course, she discovered exactly what had Sylvie so interested in golfing. It had nothing to do with the game itself and everything to do with Henry King.

"Sylvie." She hadn't meant for the word to escape her, and she certainly hadn't meant for it to have such an admonishing tone, but she didn't have to explain either at any rate.

Her aunt turned to her with eyes wide and innocent. "What? Oh, look. Vern and Henry are here."

"Indeed," Millie dryly remarked.

"Ahoy!" Vern waved one arm over his head to gain their attention. It seemed he was in a nautical mood because he and Henry had just started their game and the first hole on the course was called Hole in the Boat.

"Ahoy!" Sylvie waved in return. "Fancy the two of you being here," she said.

They stopped as they drew closer to the two men and Millie chanced a look at Henry. He appeared to be as surprised as she herself was.

"Fancy that," Henry muttered.

Millie looked this way and that, her gaze only clashing briefly with Henry's as he tried to do the same while Sylvie and Vern carried on as if this was a chance encounter. Which it wasn't.

Still, Millie couldn't call her aunt out on it in front of Henry and Vern. Some things were better endured than corrected when women were alone with one another.

"We were just about to play a round," Sylvie said, her tone overly loud and overly bright.

"You don't say?" Vern returned in much the same manner. "Why don't you join us instead?"

Sylvie didn't even glance her way. "We'd love to," she said. And that was that.

"I'm sorry about this," Henry said at the first opportunity he had. He didn't want his uncle or Sylvie to overhear, and though this golfing expedition wasn't his plan, he still felt the need to apologize to her.

He had wondered time and again what he had done wrong or poorly or whatever it was that made Millie decide they could no longer be friends. Whatever it had been, she obviously hadn't shared those feelings with her aunt or Sylvie wouldn't have conspired with his grandfather to get them together on this outing. And they'd worked on this as a team. There was no doubt. Same dumb excuses, same bad acting, and the outcome the same: Henry and Millie on one team with Vern and Sylvie on the other.

"Me too," she said. "I didn't know you were going to be here today." She shook her head. "Well, I figured you were going to be here today. Everyone is here today. I just didn't know you were going to be playing golf when Sylvie suggested it. And she didn't so much as suggest it as demand it. 'We're playing golf now.'"

He laid one hand on her arm to stay her rambling.

She took in a deep breath as he removed his hand, though his gaze still held hers.

"It's okay. I'm sorry you're . . . uncomfortable."

"Henry . . ." she started, but was interrupted as Sylvie made a crackerjack shot, obviously a hole in one from all the carrying on around them.

Someone from the office came out and recorded her name on the Wall of Fame inside the caddy shack, and she was presented with a certificate while everyone on the course clapped.

Apparently hitting only one shot on the seventh hole was a novelty. Even then, who knew hitting a little white ball into a hole would be such a big deal?

They finished up the rest of the game with Henry on one side of the course and Millie on the other, as if she were doing everything she could to avoid him. Or to avoid talking to him. There were several times during the next eleven turns that he wanted to walk across and apologize once again. Maybe she hadn't heard him the first time. But he knew she had.

He had known. Or maybe he should have known. He had been waiting for weeks, baking bread and biding his time. When he'd caught his grandfather Wednesday morning sneaking whoopie pies out of a secret container, he should have known then that Vern had been in contact with Sylvie. He should have known then that something was up. Of all of them, Vern stood the most to gain if Henry decided to stay in Paradise Springs. Vern wouldn't have to move. He wouldn't have to uproot his life.

He would have the second most to gain, Henry amended. Henry himself would have Millie. And that was a prize for certain.

There. He had admitted it. Almost anyway, but the truth of the matter was that he was falling in love with Millie Bauman and probably had been since the first time he had seen her. She was serene, caring, funny, and sweet. And she was having a baby, willing to go it alone if need be because she thought that was what God wanted from her. She was strong, bullheaded, and smart. And maybe sometimes a little dumb, seeing as how if she would give him a chance, she would see that the two of them could go this together. She wouldn't have to be alone. And neither would he.

Since Anna Kate had called off their engagement, he had never once thought about life with another. He had merely accepted it, heartbroken and sad, as God's plan for his life. Now he wondered if God had something different in mind. He just wished He would get to telling Millie. Or perhaps he wished that she would get to understanding. God was surely doing His part. The rest was up to her. But seeing as how she was standing yards from him when they could be standing side by side . . . Well. That spoke loudly, now didn't it?

But he wouldn't press. He couldn't. Millie had her own battles to fight without him adding anymore to them.

Chapter Twenty

There was a part of Millie that wished she could walk away from Vern and Henry and not look back as they made their way over to the judging stage. The announcements had started at two and carried on throughout the afternoon. There were contests for quilting, crocheting, cookie baking, pie crafting, and many other types of food, but the main event, the announcement of who had made the best whoopie pies of the year, was saved for last.

So important was the announcement that everyone around had gathered to hear who this year's winner was. As if they didn't already know.

Sylvie was smiling from ear to ear and trying her best to act as if she wasn't expecting a thing. When everyone around them knew for certain that she was prepared to win. It was all she'd talked about from Easter clear through till June, when the Festival actually took place.

"Now it's time for the announcement you've all been waiting for," Sammie Franklin, mayor of Paradise Springs, announced. She always wore a special outfit for the Festival, Millie had been told, though she wouldn't say "special" was the right word. Maybe odd. To her, Sammie looked like the little man on the Monopoly game, which was really odd, seeing as how she was a woman. But who was Millie to go challenging the ways of the English? "There was a lot of tough competition this year. Or should I say *moist* competition."

The crowd laughed obligingly at her bad joke. Sammie was a good mayor, Millie supposed. Not that she followed such political activities, but it seemed the town liked her. She was blond, forty-something, and currently serving her third two-year term.

"But in the end, there can be only one." Another bit of laughter chased around. This time exclusively among the English members of the crowd. "And the winner of this year's Whoopie Pie Bake-off is . . . Sadie Yoder!"

Applause went up all around.

Sylvie took one step toward the stage before the truth sunk in. She hadn't called her name. She had called someone else. Someone Millie had never heard of before.

"Do you know who that is?" she asked. She had meant the question to be aimed at Vern, but it was Sylvie who answered in a strangled whisper, "No."

Millie's heart went out to her aunt as this interloper, this Sadie Yoder, made her way to the stage to accept this year's trophy, along with a check for the three hundred dollars in prize money.

But Millie knew that neither one was the reason Sylvie entered. She did it for sheer love of the whoopie pie. And bragging rights.

Let not the wise man boast in his wisdom, let not the mighty man boast in his might, let not the rich man boast in his riches. Jeremiah, if she remembered correctly. And she believed the King James Bible used the word "glory" instead of boast, but it was essentially the same.

Her aunt loved the glory she received from her baking skills, but her crown had been stripped away by a woman no one seemed to know.

"She's new to town." Hattie sidled up behind them, nodding toward the stranger on the stage. The mayor was placing a blue sash around her that said Whoopie Pie Queen with the year all in glitter. Her aunt's coveted blue ribbon was going to someone else.

"What—?" her aunt stuttered.

"I wish you had been here for the judging," Hattie said. The popcorn stand was directly next to the table where the judges had been seated, but Sylvie hadn't even given them a passing look as they had gone by earlier.

"I—" Sylvie just couldn't seem to find the words.

"Would you like some water?" Millie asked.

That seemed to snap her out of it. Everyone clapped as the new reigning Whoopie Pie Queen waved to the crowd. Sadie Yoder was in her fifties, with slashing dimples and hair the color of the devil's food cake Sylvie had made for her whoopie pies. The dress she wore was different, her apron one that pulled over the head and tied around the back. She wasn't from anywhere Millie had lived. No one in Missouri wore aprons as such. Even her prayer *kapp* was strange: sheer, with two puffy sides instead of the starched and formed ones that the women of Paradise Valley wore.

As Millie watched, Sadie Yoder thanked the mayor and left the stage. Everyone started clapping again, though none as loudly as the dethroned matriarch from the last eight years. "My goodness," Sylvie said. "Isn't that something?"

Her cheeks were bright red, and Millie worried that she might overheat.

"Are you okay?" she asked.

Sylvie fanned her face. "Of course, dear. Does anyone know what the winning combination was for the year?" She looked at each of them in turn, but the men had been with them all morning and if Millie didn't know, she didn't figure either one of them would either. She turned her gaze to Hattie.

"What?" Hattie looked as if she might be a little afraid of the earnest look on Sylvie's face.

"Cake flavor," Sylvie demanded, her voice taking on a hard edge. "What was it?"

"No cake." Hattie shook her head. "Brownie."

"Brownie?" Sylvie frowned. If Millie thought her aunt looked sickly before, she looked positively ill now. "You mean chocolate?"

"I mean brownie."

"And the filling?"

"Caramel sea salt."

"Sea salt?" Sylvie sputtered. "Why, I've never heard of such a thing. That sounds like one of those ridiculous coffee drinks at that drink shack on the corner of Spruce and Main." A coffee shop her aunt had been against from the beginning.

"I guess it might be patterned after something like that," Hattie agreed. "We have a sea-salted caramel popcorn we've added this year."

"That's all well and good for popcorn. Popcorn is supposed to be salty. This—" She waved a hand about like a dying fish. "This isn't popcorn; this is whoopie pies." She sucked in a deep breath.

Millie had heard enough. Her aunt was obviously crushed over her defeat and most likely needed to get somewhere private before she said something that might embarrass her later.

"Auntie," Millie started, using her best I-need-to-lie-down voice. "I need to lie down."

All eyes swiveled to her.

"Oh my goodness, sweetie," her aunt said. "I'm so sorry. Here I am, prattling on about whoopie pies and coffee and salt and you're over there—let's go. I'll take you back to the inn immediately. You will excuse me." She wrapped her fingers around Millie's arm and started to lead her away.

"I'll walk you there," Henry said, starting to do just that.

"That's okay, Henry. You're a good man. But this is a lady's time."

Millie wasn't sure exactly what her aunt's words meant, but they stopped Henry in his tracks, a flush of red to rival that on Sylvie's face coloring his own. And she supposed that was her aunt's goal. Not making him blush, but stopping him from coming along. It may have been Millie's idea to get her back to the inn and away from the crowd, but her aunt had embraced the idea, seeing it for what it was. A lifeline to safety.

"Give it to God," Hattie called behind them. A phrase that Millie had heard the woman use a dozen times if even one. But she wondered, was it for her or Sylvie?

Millie didn't put up a fuss when her aunt helped her to the couch and told her to rest. Instead, she nodded, then grabbed her aunt's hand lest she run back out the door and start demanding to see the judges' score cards.

"Stay with me," she said, hopeful her aunt would use the time to catch her breath and, with a bit of luck, realize that losing the competition was not the end of the world.

Sylvie eased down in the chair next to the couch. "As long as you put your feet up."

Millie obediently obliged. Though she felt like she should say something, she worried that any attempts to bring up the competition would not turn out well. "What's for supper?" she asked instead.

"How can you even think about eating?" her aunt said, shaking her head.

Millie prayed it was because they had only recently eaten lunch. Though she could easily go for a snack just then. This eating-for-two business was no joke. She always seemed to be hungry. The doctor told her that was fine; it just meant the baby was growing. And as long as she ate healthy snacks, all should be well and good. "I'm hungry," Millie explained with a small smile.

Sylvie shook her head. "Where do you suppose she came from?"

Millie frowned. "Who? What?"

"That Yoder woman." Sylvie spat out the name as if it weren't her own as well. Granted, there were probably more Yoders than any other last name, but when her aunt said it like that . . .

"I have no idea where she came from. What difference does it make?" Not what she should have asked. She needed to be changing the subject away from whoopie pies and onto something less . . . charged.

"Well, I want to know. I mean, really. Brownie sides

instead of cake." Her aunt stood, cupped her chin in one hand, and looked thoughtfully at nothing. "I wonder if there's anything about that in the rules. Surely there is."

"Auntie." Millie sat up, placing her feet on the floor and grabbing her aunt's hand in order to get her full attention. "You need to . . ." Accept that you lost? Move on? Forget it and try again next year? None of that sounded like the advice she wanted to give this woman who had come to mean so much to her. "Rest." There. That should do it. Not even hardly. She shook her head at herself. "I wouldn't imagine that there's anything in the rules about it having to be cake halves. Lolly Metzger makes hers with cookie dough."

Sylvie harrumphed. "Lolly Metzger is ninety and senile. It's a wonder she doesn't make them with bologna."

Somehow—the favor of God, she was certain—Millie managed to keep a straight face. "Sit," she said, pulling on her aunt's hand, but her aunt had dug into an idea, and she wasn't about to let it go so easily.

"I mean, coming in here, new to town. There has to be something," her aunt muttered.

"Sylvie," Millie started again. But she had lost her aunt to whatever pushed her to bake.

Sylvie pulled away, muttering something about the rules being posted on the entry sheet each year. Millie was certain she was on her way to find this year's form when the front door of the B&B burst open.

Millie was on her feet in a moment, pushed by the urgency that came in with Henry as he exclaimed, "It's Samuel Raber. He's dead."

Chapter Twenty-One

It was all that anyone could talk about on Sunday after church. How Samuel had been fine one minute and dead the next. He had died of a massive heart attack without any warning, leaving those around him—especially his wife, Callie—numb with shock. Samuel had never had a health problem in all his fifty-five years. Millie supposed that just went to show that a person never knew when their time might come. And for some strange reason that made her miss spending time with Henry all the more.

Somehow she managed to get through Monday without hitching up Daisy and heading out to the farm to see him. She needed to get the Sunshine Room ready for their next guest and he was surely making good on his promise to paint the interior of Vern's house. He was doing that so it would sell better, quicker, when the time came for the two of them to move to Wells Landing. And it was that thought that got her through the rest of Monday and Tuesday as well.

"Should we invite her to join the group?" Betsy Stoll asked of the widows on Tuesday night. They had gathered once again at the B&B, Sylvie calling everyone and saying it was necessary so Millie wouldn't have to travel all the way out to Imogene Yoder's for the evening.

Millie had a couple of problems with the request. Mainly because she wasn't an actual member of the group and they should in no way change their schedule to accommodate her. But she figured that Sylvie's world had been turned on its ear and she needed to feel some sort of control over it again.

If she felt so off-kilter after losing her Whoopie Pie Queen title, Millie could only imagine how Callie herself felt, which was exactly who they were talking about. Actually Millie knew precisely how Callie felt. It was staggering when you realized life was so fragile, so easily lost.

"I could ask her at work," Imogene said. Imogene and Callie both worked at the Paradise Amish Buffet, not to be confused with the Paradise *Chinese* Buffet.

Hattie just stared at them both, Imogene and Betsy, her mouth half-open even though she had just taken a bite of tonight's whoopie pie fare.

"What?" Betsy asked, looking around the room. Betsy could be gruff at times, not as polished as some of the other women Millie had met since she had moved to Paradise Springs, but Sylvie had told her that Betsy had grown up with only brothers, and they had treated her like one and the same. "Too soon?"

"Way too soon," Elsie and Hattie said at the same time.

Betsy shrugged and took a bite of the cookie Sylvie had baked for the meeting. "I'm still not sure what this is about." She gestured with the half-moon snickerdoodle she held in one hand.

Sylvie sat up a little straighter in her seat and sniffed,

delicately, but it was a sniff all the same. "Well, I thought it would be good for a change."

"I didn't say they weren't good," Betsy replied. "Just don't know what they're about. We're not the Whoopie Pie Widows Club for nothing."

"We're not the Whoopie Pie Widows Club," Imogene said. "I don't like that name."

"I think it's kinda catchy," Hattie said. That was Hattie, ever positive.

"It's disrespectful," Elsie added with a sniff of her own.

"And here you go, serving . . . cookies." Betsy looked at what remained of the dessert in her hand. She had said the word "cookies" as if it would turn into a snake and attack them all.

Millie watched as her aunt turned an unnatural shade of red and decided that she needed to change the subject before it turned to the competition and what Sylvie was going to do now that her title was lost. And then there would be the speculation that she had baked cookies because she was going out of the whoopie pie "business" for good.

"When is the funeral?" Millie asked. "Samuel Raber's?"

"Thursday." Elsie shook her head. She was as worrisome as her cousin was upbeat. "That poor Callie. You know, they never had children. Not sure what that was about. I suppose just another turn of God's will."

A murmur of agreement went up around the room.

"They were close, those two," Hattie said. "I never saw a couple spend so much time with each other. I suppose because they didn't have any kids."

There was another murmur of agreement as everyone

munched on their snacks and thought about the husbands they had lost.

"I still think I should invite her to the group," Imogene said. "When she returns to work. Not sure when that will be. Aaron told her that she could take all the time she needed."

"She's in shock, poor thing," Hattie said.

"Maybe we shouldn't say anything to her for a couple of months. Maybe six. We don't want to set her off. She needs time to get used to the fact that she's a widow now. Like us."

Like us.

Millie had never really considered herself a widow before. She was just a woman whose husband had died. *Jah, jah,* that was the same thing. But somehow in her mind calling herself a widow was different from acknowledging the fact that her husband was dead. She wasn't sure how to explain it, but it was there, that difference. And calling herself a widow, or even just acknowledging it in her thoughts, somehow made his death more permanent.

And that brought to mind Henry King.

The truth was it didn't take a whole lot for Henry to fill her thoughts. It was as if he had a tie to every aspect of her life. And she couldn't say that they had spent that much time together, but that time had been special, connective. And now it was gone.

She wanted it back. But she had to protect her heart. As long as Henry was planning on moving back to Oklahoma after the harvest, she would steer clear of him and protect her heart.

But she missed him. Oh, how she missed him. And she would see him again. Thursday. At the funeral. She would have to prepare herself to resist him. That engaging smile and infectious manner.

Keep thy heart with all of diligence; for out of it are the issues life.

She would remember that verse from Proverbs. Commit it to memory. Surely that would help her through, for no matter how much she enjoyed spending time with Henry, now her heart was at stake.

"There you are."

Sylvie turned as Vern King came up behind her. "Here I am."

He looped one arm through hers and pulled her along with him. "We need to talk."

"If this is about whoopie pies . . ."

She'd had enough of talk about Sadie Yoder's winning recipe, idea rather. It wasn't that her whoopie pies were that much whoopie-er than anyone else's. She had just been more creative. Sylvie could have done the same thing if she had thought of it. But she preferred her whoopie pies to be constructed in the more traditional manner. Brownie halves—whoever heard of such a thing? The whole ordeal was disheartening, and she hadn't had the urge to bake even one of the tasty little cakes since Saturday's fiasco.

"Not everything is about whoopie pies," Vern growled.

"You seem to like them well enough."

"Cake and filling," he said. "What's not to like?" He had led her away from the crowd and on to a secluded corner of the house. They were nestled outside, around the side and behind the chimney.

"Why are we way back here?" she asked.

They had buried Samuel Raber, then gone back to Callie's house to celebrate his life. Most of the town had turned out. The Amish citizens anyway. Samuel was a well-liked man in their community and he would be missed by all.

"Because we need to talk, and no one else needs to hear what we're saying."

"Okay." She waited for him to begin. He was the one who had dragged her all the way around the side of the house, not the other way around. If anyone should be talking, it should be him. She shifted in place, hoping the motion would get him started.

Vern took a deep breath. "Listen," he began. "I know you're upset about this whole whoopie pie deal."

"I am not upset." She pulled on her apron, as if that proved her lighthearted mood. "But an outsider shouldn't be allowed to just come in and change the structure of a whoopie pie and—" She stopped. She had told herself she wasn't going to protest Sadie Yoder's win. Sylvie would rejoice in the success of others. Namely Sadie Yoder. And Sylvie would be grateful to God for the chance to even enter. The clarity of mind, the talent, the drive. Just because she hadn't won . . . "Continue."

"We need to do something about Henry and Millie. I want to stay here, and I'm afraid the only way I'll be able to do that is if Henry agrees to stay, and the only way he's going to do that is if he and Millie . . ."

"Is that selfish?" Sylvie murmured, half to herself and half to him. "To manipulate people's lives for the benefit of our own?"

"Now don't you go getting soft on me, Sylvie Yoder. I

need you for this. And they'll get a new love. That's good, *jah*?"

Sylvie nodded. "What do you have in mind?"

"They seemed to like the putt-putt golf well enough."

"No. They did not. They didn't even speak for most of the game."

He propped his hands on his hips. "Okay then. You come up with something."

For a moment Sylvie considered going over to Paradise Hill and visiting with Astrid Kauffman, romance writer and matchmaker, and seeing what she would suggest, but she pushed the thought away. Now she was really being ridiculous.

"I thought you wanted the two of them together," Vern said. "Was I wrong?"

"No," Sylvie murmured. "I'm thinking." She did want Millie to have love in her life. A helpmate like God intended. It was one thing to be widowed when the children were almost grown and able to care for themselves and quite another when babies were involved. Millie thought she could do it alone. And maybe she could. But how much better would it be to do it with a man she loved? A man like Henry King.

If I were her, she mused, *I would want* . . . "A romantic dinner. At a fancy restaurant."

Vern squinted at her, as if that would help him better understand her plan. "What restaurant?"

Sylvie thought about it for a moment. "That new Italian place in town."

"A romantic dinner sounds nice, but how are we going to get them there . . . together?"

She shook her head. "We're not. You get Henry to come. And I'll make sure Millie is there."

"How am I supposed to get him to the restaurant?" Vern asked.

Sylvie planted her hands on her hips. Sometimes men were impossible. Lacking intelligence and impossible. "Figure it out for yourself, Vern King. I came up with the plan. You can do this part. I can't do everything here, you know."

"It's your birthday?" Henry asked.

Vern grinned at him, hoping he didn't see through his veiled smile. "*Jah*. Absolutely."

"I thought your birthday was in November."

It was . . . really. But tonight it had been moved to . . . tonight. "Nope. And I want to go out and celebrate."

"You do?"

Okay, so maybe Vern was something of a homebody. What was wrong with that? He liked being at home. He liked the comfort and familiarity of his house, his things. That wasn't a bad way to be. But there was no need for Henry to act so shocked about it. Yet he supposed it was a tad suspicious when he up and decided to go to the fanciest restaurant in town to celebrate a birthday that truly wouldn't happen for months.

"I do." Vern gave a decisive nod. "So go take a shower and put on your best shirt. We're going to eat real food tonight."

Henry grinned. "Real food," he said dreamily. "I can get behind that."

"Then shoo." Vern waved him toward the bathroom and set about finishing his own preparations for the evening.

Sylvie had taken care of the reservations and the food. Then she promised that Millie would be there right on time. Fifteen minutes before he and Henry arrived. All Vern had to do was get Henry dressed and into town. It didn't seem like a tough chore, but it had been a little harder than Vern had anticipated. He rapped on the bathroom door. "Don't dally," he told Henry through the wood. "We have a reservation for six forty-five."

"Got it." Henry's voice was muffled through the sound of running water and the thickness of the door.

"Good," Vern said.

Once they got to the restaurant, he and Sylvie would leave the couple alone to eat, enjoy the food Sylvie had already ordered, and reconnect. Fall in love perhaps. Vern wasn't sure that was exactly how it worked, but he did know one thing: They couldn't fall in love if they were never in the same room together for more than five minutes—church aside.

Sylvie promised that everything was taken care of, from the candles to the dessert. Something called tara-mizzou. Or something like that. Now Vern had to do his part: get Henry into town.

He rapped on the door once more. "Six forty-five," he reminded Henry once more but didn't receive an answer. No matter. Henry would be ready and Vern would too. He headed out to the barn to hitch up the horse.

His *dawdi* knocked on the door a second time and reminded him of the time. Henry might have rolled his eyes at the man, but he was too busy trying to wash the paint from his hair. And his arms, his face, his neck, and his hands. He had seen people who could paint an entire building and not get one speck on them. He was not one of those people. Every time he painted, he ended up with paint everywhere.

And now, after a day of craning his neck back to paint the ceiling in the bulk of the house—and that was after he had already painted the walls—his grandfather wanted to go into town and eat at the fancy Italian restaurant for his birthday.

Henry was exhausted and would rather have a nap and a can of ravioli than go out, but since this was a special occasion, what else could he do? A little advance notice would have been good. If he had known they were going out tonight, he might not have worked so hard today. See, once Henry got the walls painted, he could tell just how bad the ceiling looked, and what choice did he have but to paint that too? It wasn't as noticeable in the kitchen, with its natural wood cabinets, but wall to ceiling it was obvious.

Henry scrubbed at his face some more, paying special attention to his eyebrows. How had he managed to get paint in his eyebrows?

He would have sworn on anything and everything that Vern's birthday was in November. He remembered birthday cake at Thanksgiving as clear as day. But it must have been someone else's special day he was recalling, not Vern's.

And he couldn't help feeling it was a little strange that Vern wanted to go out. Henry had never seen another man more contented to be at home resting, reading, and just being. But he supposed that everyone got the urge to go out every now and then.

Then there was the thought of Italian food. Made fresh, not out of a can or a box. That sounded like a slice of heaven on a plate. His mouth watered just thinking about it. Getting out and having a good meal sounded like the best plan a man could come up with—especially a man, or men who had been fending for themselves these last few weeks. No matter how bone-tired they were.

He dried and dressed and combed his wet hair. It could dry on the way, he supposed. Vern seemed to be in a hurry. Henry wasn't entirely certain how reservations worked, but he expected that they wouldn't give their table to someone else just because they were a little late arriving. But Vern didn't seem willing to chance it, so Henry hurried.

Before long they were bouncing along toward town.

"I don't think I've been out this late in a buggy since my courting days," Vern said. He looked around, as if all the sights had changed from earlier, like the scenery on the side of the road was different once evening hit.

But Henry did like the way the sun was going down and the lavender light it cast around, bathing everything in a mellow glow.

"It's been a while for me too."

"Good," Vern said. "Then this will be worth it."

Henry frowned, turned toward his *dawdi*, and eyed him carefully. "What do you mean, 'worth it'?"

Vern shrugged. "Nothing. Just going all the way into town to eat. You know."

"I thought you wanted to celebrate your birthday." He

was beginning to get even more suspicious that something was going on.

"Oh, right," he said with a small chuckle. "I do. Celebrate. That's tonight."

And that suspicion didn't go away as they rode into town and over to the Paradiso Italia Restaurant.

There were hitching posts scattered all around Paradise Springs. Vern found one, tied up their horse, and together they made their way to the restaurant doors.

"Is this one of those places that will sing to you if you tell them it's your birthday?" Henry asked as they stepped inside.

"Do not tell them it's my birthday," Vern said. His tone brooked no argument, but Henry had already made up his mind to catch the waitress and let her know as soon as he had the chance to do so without Vern finding out. That was what made it fun.

The hostess checked them in and led them into the restaurant. It was dimly lit, romantic one might even say. With candles flickering on every table, white clothes draped over the tops, and silverware and plates all precisely laid out in a way that made him want to give up and eat with his hands.

"Do not," Vern said again.

"Fine," Henry grumbled his lie. "I won't, but—" The words stopped in his throat as he caught sight of her sitting there. Her back was to him, but he knew it was her. As sure as he knew his name. As sure as he knew in that minute that he loved her and didn't want to live without her. Millie.

"Millie." He breathed her name. his heart nearly stopping in his chest. What was she doing here?

Chapter Twenty-Two

Millie looked from her aunt toward the so-familiar voice. "Henry," she said.

She turned back to her aunt. Sylvie's eyes grew comically wide as she pretended to catch sight of the two men. "Vern and Henry!" she exclaimed. "What in the world are you two doing here?"

"We came out to celebrate," Henry said. "It's Dawdi's birthday."

"It is?" Millie looked from her aunt to the two of them. Maybe she had read the situation wrong. When she had seen them, she had known that her aunt was up to her old tricks once again. Losing the Whoopie Pie bake-off had set her back a little, but it seemed that she had made a full recovery. Or close to it, if she was trying her hand at matchmaking once again.

But if it was Vern's birthday, perhaps she had misinterpreted what was happening around her.

"*Jah. Jah.*" Vern hooked his thumbs under his suspenders and rocked back on his heels.

"Well, now, that's special." Her aunt's voice seemed a little strained as she shifted in her seat. "Why don't the two of you join us?" Sylvie offered. "We're just about to order."

Henry opened his mouth to protest, she was certain, but before he could utter one objection, Vern had pulled out a seat and settled in.

Millie looked to Henry.

I'm sorry, he mouthed.

She shook her head, so very happy to see him even as she knew she would have to steel her heart against the many charms in his warm brown eyes.

Henry sat as well, though more reluctantly than Vern by far.

"Your birthday, huh?" Sylvie asked as Vern shook out his napkin and draped it over his lap.

"*Jah. Jah.* Birthday."

"But he doesn't want to tell the waitstaff that it's his birthday," Henry informed them. "He doesn't want anyone coming by and singing to him."

Millie gave an exaggerated pout. "Aw," she said. "That's the fun part."

Sylvie shot her a look that Millie didn't quite understand. It seemed to be half exasperation and half *shut up, will you*? "If that's not what Vern wants . . ."

Millie nodded. "Of course."

Her aunt looked around. "Where's our waiter?" she asked no one in particular. "We need to get the two of you some menus."

"You can use mine," Millie said, closing it and handing it to Henry.

He took it and her gaze snagged on his. Why, oh why did she have to fall in love with someone so impossible for her to be with?

No. Not love. She almost shook her head at herself but managed to stop the motion before it could be carried out. She wasn't in love with Henry King. She might be well on her way to *possibly* falling in love with him. But Joshua hadn't been gone very long. Just a few months. Less than a year. And she didn't believe herself callous enough to move on so quickly after losing him. Though in all honesty, most times it felt like he had been gone forever. That her life with him and without him were centuries apart. Almost another life entirely.

"I'll go see if I can find him." Vern stood, tossed his napkin down in his chair.

Sylvie shook her head and stood as well. "You don't even know what *she* looks like," she corrected. "I'll go with you."

Vern nodded, then gave her aunt a grin that Millie didn't quite understand. It seemed as if he had a secret he was keeping. Or maybe the pair of them were planning something. Maybe that's why they were even here at all.

She watched the two of them wind their way through the tables in search of their server, then turned back to Henry. *Have we been set up again?* she wanted to ask, but she couldn't bring herself. Instead she took a piece of bread from the basket and made a show of dipping it into the small saucer of olive oil and herbs the waitress had brought over when they had first arrived at the restaurant. She didn't mean to be so elaborate, and maybe she hadn't been. But it felt like it.

"How've you been?" Henry asked her just as she took a bite.

She nodded her head and chewed, thankful to have a little time to answer him but wishing he wasn't sitting there so patiently waiting for her to respond. It was awkward somehow, as if she were stalling in her answer, not merely chewing a piece of food.

"Well," she finally managed. She used one hand to cover her mouth as she spoke, traces of the bread still hanging around inside. Why was her tongue so dry and her teeth suddenly sticking to her lips? She snatched up her water and took a large drink. What was taking Vern and her aunt so long? The restaurant wasn't that large. How many waiters and waitresses could there be?

He nodded. "I'm glad."

She managed to get enough water into her that she felt she could speak without sand flying out of her mouth. "How about you?" she asked in return.

"I've been all right."

For a moment she thought he might say more, then he picked up his own piece of bread and made a play at dipping it just so.

But at least it reminded her of a safe topic she could discuss with him. "Thank you for the bread you sent over last week."

He nodded. "It wasn't as good as this." He gestured with the half-eaten piece of bread he held in one hand.

"It was pretty tasty, though," she countered. "I never knew you had a talent for baking."

He shrugged. "Neither did I until I started doing it."

She wanted to ask him why he had started baking and if he had ever tried his hand at anything other than bread, and why were they talking about an inane subject like bread when it seemed like so much was hanging, unsaid, between them?

He must have felt the same, for he looked around the

room. Millie allowed her gaze to follow his, noting the other patrons all seemed to be smiling at them, as if there was some big secret the two of them were yet to be let in on.

And she tried to think of something to say. Something that wasn't about bread or falling in love. But nothing came to mind.

"Are you ready to order?" the waitress asked, suddenly appearing at their table once more. It was the same girl as before. Or so Millie thought. She had short blond hair, which hung to her chin on one side of her face but was cut very short on the other. She had an earring that went diagonally through her ear and a tattoo on the inside of her wrist. There couldn't be two of them just alike.

"No," Henry said. "Our companions went to find you and get a couple more menus."

"They did?" She frowned. "An older man and woman?" she asked. Then she continued, a little reluctantly. "Amish like you?"

Henry nodded. "That's right."

She gave him a relieved and apologetic smile. "They told the hostess something came up and to tell you both that they would see you at home if you asked."

Millie was staring at the waitress, but she felt Henry's gaze when it fell to her. She didn't want to look at him. Didn't want to acknowledge what had just happened . . . again.

"They're still here, though," Millie said.

It wasn't quite a question, but the waitress answered anyway. "Uh, no." She seemed reluctant to divulge that little bit of information. "Is that a problem?"

"No," Millie said automatically. The young girl was

apologetic and uncomfortable, and Millie didn't see any reason to make her feel even more so.

"They set us up," Henry said, a little under his breath but loud enough that both Millie and the waitress could hear.

"So are you ready to order?" she asked again. She looked from one of them to the other and back again.

"Can you give us another minute?" Millie asked. She was as thrown by the whole setup as Henry was, but she seemed to recover a little more quickly. Perhaps because she'd had to be on her toes all week where her aunt was concerned. Extra vigilant because Sylvie had lost the whoopie pie baking competition.

"Of course. I'll be back." She sent them both a dimpled smile and made her way across the restaurant to check on the other customers.

"I don't know what to say," Henry said. "I don't know which one of them came up with this idea, but I'm really sorry."

Millie shook her head. "It's okay. And it really doesn't matter which one of them came up with the plan. They both carried it through."

He nodded. "I suppose." He took another piece of bread from the basket and dipped it into the oil-and-herb mixture. "So what do we do now?"

She looked around. The other diners were still glancing their way every so often. "I guess we have two choices,'" she said. "We could leave or order." She couldn't help but wonder what everyone would do it they did indeed get up and walk out. It almost seemed as if everyone around them knew why the two of them were there. She supposed she could be a little sensitive to being set up once again.

But she really did feel like she was on display, right there in the middle of the Paradiso Italia.

He took a deep breath and thoughtfully chewed, though she couldn't tell in the least what he might be thinking they should do.

A part of her—a big part—wanted to go back to the inn and give her aunt a piece of her mind for putting them in such an uncomfortable situation. Another part of her— not quite so large, but still enormously powerful—wanted to stay there, see how Henry had been doing. Maybe test out her theory as to whether or not she could be falling in love with Henry King after only being widowed for a little over six months.

But was that something she was willing to chance, that she might fall in love with him?

If he moved back to Oklahoma in October, what would she do? He was sure to take her heart with him. And she knew once Henry had it, she would never see it again. And no amount of prayers would change that fact. She knew it for certain.

"Is it really your grandfather's birthday?" Millie asked. Why she felt compelled to ask she wasn't sure, but some-how she figured it was important enough to know.

Henry shrugged. "I have no idea. But I don't think so."

"So that was an excuse to get you to the restaurant?"

"I suppose."

"Sylvie told me that she wanted to start cooking suppers at the inn. She thought Italian food would be a good place to start."

He laughed. "Italian food? Like Amish lasagna?"

"I suppose, but she's not been quite the same since the

judging." She didn't have to say any more. He understood. She could see it in his eyes as he nodded.

"I would imagine that country cooking favorites would be what people would expect from an Amish-owned B&B."

"That's what I told her," Millie exclaimed. "But she insisted on Italian." Now she knew why.

"Do you think she's really going to start serving suppers?" Henry asked quietly.

Millie sighed. "No more than you believe it's Vern's birthday."

"So we agree this was a setup?"

She nodded.

"Do we stay or go?" he asked. "It's up to you."

"Don't make me—"

Henry stopped her words, laying one hand on top of hers where it rested on the table. "I'm leaving it up to you because I want to stay. I want to have this dinner with you and more. If I'm truly being honest, I believe I want to have every dinner with you for the rest of our lives, but I know—"

"You mean that?" she asked. Tears filled her eyes. Hormones, she told herself, but she knew she was not fooling anyone. She was dangerously close to falling in love with Henry King, but she didn't want to be in love alone. But if what he was saying was true . . .

"With all my heart," he promised.

The tears broke free and spilled down her cheeks.

"We can take this slow," he told her. "It's not about rushing, it's about the time we're spending together. But I'll be truthful: I don't want to waste any minutes wondering whether or not this is real."

She shook her head, her vision blurry as she squeezed his hand and smiled at him. "I would never."

"I know. But some pains are hard to forget."

Like she didn't know. "Let's make a deal," she said, pulling her hand away to wipe at the steady stream of tears racing down her cheeks. "I'll promise it's real if you promise to hire someone to reroof the inn or the house or wherever we're staying when the time comes."

He smiled at her in return. "That's a fine deal, Millie Bauman. I accept."

Once the waitress came back and started to take their order, the folks around them started to clap. It seemed everyone but them knew they were destined to end up as a couple that evening. And as far as Millie was concerned, that was simply fine with her. Henry didn't seem to mind either, not even when he found out that Vern had left money to pay for the supper with the hostess.

"Where to now?" he asked as they walked out of the restaurant.

"What would you like to do?" she asked in return. Though she didn't admit it, she wasn't quite ready to go home yet.

"We could take a walk . . ." he said.

Their buggy was still in the parking lot at the restaurant, which meant either Vern had gone back to the inn with Sylvie or he'd found someone to take him home. Probably the former, she suspected.

"A walk sounds perfect." She smiled at him. Everything since they had made that promise to each other had been perfect.

"I've got to ask," Millie said quietly as they walked toward the town square in the center of Paradise Springs.

Aside from the park, the courthouse, and the putt-putt golf course, there was a statue of Moses Miller, the founder of Paradise Springs, standing in the middle of the green grass surrounding the main city building.

"*Jah?*"

"Does this mean that you aren't going back to Oklahoma?" Her voice held a rough edge. She hated the way it sounded, like some rusty old thing that had been left out in the rain too long.

He stopped, right there in front of the statue of Moses Miller. Henry took her hands into his and dropped to his knees in front of her.

"Henry," she screeched. "What are you doing? You're going to ruin your trousers."

"It's an English custom," he explained. "They get on their knees to ask someone to marry them."

"We get on our knees to—" Whatever she had been about to say was quickly lost when the weight of what he had said hit her fully. They had danced around the topic all evening, but nothing definite had been said. Even with all the promises they had made. "Marry them?"

"Me," he corrected. "Millie Bauman, will you marry me?"

Tears welled in her eyes, blurring her vison. She almost poked him in the eye as she reached for him, cradling his face in her hands. "Of course. Of course." She cried, laughing all the while tears trickled down her face. She had never been happier. Never more excited as she was in that moment. "Now please, get up. You're my partner, my love, you shouldn't be down on your knees in front of me."

"I wanted to show you how much I care," he replied. "I want you to always remember that."

"I will. I will," she said. "Now get up before I have to get down there with you. Because if I get down there, I'm not sure I'll be able to get back up without the help of a crane."

They were both laughing as she finally urged him to his feet.

"I never expected this," he admitted as they walked around the edge of the park on the track used for just that. But since it was well past dark, there weren't any walkers out. In fact, it seemed as if they had the whole park to themselves. Like they were the only ones there. Like it was all for them.

That was how it felt. Special. Like they were the only two people in the world and the night had been made exclusively for them.

To say the thought was fanciful was an understatement, but it made her smile anyhow.

"You think that's funny?" Henry asked, and Millie realized that she had drifted away in her own thoughts. That was one of the worst side effects of her pregnancy. There were times when she couldn't keep her focus. It didn't matter how important the conversation was, her concentration simply wasn't there.

"I—" she started, but he plowed on ahead, saving her from having to acknowledge that she hadn't been listening.

"I never expected to feel this way again," he admitted. "In love. And yet here we are."

She smiled. "Me either." She wanted to tell him how devastated she had been when Joshua was killed, but she couldn't bring the words out, afraid they would somehow sour the near-magical night that surrounded them.

He gestured toward the swings, as if inviting her to sit and enjoy herself, but she placed one hand on her stomach and shook her head, without words telling him that swinging was not a good idea.

Instead he led her over to the merry-go-round and they sat down side by side, using their planted feet to push themselves back and forth, only as far as their legs were long.

"I think taking it slow is best," he said. "Once the baby comes, we can figure it out. By then, you'll be finished with your year of mourning and—" He shook his head. "I'm too excited," he admitted. "Too happy."

"Is there such a thing?" she asked. But she felt the same.

"When you said you didn't want to play along with your aunt's matchmaking attempts . . . I thought my heart had stopped."

"It wasn't easy," she admitted.

He smiled, the wind ruffling his hair where it poked out from underneath his hat. "Did I tell you that I'm glad you changed your mind?" he asked.

"Not yet," she teased in return. "Are you?"

His eyes grew serious, intense. "More than you will ever know."

Chapter Twenty-Three

What had started out to be a false birthday celebration ended up being the best meal of Henry's life. Not that he could remember what the food tasted like the next day, but he knew every nuance of Millie's every expression throughout every minute they'd spent together.

He should have known. It had always been that way with her. She had gotten under his skin—in a good way. She had burrowed in and wasn't letting go. He hadn't minded until she decided that they couldn't even be friends. That was when all the problems started as far as he was concerned. But that time was over, short-lived and gone.

Now Henry would forever remember that night as one of the best he had ever spent with anyone. Anytime. Ever.

They had taken their time, strolling around the park, talking about this and that and nothing in particular, just enjoying being with the other. They talked a little about second chances and how they felt that God had somehow led them together.

When they finally made their way back to the B&B, they found Vern and Sylvie anxiously awaiting their return. It seemed they had already called the restaurant twice to see if they had finished eating. When they were told the couple had left Paradiso Italia, they had expected them to come straight home. Now the pair wanted a play-by-play. But Henry wasn't willing to share their evening with anyone else. Not yet anyway. Maybe later. Maybe in a couple of weeks. For now, he wanted to keep it just between them. Something that only the two of them shared and no one else.

He supposed that Millie must have felt the same for she didn't offer to share any of what they had talked about. Only that they were glad that they had supper together and they hoped there would be many more in the future.

Let his *dawdi* and her aunt make what they would from that. With the imaginations both of them had, they would definitely have no problem coming up with a scenario, and with the evening that he and Millie had . . . well, he was certain their kin would get it right. But it would be a while before they would be sharing their love with the world. That much they were in agreement on.

And until then, this new romance would stay just between the two of them.

"I don't understand," Vern said two days later. "She didn't say anything once we left?"

Sylvie slid a plate full of cupcakes in front of Vern and shook her head. "No. For the third time. She didn't say anything. Just smiled at me like she was the cat who swallowed the canary and went on up to bed."

"And nothing this morning?"

Sylvie bit back a sigh. She grabbed her coffee cup and eased into the seat across from Vern. He had come over just after breakfast and wanted to know what all Millie said to her after he and Henry had gone home. So Sylvie had grabbed him a plate of the cupcakes she had made yesterday afternoon and the two of them had settled around the worktable in the kitchen. But she didn't have anything to share.

Neither did he, it seemed. The couple—Millie and Henry—weren't willing to divulge any details about their date. At least not the ones Sylvie and Vern wanted. Like what happened between the two of them after Vern and Sylvie had left.

Truth be told, Sylvie had half expected Millie to come storming home the minute she discovered that she and Henry had been set up. But she hadn't, and as far as Sylvie was concerned that was a good sign.

Now whether or not they could get the pair to tell them about it was another matter altogether.

"I wish I knew what was going on."

"Something good," Vern said with a nod. His mouth was full of banana rum cupcake, which he seemed to like. It was a new recipe. One Sylvie had been meaning to try out on whoopie pies, but after the competition . . . well, she just didn't have it in her to bake any whoopie pies. Not now anyway. Maybe in a day or so, or a week or two, she would feel differently about the entire matter. Until then she was baking other recipes. Ones she had been collecting for years before she had been crowned—and dethroned—as Paradise Valley's whoopie pie baking queen.

"You sound very sure of that," Sylvie said. She took a sip of her coffee, then picked up one of the cupcakes and peeled the paper wrapping from the bottom. One bite and . . . yum! Fantastic! Even if she did say so herself.

"I am sure of it." Vern swallowed down half the second cupcake and reached for another.

"Because . . ." she prompted.

"Because he hasn't baked a single loaf of bread in two days."

Maybe . . . but she wished she had more definitive proof, like Henry telling Vern that he had asked Millie to marry him.

But if what Vern was saying about Henry walking around with his step light and his head in the clouds without baking a single loaf of bread were true . . . then when coupled with Millie acting the same way—well, with steps as light as the steps of a woman who was seven and a half months along could be—then a romance had to be brewing between the two of them.

"I suppose you'll be happy then," she said, "being able to stay here in Paradise Springs."

"You know what would make me even happier?" he said. His eyes twinkled over the wiry gray strands of his beard.

"More cupcakes?" she asked dryly. That was just like something Vern would have spouted off, but when she said it for him, he looked positively crushed.

"No, actually I was going to say something else."

Sylvie stared at him a moment. First he had come in and plopped down, wanting to know if she had any snacks; now when she teased him about it, he wanted to act all hurt. One thing she had learned about Vern King in these last couple of months was that he had a tough hide. One that he wasn't showing today.

"What's wrong with you, Vern?" she asked.

He shrugged, casting a longing look at the cupcakes,

as if he wanted another but now wouldn't dare actually take it lest she make fun of his appetite again. "Nothing. Just to hear you talk, I only come around to get food and for no other reason."

She frowned at him. Now what was he talking about? "What are you talking about now?"

"This," he said, gesturing toward the table and the two of them, like that explained anything at all.

"Can you be a little more specific?"

"Fine." He stood in a huff, so quickly that he knocked his chair over behind him. "Maybe I came here because I like spending time with you, Sylvie Yoder. You ever think of that?"

"You like spending time with me?" The words escaped her, a little more than a whisper of awe.

"Well, maybe I do and maybe I don't. But why would I tell you something like that now if you want to say I just come to get cupcakes and such, huh?" He reached out to set his chair back right, but only knocked it over again.

"But . . ." Sylvie wasn't sure what to say to that. That she liked spending time with him too? That she wanted him to mean those words. She wanted to spend more time with him. But she couldn't be that forward. Not at all. So she said the only thing she could. The only thing that popped into her head. "We're friends, *jah*?"

He nodded, and having finally set his chair back to rights, he braced his hands on the back of it as he stared at her. His gaze was intense. His knuckles white where they gripped the wood.

"Well, good." She gave a decisive nod. "Friends can tease each other and friends can get their feelings hurt. But friends can also apologize."

He wiped one sleeve across his mouth. The grip of his other hand had loosened, but he still looked at her with intense blue eyes, like those English laser beams the young male guests were always talking about. "Are you trying to say you're sorry, Sylvie?"

She nodded. "I am. Will you accept?"

He nodded in return, pulled the chair back out, and sat once again.

Her heart was racing. Her breathing labored. She would never intentionally hurt his feelings. Not on purpose and definitely not over something as foolish as cupcakes. But what had her stomach in knots and her jaw clenched in anticipation? Had she thought he was going to walk out and never come to see her again? How ridiculous was that?

That he would walk out and never return. Not when they both knew as sure as everything that Millie and Henry would be getting married soon. Oh, they hadn't said as much, but a woman had eyes. And her niece was in love. And now that Henry was staying in Paradise Valley, there was no reason for him and Vern to return to Oklahoma.

Just the thought of that set her emotions on their head.

What was wrong with her?

She hadn't acted like this since—

No! It couldn't be. She wouldn't accept it. She couldn't accept it.

But it seemed that she would have to.

She had gone and fallen in love with Vern King.

The thought plagued Sylvie long after he left. Well, he had eaten two more cupcakes and *then* he left. But thankfully he hadn't noticed how distracted she was. He kept talking about how delicious the cupcakes were and how glad he was to be staying in Paradise Springs. Sylvie wanted to ask him how he could be so confident that Millie and Henry would get married, but in the end she let it go. She didn't want to take that smile from Vern's face. She had never seen him happier, and that joy made him even more handsome than before.

She still couldn't figure out why she had never noticed in the past. Probably because she hadn't really known him then. It was true: A person you cared about appeared more attractive after you got to know them. And that was exactly what had happened between her and Vern.

Now she had to wonder if he felt the same.

He liked her cooking, that much was apparent in the way he shoveled down whatever she set in front of him. But some of that could be because since Johnny B's accident, Vern had been eating his own cooking. She knew that a great many English men were cooks—chefs, they called themselves—but she hadn't known many an Amish man who would get in the kitchen and make himself at home. They had other things to do besides learn to prepare food. That fell to the women.

She had heard enough talk among the English women who visited the B&B to know that they considered this to be a sexist approach to life and chores, but she figured the ax swung both ways. Wasn't it sexist to expect the men to bring in the money to buy the food to put on the table? Men did most of the planting and harvesting of crops. The men took care of the animals when there was trouble. They ran the church, moved the benches from location to location, preached, counseled, and well, a whole bunch of other stuff. Women took care of the house and the children. That wasn't sexist. As far as she could see, it was simply a division of chores.

And with that division came issues when one spouse died and the other was left alone to take care of both sets of chores. Most women were ill equipped to make the money the men did, and most men had no idea how to get around in a kitchen or how to change a diaper.

Maybe that was why so many of the widows and widowers in Amish communities remarried quickly after losing their husband or wife. Sylvie herself had opened the B&B when her Andrew died. And though she missed him every day for years, she had what she needed there to support herself. Not everyone was so fortunate.

But she had looked into Vern's eyes. And in them she had seen more than the enjoyment of the food she had prepared. Hadn't she? Or was she just being hopeful once again?

"Auntie?"

Millie called her name loudly, and Sylvie realized she had been waxing the same spot on the buffet over and over again while she had been thinking. "*Jah*?"

"You're half the county away today. What's going on?"

Could she tell her? Should she tell her?

No, Sylvie decided. What difference would it make? It wasn't like Vern had declared that he had feelings for her. She had fallen in love with him, not the other way around. And that love could go years unrequited. Maybe even a lifetime.

"Nothing, dear. You doing all right?"

Millie eyed her carefully. "Are you sure? I called your name three times before you answered."

She had?

"I'm fine, dear." Sylvie stopped, smiled, then turned away, a little antsy now, filled with this new development.

She didn't want to look at Millie too long lest her niece learn her secret through the light in her eyes alone.

"The Blue Room is all clean and ready," Millie said, thankfully dropping the previous subject. It wasn't something Sylvie thought she could talk about yet. If ever.

"I do wish you would slow down," Sylvie admonished. "You need more rest."

Millie smiled and rubbed her hand over the mound of her belly. "I feel fine. Everything's in order and . . . fine. There's no need to worry."

Yet she couldn't help but worry a little. After all, with babies anything was possible right up until the end. And she wanted only the best for her niece and the little one on the way. "You say that, but promise me that you'll take the afternoon to put your feet up."

"Auntie."

Sylvie held up one hand to stay her niece's protests. "Hup," she said with a shake of her head. She closed her eyes as she did so, telling Millie without words that she wasn't listening to any more protests.

"Okay," Millie finally agreed. "I'll take the afternoon off."

Sylvie smiled. "Good. Good," she said. "Won't be long now."

Millie smiled. "The doctor said any time."

"Have you called the midwife?" Sylvie asked.

"I've talked to her once, but we never settled on anything."

Sylvie shot her a pointed look. "If you want to have the baby here, then you'd better. Otherwise you'll end up at the urgent clinic." Which was perfectly okay for cuts, scrapes, and bruises, but not the most . . . cozy place to have a baby. Not like some of the English birthing rooms she had been hearing about. She and Millie had agreed long ago that she should have the baby right there in the B&B. Sylvie couldn't think of a finer thing to have happen under that roof.

"And be sure you talk to her about accessories," Sylvie continued. "That's not the word she used, but Sarah Esh was saying something at church not too long ago about birthing pools and birthing balls and all sorts of unusual items with the word "birthing" in front of them. If you don't want anything weird like that, you had better let her know."

Barbie Troyer had been the midwife in those parts for as long as anyone could remember. She was old, wizened, and had brought more babies into the world than any of the doctors out at the Paradise Springs Urgent Care Center. Not that the statement was truly saying much. Not many people stayed in town to have their babies, preferring to drive to one of the larger, neighboring towns to bring their child into the world. Which was nice if you had the time, but with Amish buggies being what they were, it was better to have the midwife than chance making it to the next town before having the baby in the backseat.

"She didn't say anything about accessories," Millie said, making a face. "At least not the last time I talked to her."

"Good." Sylvie gave a firm nod. "Maybe she's over all that newfangled nonsense."

"Maybe," Millie murmured, but Sylvie could tell that she was a little concerned.

"I did hear that a birthing pool was nice," she said to smooth things over.

Millie gave a small nod. "I don't think we have room for any of that anyway."

Sylvie looked around the front sitting room. It was spacious enough. Maybe even big enough for a birthing pool, but it was also less than ten feet from the door. Having the baby at "home" was one thing, in the middle of a bustling house full of strangers another. "You're probably right. And Barbie knows that you want to have the baby here?" Sylvie asked.

"*Jah*," Millie said.

Quiet and simple.

She didn't say the words. She didn't have to for Sylvie to hear them. That was Millie, quiet and simple. Though these last few weeks had been anything but.

"Did you make some snacks for later?" Millie asked.

"I made some cranberry-orange scones," Sylvie said, completely proud of herself for the change. The picture in the recipe book looked too good to pass up. Never mind that it was a recipe under the Christmas section.

"Isn't that sort of Christmassy?" Millie asked.

"No." Sylvie waved one hand, as if to wipe that comment from their memories. "You can eat cranberries anytime." And that was the truth, though something about cranberries just said winter holidays. Mix it with orange and that seemed exactly where it belonged.

But why? Sylvie thought. People ate peppermint year-round. Made sugar cookies with icing. Maybe not in Christmas shapes, but the same recipe. The icing tasted the same whether it was pink and yellow or green and red.

"I thought you might make some whoopie pies today," Millie said almost shyly.

Just the mention of the words "whoopie pies" and her heart constricted. Sylvie sucked in a deep breath and pushed those emotions down inside. Way down deep inside. She wasn't going to deal with all that just yet. She didn't understand why the subject was so charged for her, but it was. And she was dealing with it the best way she knew how—by avoiding it entirely.

"Nah." She flipped her hand again, realizing only after she had completed the motion that it was telling more than she wanted it to. She wanted to show that it was no big deal. Whoopie pies or cranberry-orange scones, someone as smart as Millie would surely pick up on the crack in her voice and the overuse of her hand, flopping there between them like a drunken butterfly.

She stuffed the offending hand into the waistband of her apron to keep it still and tried again. "I have so many recipes, I thought I should try something new."

"You're sort of known for whoopie pies," Millie said.

"I *was* known for whoopie pies." Now that honor went to Sadie Yoder.

"The guests have been asking for them," Millie continued.

"I didn't hear any complaints about yesterday's cupcakes."

Millie shook her head. "I didn't say anyone was complaining. Just wondering what's happening to the whoopie pies at the Paradise B&B."

"That's just it," Sylvie said with a decisive nod. "We want to be known as the B&B with the best food, not just the best whoopie pies, *jah*?" She nodded with more enthusiasm, gaining momentum with the idea.

Okay, so it wasn't exactly what she had been thinking when she stopped making whoopie pies, but she wasn't ready to tell the truth—that she was so heartbroken over not winning the competition that she wasn't sure she would ever bake another whoopie pie again.

Sure, chances were that she would indeed bake some, sometime, just not right now. Not until her pride healed and her ego recovered. She hadn't gotten to try Sadie Yoder's award-winning brownie pies—she wouldn't say "cake." Cake and brownies were two entirely different things—but she had heard enough people talking about them to know that they must have been scrumptious. And she supposed that was what hurt the most. It wasn't that she had gotten distracted and accidentally added salt instead of sugar like she had a few weeks ago. She had made delicious whoopie pies in their own right. But they had been edged out by someone more innovative and creative and . . . young.

That was it. That was what was really bothering her. She was turning into that old woman who had gotten stuck in her ways and couldn't see the need for change. She didn't want to be that lady. She wanted to shine. She wanted to be creative, fun, and admired.

That isn't what God wants from you, she told herself. And she knew. But it had been hard to find her place after Andrew died. She had done it by making the best B&B in the valley, and by making the best whoopie pies anyone had ever tasted.

Until now anyway.

Too much of her identity was tied up in her baking skills. She knew that. The endeavor had become too important to her. If she could, she would stop, but she couldn't put all that onto Millie with the baby so soon to come. And she certainly couldn't *not* serve afternoon snacks. So she was stuck there, trying to sort through it all, make sense of it all, and get through it all, and until she could do that, whoopie pies were off the menu.

Chapter Twenty-Four

It was a pain unlike any other.

Millie placed a hand on her abdomen, but only lightly. She could barely stand to touch it.

She eased her feet onto the floor of her bedroom and tried to stand. But the effort seemed to take too much energy.

Quit being dramatic, she told herself.

She had been prepared for tearing, searing pains that seemed like they would split her in half. She had heard enough *mamms* talking to know that was the consensus on what childbirth felt like, but this was nothing like that. This felt as if she had been bruised, deep inside. Run over by a car. Left on the roadside to . . .

Die . . . have the baby . . . maybe both.

But she needed to stop wallowing and get herself downstairs. The pain might not feel like she thought it would, or even what she had been led to believe it would, but it was obvious that she was in labor. She would have this baby today. Or tomorrow. With any luck today. She surely didn't want to endure this kind of pain any longer than she had to.

Cautiously, she pushed herself to her feet and grabbed her robe from the foot of the bed. Normally she would use it to get to the bathroom and back to her room so she could change into her dress for the day, but today was not a normal day. And she was headed downstairs to tell her aunt the news. The baby was on the way!

Except getting down the stairs was harder than she had anticipated it to be. Sure the stairs had been a challenge the entire time she had lived here, or rather as her stomach had started to grow and grow. But this was something entirely different. Each step felt as if it was pulling her in half. The pain took her breath away. Halfway down she wasn't sure that she would make it. Then what? She would have the baby right there on the stairs?

Lord, give me strength to overcome this pain.

She took another step, caught her breath, and prayed again.

The Bible told them of Eve's punishment for disobeying God in the Garden of Eden. She was to bring forth children in pain. But Millie had no idea it was this sort of pain.

She thought she had been prepared, but she was mistaken. This was nothing like what she had imagined it would be. She had pictured herself working through the contractions, using the breathing techniques the midwife had taught her. She had learned to picture a happy place where the sun was shining and the breeze tickled everything it touched. She just hadn't had to do that when her body felt like it was being torn in half by . . . she didn't know what. She couldn't think. Something terrible.

She inched down another step, nearly falling back, and the white-hot pain seared through her again.

Lord, give me strength, she prayed. Not her best prayer, but all that her red-clouded thoughts could produce. She had to make it to the bottom of the stairs. Once she was there, everything would be all right. Somehow. Some way.

"Millie?" Her aunt's voice seemed to come to her through a fog.

"Sylvie," she managed in return. "Baby," she said, then everything faded to nothing.

Millie woke on the couch in the sitting room. She took note of where she was and closed her eyes once more. She was still alive. She was lying down, though she had no idea how she had gotten there. She must have walked. There was no way her aunt could have carried her. So the time she spent asleep must have been her mind blocking out the excruciating pain.

Part of her wanted to push herself up. She hated the helpless feeling that surrounded her, pressed her down, but she couldn't find the energy or even the will to do so.

The pain was still there, though since she had stilled it had reduced to a throbbing ache like a thousand tooth-aches instead of the searing stabs that were trying to kill her earlier.

"This is beyond my expertise," an unfamiliar voice said.

Who was that?

Millie opened her eyes and peered over to where her aunt was talking to a young woman Millie didn't recognize. She was Amish, so most likely not a guest at the inn, but other than that quick detail she didn't have the focus to assess much more.

Her aunt needed to call the midwife. Barbie Troyer looked to be older than anyone Millie had ever met, but she was sharp. She had keen eyes and soft hands and she would know what to do. To hear the people of Paradise Valley talk, Barbie had delivered over half the souls on both sides of the Paradise line.

"Midwife," Millie said, though the word never seemed to materialize. Her throat was dry, her lips parched. She tried again. "Midwife." Her voice sounded like the croak of a frog, but it was close enough to a word that it drew her aunt's attention.

"She's awake." Sylvie bustled over. Millie heard her movements rather than saw them. Holding her eyes open was becoming such an effort and the pain, though it had changed, was leeching the energy right out of her. "What's that, dear?"

Millie felt a cool hand on her forehead, her aunt's gentle touch. A smile played at the corners of her lips. Everything was going to be okay, and until that time she hadn't realized how worried she had been. Under all the pain and foggy thoughts, she had been worried that something would happen to the baby. But everything was sure to be okay now. Once her aunt called the midwife.

"Barbie," she whispered.

"I think she said Barbie," the unfamiliar voice said. Millie now knew it belonged to the tiny Amish woman who looked to be no more than a teenager, though she still didn't know who she was. It didn't matter. Her aunt would get Barbie, and she would know what to do to get her through this unexpected pain.

"Barbie's not coming," her aunt said. "This is Annabelle. She's a midwife."

She couldn't be. She was too young. She wouldn't know all the things that Barbie knew. She couldn't. She hadn't had the time to learn them.

She was about to say just that when another pain gripped her and refused to let go. She gasped, then held her breath, sending out prayers though she had no idea if God could even tell what she was saying. This wasn't right. Barbie was supposed to help her. No one had told her the pain was going to be like this. No one had explained to her that she would feel like she was dying.

Fear gripped her. Not for herself, but for her child. If she died, what would happen to the baby?

Lord, please, she prayed, though she didn't add anymore. She didn't know what to say. She didn't know what she wanted, only that something had to change.

"Please," the girl said, echoing her prayer. "We have to get her to the hospital."

Sylvie paced behind the line of chairs that sat facing a television. The sound was turned down so there was no noise other than the squeak of her shoes against the overwaxed tile floors.

Every hospital she had ever been in—and truthfully, she hadn't been in many—they overwaxed the floors. She had lived a full life. Long enough that whoever was waxing the floors had gone on to something different, and yet the overwaxing remained. Why was that? So people like her wouldn't pace?

She drew a couple of exasperated looks from the other people waiting there with her. They had taken Millie into emergency surgery and this was the waiting area for the surgical patients, but how many of them waiting were here on an emergency? None by the way they lounged around, eating chips and watching the television that had no sound.

And how was she supposed to sit down, knowing that Millie might be—well, not knowing that Millie might be—

How was she supposed to sit down with so much going on?

As soon as she had gotten to the hospital, she had called out to the Beachy farm. They were perhaps the closest neighbors to Vern and Henry who had a phone. Sylvie hated giving Malinda firsthand gossip about Millie, but she wanted Vern and Henry there as soon as possible. She needed them there. This was big, scary, nothing like Sylvie had ever dealt with before, and she needed Vern's support and Henry's calm demeanor. Plus Malinda would find out soon enough anyway. She always did.

"What's happening?" a deep, familiar voice asked.

Sylvie stopped midpace and turned to find Vern striding toward her, Henry at his side. They wore identical expressions of concern and hope.

"I'm so glad you're here," she said. She wanted to throw her arms around Vern and hold him close. Around both of them and absorb a little of their strength to get her through, but it wasn't appropriate, so she pulled on her apron instead.

"How's Millie?" Henry asked.

Sylvie shook her head. "I don't know. They took her into surgery hours ago." She looked to the clock hanging opposite the television. "Forty minutes ago," she corrected herself. It had only seemed like hours had passed. "I don't know what's happening."

"Did they say what was wrong?" Henry asked.

Sylvie shook her head, but that was a lie. The doctors had said something about the placenta, and from there it all went over her head. She was an innkeeper, not a doctor or even a midwife. She didn't know about such things and she certainly wasn't talking about such delicate matters with two men, even if those two men were the most important men in her life at the moment.

"But she's having the baby?" Henry asked. His eyes shone with worry. The corners of his mouth were pulled down with concern, but when he said the word "baby," they tried to raise a little. That was what they had to keep in mind. A baby.

"*Jah*." Of that she was certain. Millie had been in labor when she had found her at the bottom of the stairs hunched over in pain. And though Sylvie herself had never been blessed with a child, she had heard enough talk to know that something was wrong. Just how wrong was still a mystery to her.

"We should pray," Vern said, and Sylvie felt a gush of love for him.

Jah, she loved him. What a time to realize such a thing. Or perhaps she had realized it long ago and was just now admitting it to herself.

He put his hand in hers and squeezed her fingers as Henry clasped her other hand. They stood that way, in a circle, with hands joined as they bowed their heads.

Sylvie's prayers were like a dog chasing its tail. She didn't know what to say, so her words went round and round. Her entire life she had been taught to respect and accept God's will. It was almost as much a part of her as the color of her eyes. But this was different. She instinctively prayed that God's will be carried out, then automatically asked for God's will to be her own—that Millie and the baby live and thrive.

She hadn't wanted to let herself believe that Millie might not survive the birth. Would things have been different if Barbie had shown up and not her apprentice, Annabelle? No, that was too much like assigning blame. And that was not something she did.

So as much as she prayed that God's will be done, she turned right around and prayed that Millie and the baby would be fine, healthy even. Whole and safe and . . . safe.

"Sylvie Yoder?"

Sylvie raised her head without even saying amen. "I'm Sylvie Yoder."

A small woman in one of those sickly green-colored hospital uniforms came striding toward them. She had eyes that tilted upward at the corners and silky black hair just visible from under the matching green cap she wore. Sylvie noticed that her pristine white shoes were as squeaky against the tiles as her own well-worn black walking shoes.

"Dr. Nguyen," she said. She reached out a hand to shake. "I was the attending physician for Millie's surgery."

Sylvie didn't understand much of what that meant, except that this woman had been there for Millie's operation. "How is she?" That was all Sylvie cared about. Her niece and the baby.

"Resting. She and the baby are fine for now. Though we're not through the woods yet. Can you come into my office where we can talk more privately?"

Sylvie nodded and started after the doctor. Vern and Henry moving after her.

The doctor stopped. "I apologize, but the two of you should remain here."

Henry took a step forward. "I'm her fiancé," he said.

They had never stated their intentions before, and though Sylvie knew in her heart of hearts that the two of them would get married someday, it was a joy to her to hear him say as much.

The doctor made an apologetic face. "I'm sorry, but regulations state that I can only share the information with the person or persons listed on the patient's form, and there's only one listing. Sylvie Yoder." She looked at the clipboard she carried, as if double-checking her information.

"I'm her fiancé," Vern said, stepping forward. He cleared his throat. "Sylvie's. Not Millie's. He's Millie's man."

Any other time Sylvie would have been gushing with happiness mixed with a good deal of annoyance. Vern was her fiancé? When had that occurred? He certainly hadn't told her about it, and yet here he was, announcing his intentions for the first time to a stranger and not to her.

"I'm very sorry," the doctor said.

"Stay here," Sylvie grumbled. "We'll talk about this later." But she was too concerned for Millie and the baby to say much else.

Her palms were wet and her mouth dry as she squeaked her way behind the doctor. The woman led her down one hall, then another, before opening a faux wooden door that had her name at eye level. Sally Nguyen. She didn't look like a Sally, Sylvie thought. Then chastised herself for her silly thoughts. It was just she was so nervous, so worried, and she needed to hear what the doctor had to say.

"She's not out of the woods yet." Sylvie rushed before the door even closed behind her. "What does that mean?"

"Please." Dr. Nguyen gestured toward the chair placed in front of the faux wood desk. Then she made her way around it to sit in the large leather chair on the other side.

Sylvie perched on the edge of the chair she had pointed to and waited for the doctor to answer her question.

"Your niece had a placental abruption. It's a fairly uncommon condition where the placenta detaches from the uterine wall. That caused the pain she was experiencing when she came into the hospital and excessive bleeding, which in her case was internal."

"What does this all mean?"

"Millie's resting. The baby is undergoing a few tests, and we'll have to see from there."

"But for now?"

"They're both stable." The doctor leaned back in her big leather chair. The size of it seemed to swallow her, and Sylvie wondered if it had belonged to someone else before she had taken it for her own. "We were extremely fortunate. One of the top obstetricians in the state just happened to be in the area visiting family and agreed to come in and perform her surgery. Otherwise we might have had to life flight her to Kansas City. But we were able to take care of everything here."

"When can I see her?" Sylvie tried to relax herself, but she had a feeling there was a lot more the doctor wasn't saying. Because she was Amish and might not understand? Because she wasn't the patient? She had no idea. Or maybe she was just being overly worried because they'd had such a scare.

"We'll have her in a room shortly. A nurse will come

and get you then. If you're hungry, you can go down to the snack bar and get a little something while you wait. It may be a while before they can go home."

That didn't sound good. But at least the doctor had mentioned going home. She had to look on the bright side wherever she could find it.

"Thank you," Sylvie said.

The doctor stood and reached out a hand to shake.

Sylvie took it into her own, a dozen questions circling around inside her head. They would have to wait for now. She had enough information to digest before moving to the next. And for now she only wanted to make sure that Millie was okay.

But one question wouldn't wait. "The baby . . ." she asked.

The doctor smiled. "It's a girl."

A girl. Henry couldn't believe it when Sylvie told him. She had come out of the doctor's office with very little information on what had happened during the birth. But Henry didn't press. The main thing was that Millie would soon be in a room where they could see her. She would most likely have to spend a couple of days there in the hospital, recovering from whatever surgery had been performed to bring the baby girl into the world. A C-section, he believed they were called, though Sylvie didn't name it.

Now they were eating sandwiches they had bought in the cafeteria downstairs and waiting for news on Millie. He just wanted to see her.

He wasn't too proud to admit that he was a little hurt that he hadn't been named on Millie's form to receive information concerning her medical condition. Doctors—female or not—weren't opposed to sharing womanly information with men, as long as your name was on the form.

But he wasn't letting that small detail take away from the joy he was feeling. A girl. He might not be the biological father of the child, but she would be his. He and Millie would raise her and other children they would make together and have one big, happy family. It was all he had ever dreamed of. But he had put that dream aside when Anna Kate had walked out. He thought his time was up. He was already thirty. And who was he going to marry in tiny Wells Landing? He was practically kin to everyone there. Okay, that was an exaggeration caused by grief. He knew it, but it had taken a trip to Missouri to help him see that starting over was in God's plan for him. The thought made him smile.

"What are you grinning about?" Dawdi asked.

"A girl," Henry returned. "A baby girl."

Vern matched Henry's smile with one of his own. "That's something else, *jah*?"

His grin deepened. "*Jah.*"

"But I have a feeling there's more to it than that," Vern continued.

Henry shrugged. The two of them were sitting in the waiting area alone; the other family who had been there had gone on and Sylvie had excused herself to go to the ladies' room. "Maybe."

"No maybe about it."

Henry shrugged again, feeling a little like one of those puppets on strings. "I keep thinking about how I never expected to find love again and here I am."

Vern nodded. "I understand. I feel the same."

"I guess I should start looking for a house," he said. "There's no way we're going to be able to fit all our kids into the inn and still have room for guests."

Sylvie picked that time to squeak up behind them. "You better do her right, Henry King. Her father might not be here, but I am."

"You know me better than that." And she did, but he knew she loved her niece with all her heart. Just as he did. "Do you think the bishop would approve us getting married this fall? I know it's before the year of mourning is over, but . . ." But he couldn't wait to start his life with her.

"Maybe," Sylvie said. "But for now, let's concentrate on getting the two of them home."

Chapter Twenty-Five

Millie looked down at the child she held in her arms and contemplated the wonder of it all. Babies were miracles. That much she knew as surely as she knew her own name. Her scare at the hospital was proof enough of that. And though they had told her of all the complications that could still arise even though she and Linda Beth were home from the hospital, she had faith.

But not enough that she would see Henry. Faith in God was one thing. Faith in man was another. It wasn't that she didn't trust Henry. It was more than that. What would happen if she let him back in and something happened in these crucial twenty-eight days the doctor had told her about?

The placental abruption came with more complications than she could have ever imagined. Linda Beth could have lasting effects from the episode. Millie didn't like that word, but she didn't know what else to call it. Linda Beth had to be monitored closely for the first twenty-eight days. She was at a greater risk than other babies for problems, even death during this time. Millie wanted to spend every second with her. She needed to care for her, soak up her presence, and not let those around her fall in love with her lest the worst happen.

It had been a week, and somehow she had managed for her and Linda Beth to be unavailable when Henry and Vern showed up to check on them.

But she knew her aunt was getting suspicious. Soon Millie would have to tell her the truth. Yes, she was concerned about the problems that could occur during that twenty-eight-day window, but it was more than that. Bigger. And she hadn't dealt with it yet. How could she share the horrible news with her aunt when she couldn't even allow it in her thoughts?

She kissed the top of Linda Beth's downy head and smiled. How was it possible to love a person you had just met so much? A miracle, yes. And the only miracle she would receive.

A soft knock sounded at her door a second before her aunt gently pushed inside. "They're gone now." She moved easily across the room and sat on the edge of the bed, close to where Millie sat in the rocking chair holding Linda Beth while she slept. She knew she should put her down, but she didn't have it in her yet. Maybe tomorrow.

"*Danki*," she said quietly, so as not to disturb the sleeping baby.

"You can't avoid him forever," her aunt said for what could have been the millionth time. At least the hundredth.

Can't I? "I know," she murmured.

"Or me," Sylvie continued. "Are you going to tell me what's wrong?"

Millie breathed in and let the air out on a sigh. She wanted to. She wanted to release herself of this burden, but she wasn't sure how. What if she said the words out loud and they were made even worse for having been spoken?

"I talked to the doctor about what happened," Millie said, hoping that whatever she said would deflect from the topic her aunt wanted to discuss.

"The placenta issue?" her aunt cautiously clarified.

Millie nodded. "He said most times it's caused by a trauma. Like a fall or a car wreck."

"But you didn't have anything like that," her aunt said.

"He also said it could have been stress."

There was no denying that she had been under a great deal of stress during her pregnancy. Everyone had hoped that the move would help, but moving didn't take away the fact that her husband had died and she had been left alone to raise a child who wasn't even born yet.

"And?" her aunt prompted. Millie knew what Sylvie wanted her to say. Could she say it?

"And nothing." She smiled, but she could see that her aunt wasn't going to accept her stall tactics any longer.

She tried her best to grab the words as they raced around in her head. Yet they were slippery as buttered eels and squirmed from her grasp. If she left them alone, she wouldn't have to deal with the truth, but if she hunted them down . . .

Millie sucked in a deep breath. She couldn't allow the fear of the truth to overcome her. She had Linda Beth to think about now.

She had Linda Beth. Her own miracle. Her only.

"There were a lot of complications," Millie told her. "I'll never have any more children."

* * *

"Oh, my love." Sylvie crossed the room and knelt before her niece. She clasped her hand into her own and gently squeezed her fingers. Tears rose into her eyes. "Perhaps—"

But Millie shook her head. "No."

And now, more than ever, Sylvie wished she had pressed the doctor harder to share this news with her. Sylvie might have been listed as next of kin, but now she was beginning to believe that Millie had asked the doctor not to share this devastating news. Oh, the burden!

She gave Millie's hand one last little squeeze and pushed back to her feet. "There's more to life than children," she said. "And you already have the best one ever . . ." she teased, hoping to bring a smile to Millie's lips.

"He wants a family, you know."

To her dismay, tears rose in Millie's eyes and trickled down her cheeks. The whole time she had been home, Sylvie hadn't seen her cry once. Her expression had always been sad and a little far away. Now she understood why.

"And he'll have one." She gestured to Linda Beth where she rested in Millie's arms.

"No, a big family. Lots of kids, a dog, a cat, a bunch of chickens."

"I was never blessed with children," Sylvie said. "But I learned that sometimes God's plan doesn't line up with our own. Still, that doesn't mean it's not a good plan." She smiled for reassurance.

Millie shook her head. "Maybe if we were already married, but this is different. If he marries me now, he'll have to give up everything he wants from life."

"That's not true. He wants you. He's been by every day

since you've been home. And every day you've refused to
see him."

"I can't tell him yet," she admitted with a small sniff.
At least her tears had stopped for now. They were beginning to weaken Sylvie's resolve. "I just can't."

"Can't tell him what?" Sylvie asked. "That you're not
going to marry him or . . . the other?"

"I can't marry him." Millie's voice rose and the baby
in her arms stirred, fussed, then let out a wail of her own.
Millie shushed her. She cradled her closer and kissed her
forehead. Linda Beth settled back in her mother's arms,
content once again.

That was when Sylvie realized that Millie hadn't put
the baby down once since she had come home. Maybe at
night, but every time she had checked on the two of them,
Millie had been sitting up, holding the baby close while
she slept.

"Maybe you should talk to someone," Sylvie said gently.
She didn't want to alarm Millie more than she already was
about life, but something was wrong.

"I'm talking to you," she said.

Sylvie shook her head. "No, about your . . . feelings."

"I can talk until I'm blue in the face and it won't change
the fact that I can't give Henry what he wants from life,
from a marriage."

"How do you know what he wants?" Sylvie countered.

"We've talked about it." Millie's voice had an edge. She
was getting tired or frustrated or both.

"I'm sure he wants a lot of things from a marriage. But
it seems to me the number one thing he wants is you."

"You don't know that," Millie said.

"Neither do you. And yet you've not given him a chance

to tell you himself what's most important. Don't you think you should?"

Her niece stopped rocking, a look of panic and resignation taking over her sweet face. "I—"

"You should and you know it."

"Maybe," she murmured, obstinate as ever. Millie could be that way, stubborn as a mule. Sometimes it was frustrating, but Sylvie knew that it was her tenacity that got her through losing her husband and starting over. It would get her through this time as well. If she could only get her to talk to Henry and tell him the truth, surely everything else would fall into place.

"No maybe. And I'm warning you now. When Henry comes by tomorrow, I'm letting him in."

"Auntie," Millie protested.

Sylvie held up a hand to stay her words. "Nope. One way or another, that man deserves to know the truth."

P-o-s-t-p-a-r-t-u-m d-e-p-r-e-s-s-i-o-n.

Henry typed the letters one by one into the computer at the Paradise Springs Public Library. He had never heard of such a thing, but as chance would have it, he was in the apothecary looking at some new oils, hoping to find something useful to take to Millie, when Betsy Stoll had asked him about the baby, and as much as he tried to be vague and not really say anything, Betsy figured out that he hadn't even seen the child yet. She must have been keeping track because she told him that as far as she knew, no one had been in to see the child, and she mused that Millie might be suffering from postpartum depression.

And that was how he found himself at the library with

a spray bottle filled with essential oils that Betsy called Mommy Revive Blend, trying to figure out what was wrong with the woman he loved.

It was obvious that *something* was wrong. She had been home from the hospital a week and she hadn't let him in to see her once. He hadn't even seen the baby. Whatever it was that was bothering her . . . well, they could get over it. But he couldn't help if he didn't know what it was.

He pushed Enter on the computer like the librarian had shown him to do and sat back as the screen changed and a page full of listings about postpartum depression popped up on the screen. He chose the first one and started to read.

Maybe, he thought. Maybe that was what was wrong with her, but he hadn't heard Sylvie say anything about her not wanting to care for the baby or not having any interest in the child, or even life. Every time he had gone to the inn, Sylvie had told him that they were sleeping, or Millie was feeding the baby, or bathing her, or something. But never that she wasn't taking care of little Linda Beth.

He loved the sound of her name. Sentimental marshmallow. That was what he was, but he had been waiting for this time. Waiting to see this child that had been growing inside Millie the whole while he had known her.

That child was a part of her, and though he hadn't met her yet, he loved her in the same way he loved Millie— completely, wholly, without question.

Now if he could just figure out what was going on with Millie that she didn't want to see him . . .

He drummed his fingers on the table where he sat, accidentally hitting a couple of the computer buttons, and a new picture popped up on the screen in front of him. More words, more articles, these about anxiety.

He started to read, and the more he read, the more he thought about Millie, shutting herself off. Then he had an idea.

P-o-s-t-p-a-r-t-u-m a-n-x-i-e-t-y.

He hit Enter. A host of new choices appeared before him. Pleased with his ingenuity, he chose an article and started to read once more.

An hour and a half later he let himself into the inn and went to find Sylvie. Of all the things he had read on the internet that morning, he was concerned that Millie had some sort of depression or anxiety. Either one could potentially alter her thinking enough to keep her from taking proper care of the baby. She needed help. Sylvie needed help. And he was just the person to give a hand to get them through. After all, he was marrying Millie just as soon as possible. This last week, not being able to see her, just showed him how much of life he was missing not sharing it with her. It might be soon for her, but he wanted to show her life was good. God was good. And they could have their best life together.

If he could get in to see her.

Of course he found Sylvie in the kitchen making . . . something.

"What's that?" he asked, momentarily distracted.

She smiled, obviously pleased with her efforts. "Pastéis de Nata."

He waited for her to continue.

"Custard tarts from Portugal."

Ever since her loss at the Whoopie Pie Festival he hadn't seen Sylvie make one single whoopie pie of any flavor. But he surely didn't know what to push into the library computer to help with that. So he held up the papers the librarian had helped him to print. "I found out some things today and I feel Millie needs some help."

Sylvie sighed, her joy over the new dessert seeming to leak right out of her. "I know."

"And I'm not leaving until I see her," he continued, gaining momentum. "If I have to wait until after she feeds her and changes her and bathes her and dresses her again, so be it. But I want to see my girls."

Until that moment he hadn't realized he felt that way about them, but that was what they were: Millie and Linda Beth, his girls.

Sylvie sighed again. "Would you like to try one?" she asked. "These over here are cool enough." She pointed to a tray off to the side of the kitchen worktable.

"I want to see Millie," he said.

"I know." She dried her hands on her apron and turned toward the door leading into the rest of the house. "This way."

Henry took one last look at the Portugal tarts—whatever they were—before grabbing one and following behind Sylvie through the foyer and up the staircase.

As he passed the closed doors, he saw that each had a plaque screwed into the wood telling which room it was. Strange, but he didn't remember that from the first time he had come here, the day he and Vern had worked on the sink in one of the suites. The rooms had funny names, like the Lavender Room and the Blue Room, each sign matching the color it listed. He was about to ask her if

all the rooms were done by color and what exactly that
meant when she stopped at a door with a white sign the
same color as the door. This one read PRIVATE.

"Stay here," Sylvie said.

He started to protest. He wasn't leaving until he got to
see Millie and that was that.

But before he could say a word, Sylvie cut him off. "I
know. But I have to give her a warning first, okay?"

Henry nodded, though he wanted to burst through the
door and make sure that Millie and the baby were okay.
And not just because Sylvie had told him so but because
he had seen them with his own eyes.

Sylvie gave a quick nod in return, then rapped lightly
on the door before letting herself in.

Henry waited outside. He took a bite of the dessert he
had snatched from downstairs. It wasn't that he really
wanted it, but he was nervous and needed something to
do while he waited.

It wasn't bad, this little pie-looking sweet from across the
world. It wasn't a whoopie pie for sure, but it wasn't bad.

He could hear their voices as he stood there eating the
dessert he didn't really want and waiting once again. But
he couldn't understand what they were saying.

After what seemed like forever, Sylvie came back out.
"You can go in now."

His heart jumped in his chest. Millie.

He eased through the door, hardly aware of the fact that
Sylvie closed it quietly behind him. He could only focus
on the scene before him. Millie and the baby.

"Hi," he said, suddenly self-conscious and a little nervous. This was what he had wanted. This was what he had

been waiting for. And now that he was here, he wasn't sure exactly what to do.

"I brought you a present." He held up the little paper sack from Paradise Apothecary. "It's supposed to help with mommy exhaustion." Whatever that was. He was learning more than he ever imagined in these last couple of days. "That's what Betsy said anyway."

Millie smiled, but the action seemed more sad than joyful. "If anyone would know it would be Betsy."

Henry wasn't sure what she meant by that but nodded anyway.

"I—" They both started at the same time, then laughed and shook their heads.

"You first," he said.

"No," she countered, "after you."

"I've missed you," he said. He had lost the thread of his earlier speech. Just seeing Millie after so long and after so much worry had about done him in. Being so close to her now . . . he just wanted to soak in her presence and gaze at the tiny bundle she held. "Is that—"

Millie smiled, and this one was more like the Millie smiles he had seen before. "This is Linda Beth."

Henry inched into the room, almost afraid that his footsteps might disturb the sleeping baby. He wanted to hold her and yet he was scared. She was so little. He remembered people in the community back home having babies, and he was sure they were the same size as the child before him, but they hadn't seemed so delicate to him. So fragile. So tiny and sweet-smelling.

"Hi, Linda Beth," he murmured. He reached out a hand but didn't touch her. And for a moment he almost thought Millie had moved Linda Beth away from him. But that couldn't be right. "She's amazing," he said, completely in awe of this perfect little creature.

"*Jah*," Millie said.

"And how are you?" He asked the question cautiously. He didn't want to pry, but he needed to know. Still, women and men—even married ones, or soon-to-be married ones—didn't talk much about such matters as childbirth.

"Henry, I can't marry you."

Her words fell between them hard and fast. So quickly that Henry thought he must have imagined them. That was what it was. He had heard her wrong. She wouldn't be telling him that. "What?" he asked so she could repeat what she had actually said instead of those horrible words he had thought he heard.

"I can't marry you."

All the air seemed to be sucked from the room. He couldn't breathe. This wasn't right. His hearing was off. This was more than anxiety or depression. This was not happening. "What are you saying, Millie?"

She pressed her lips together and shook her head. "Are you really going to make me say it again?"

So he had heard her correctly. "*Jah*," he said, anger and confusion rising up in him. "I am. What was that?"

"I am calling off the wedding."

"We don't have a wedding planned."

"The engagement, then," she corrected herself. "We are not getting married."

"You're just depressed or anxious," he said. Then, remembering the papers he had printed out at the library, he held them up in one hand. "I've been reading about it. Lots of women—"

"I'm not not marrying you because I'm anxious or

depressed. I'm not marrying because I can't have any more children." The words came out on a single rush of air, as if she had to push them from her body in order for them to be heard.

"What?" All the steam had gone out of him. What was she talking about now? His head was going in circles, like a puppy trying to find a good place to lie down. "You can't—" He couldn't finish.

She seemed to shrink there, sitting in that rocking chair, to half the size she had been before. "I can't," she reaffirmed. "I know how much a family means to you, so I'm releasing you from our agreement so you can go find or make the family you've been dreaming of."

Henry shook his head, partly to tell her that he disagreed with her and partly to rattle his thoughts around so they hopefully lined up and started to make sense. "I've only dreamed of being with you and . . . and . . . Linda Beth. Even before she was born." That was all he had allowed himself to dream about since Anna Kate walked out, and only then because he couldn't help himself. He and Millie were supposed to be together. His time with her had shown him that. And if Anna Kate hadn't gone to Belize, he would still be in Oklahoma and he wouldn't have ever met Millie. But that wasn't what God had planned for him. For them.

Now Millie wanted to go messing with God's handiwork.

"I can't do this to you, Henry. You need to go now."

What? What was she saying now? Why couldn't he get his mind around all this? He felt as if he had been conked over the head with a lead pipe.

"Why do you get to say?" he finally asked. "What about what I want?"

She smiled at him, and tears rose into her beautiful blue eyes. He had never seen her look lovelier, or sadder, than she did at that moment. "You don't know what you want. Not really. And we might be okay for a year or two, but I couldn't live with myself, knowing that you could have had all your dreams and instead you're stuck with me."

Henry felt the sting of tears in his own eyes. He blinked furiously, trying to hold them back. He didn't want to cry in front of Millie. He had never cried when he and Anna Kate had parted ways. She had shed many a tear, apologizing and promising that he could come too. But he had held her close, kissed the top of her head, and told her goodbye.

He wasn't even going to be able to do that with Millie. And he was angry. He hadn't been angry before. But she was telling him what he wanted from life, what he needed. And she wasn't giving him a chance to say. And when she did, she told him it wasn't the truth. The real truth.

Stubborn woman.

"You don't know what you're saying," he said. "Let's give it some time, *jah*?" Finally he managed to blink the tears back. He sniffed and waited for her to answer.

"No," she said. "I've been thinking about this all week. This is it. We're through. Goodbye, Henry."

Chapter Twenty-Six

"What did you call these again?" Vern asked the following day.

Sylvie had been working all morning, searching for a new dessert to take with her to the widows' group meeting. Well, not exactly take. She had asked if the meeting could be moved to the inn this week and until further notice, so she wouldn't have to leave Millie alone to attend. Seeing as how hosting the meeting was a big chore, no one protested.

But finding something besides whoopie pies to serve . . . well, that was another matter altogether.

"Beignets," she said. "At least that's how I think you're supposed to say it. They're French."

Vern held up the light and fluffy square of baked dough sprinkled with powdered sugar. "It's like a doughnut."

"Maybe," she said. "But these are baked. Not fried." Though she did have a recipe for fried ones. It was just that she was a baker and she liked to bake things. Not fry them. "And they're French."

Vern took another bite and chewed thoughtfully. "A French doughnut."

Sylvie rolled her eyes. "Not the point, Vern King. And not why I asked you to come here today."

"I believe I called you," he said.

"Well, I was about to call you," she countered. "We've got to do something."

Thankfully he didn't ask about what. "I don't think there's anything that can be done," he said. "According to Henry, she's got her mind made up."

"So he's giving up then?"

Vern brushed the powdered sugar from his beard and reached for another of the treats. "I didn't say that, just that he seems to believe that she's not willing to change her mind."

"That's the same thing."

"Not hardly." He took a big bite of the beignet. "You know, if you could figure out a way to get Bavarian cream on the inside of these—"

"Not a doughnut, Vern. Now focus." She moved the plate away from him, across the table, hoping that would set his thoughts on the right path. These days it seemed all he cared about was eating. "Henry's not baking bread, is he?"

Vern studied the little pastry. "Nope. And that just goes to show you. He's letting her go."

"But why?" Sylvie asked. "They were good together. They need each other." And we need them, she silently added. For if Henry decided to move back to Oklahoma, it was certain he would move Vern with him.

Sylvie reined in those thoughts. That wasn't the most important part. That was just the part that affected her directly. Moving or not, Henry and Millie belonged together. And that was all there was to it.

"Best I can figure, a man can only take so much heartache; then he's had enough. Seems like Henry has had his fill of heartache in this life."

"We have to do something," Sylvie said.

"What?" Vern asked.

"I don't know," she retorted. "We need to think of something."

"Like what?"

"Vern King, if you don't—" She didn't know how to finish that. She didn't have any ideas for how to get Henry and Millie back on the road to marriage. Why did she expect Vern to have any? Because they needed one. Desperately. "This is going to be really awkward at Christmas," she mused.

Vern shook his head. "I won't be here at Christmas, I expect."

The thought sent a flash of pain through her heart. She had gotten used to having Vern around, trying her recipes and otherwise making her crazy. In a good way, if that even was a thing. She wanted him around more. And that was a new feeling in her. But if he had to move to Oklahoma . . . it wouldn't just be that he would be leaving. He would be leaving *her*. And whatever this was budding between them would never have a chance.

Just like the love between Henry and Millie.

There. She had called it by its name. Love. *Jah*. She was in love with Vern King. As crazy as the idea sounded, she liked it. But not if he was moving away and never coming back.

Vern leaned across and started to take another beignet from the plate.

Sylvie snatched them out of his reach. "No," she said

emphatically. "No more treats. In fact, get out of here, Vern King, and don't come back until you have a plan on how to get these kids back together!"

One week passed and then another. And Sylvie was no closer to figuring out this dilemma. Unlike the days just after the birth, Henry had stopped coming by the B&B demanding to see Millie.

Sylvie had seen Vern at church the Sunday before and it seemed as if he had avoided her. Millie of course stayed home with Linda Beth, as was expected, and though Sylvie prayed then and every day actually for some sort of solution, some idea on what would bring Henry and Millie back together, she had none.

Except to invite Henry to the B&B and see what happened next.

She could pray that God would step in and the two people who belonged together most in this world would find their way back to each other.

Henry pulled his buggy into the drive at the Paradise B&B and stopped. Stopped the horse and carriage. And just stopped.

This would be the first time he had seen Millie since she had told him goodbye. The truth was, he didn't know for certain that he would see her, but when he had accepted Sylvie's invitation to come have afternoon tea with her at the inn, he had automatically assumed Millie would be included. Okay, that was wishful thinking on his part.

Sylvie had made no mention of Millie and he hadn't asked. But at least being at the inn for tea brought him one step closer to Millie. Or the chance to see her.

How pitiful was that? She had told him that she never wanted to see him again and he wanted to simply be in the same building with her? The strangest part of all was he never felt that way about Anna Kate. Or if he had, the feelings were much more watered down, not as intense as the pain over losing Millie and Linda Beth.

And despite the fact that she told him that she didn't want to marry him and didn't want to see him, he was desperate to see her. Not that he would let anybody know. A man had his pride. He had acted like it was no big deal, that he wasn't heartbroken, devastated, or even destroyed from losing love once again. And not just any love, but Millie.

And so he had accepted the invitation to tea so he could play it cool and perhaps get one more look at the love of his life.

He wasn't sure what that meant. Tea. He drank tea a lot. Had his whole life. Usually Sylvie was pressing a glass of lemonade in everyone's hand, but it didn't matter what they drank. Being at the inn put him that much closer to Millie, and that was all he cared about.

He had been listening at church to what the ladies were saying. Okay, so he was eavesdropping, but he needed to know that Millie was okay. And now that she'd had the baby, they were the biggest talk in the community, usurping Samuel Raber's death at the Whoopie Pie Festival and Sylvie's topple from whoopie pie stardom.

As far as he could tell, both mother and baby were doing fine. But if he was able to see them today . . .

Yet now that the possibility could come about, he was reluctant. What if she didn't want to see him at all? He wasn't sure he could handle that. Missing her was one thing, but knowing that she didn't want to see him again, ever, was another all on its own. He had been trying to be patient until she got over whatever this was, Postpartum I-Can't-Marry-You. He wondered if there was such a thing. He hoped so and it would pass like the internet had said the other conditions that happened after having a baby would.

The truth was, he missed her. He missed his friend. He missed talking with her and laughing with her, even discussing the issues they faced. Nothing seemed too big when he was with Millie. It was as if all the world's problems shrunk down to nothing when she was by his side.

Yet he had promised Sylvie that he would come visit today and so he would. He had wanted to come first thing, right after he got up and dressed. But Sylvie told him that tea was to be served at three. He'd never heard of such a thing but didn't argue. So he'd prowled around the house, too antsy to do any work and too nervous to sit down. Now, finally, it was time.

Henry hopped down from the buggy and tied his horse's reins to the hitching post; then he made his way through the back door that led into the kitchen, like Sylvie had instructed him to.

The kitchen was as immaculate as ever, near gleaming, though the faint scents of bacon, yeast, and sweetness hung in the air just beneath the scent of lemon cleaner. But Sylvie was nowhere to be seen.

He shut the door behind him and made his way through the room, past the worktable that sat in the middle of the space and to the swinging door on the other side.

"Henry?" Sylvie called to him. "Is that you? In here. The dining room."

The dining room? The only time Henry had been in there had been when he and Vern had come to supper when Sylvie had thought something was wrong with one of the sinks upstairs. At the time he and Millie hadn't been friends, but he had enjoyed her open smile and sweet demeanor. What he wouldn't give to go back to that time. Maybe start over. Figure out a way to convince Millie that she and Linda Beth were enough family for him.

With a shake of his head to clear his thoughts, he pushed into the dining room where Sylvie waited.

He did his best to temper his expression. He was immediately disappointed that Millie wasn't there as a wonderful surprise for him, and that all had been forgotten. He wouldn't want Sylvie to think that he was dissatisfied with her. That wasn't the case at all. He just missed Millie. Plain and simple.

Sylvie smiled at him, and he nearly breathed a sigh of relief that his deception had been successful. "She's not here," Sylvie said. "I mean she's *here,* just not here. She's upstairs with the baby. But she'll be down in a bit."

Henry eased into the room, almost cautiously, as if she might jump out from behind one of the chairs to spook him. "What's all this?" he asked once it became apparent that Millie wasn't leaping out from anywhere and he could relax for a moment. This was his chance to get himself together while "a bit" passed and he would be ready to see Millie once again.

"Tea," she said simply.

Tea. Maybe that was something else he needed to look up in the computer at the library. Last he knew, tea were leaves that were steeped in water to make a drink that could be consumed hot or cold, sweetened or not. But this . . .

This was a dessert cart from a fancy restaurant, like Paradiso Italia. In fact this spread looked even better than the one they had been offered when Henry and Millie had eaten there.

Why was it that every memory that passed through his mind had something to do with Millie?

Sylvie half stood and started naming off each treat, pointing to it as she did. "Brown butter rum cannoli, Pavlova with blueberry jam, coconut crème crepe cake, and chocolate peanut butter caramel mousse pie."

Everything looked absolutely scrumptious, but decadent and sweet. Very, very sweet. And there wasn't a whoopie pie in sight.

She's trying too hard, he thought. And he tried to remember the last time he had eaten one of Sylvie's whoopie pies. Before the competition, he was sure. It seemed that losing her title may have affected her more than anyone realized. They had all been too wrapped up in their own lives and their own problems to notice. He started to say something; what, he had no idea, but he was saved from having to come up with something in that moment as Millie came into the room.

"Auntie, I—" She stopped right there in her tracks and stared at him as if she had never seen such a creature before. And she wished never to again—half surprise, half horror. "Henry." Her hand flew to her head. She wore a kerchief instead of a prayer covering, something he had seen his mother and sisters do when they were cleaning or doing yardwork. But they would never have greeted a guest in such a manner.

She didn't know I was coming.

"Hi, Millie." He smiled apologetically. And yet he wasn't sorry. He had wanted to see her for weeks now, had been trying to come up with a reason that she had to see him, but this was better, he was sure. Maybe because he had no reason why she should see him other than he loved her and she loved him. She might not want to marry him, but he wasn't about to start believing that she didn't love him. His heart couldn't take that kind of blow.

"I—" she stuttered, her speech reflecting his own thoughts. He had so much he wanted to say to her. He wanted to convince her to see him again. Give him a second chance. Give them a second chance. He wanted her to sit down with him, eat some of the yummy-looking desserts that Sylvie had prepared. But there were so many words running around in his thoughts, they had started to tangle together.

"Where's Linda Beth?" he asked. It was the only co-herent sentence he could form.

"Sleeping." Millie seemed to shrink just a bit, as if she had been holding her breath and releasing it had decreased her size. Or maybe she had just relaxed. Maybe talking about Linda Beth was safe to her and didn't make her nervous.

If that was the case, he would talk about the baby all day long, even when he wanted to talk about more. So much more.

Take it slow.

He was in the same room with her, and that hadn't happened in weeks. Surely this was a start in the right direction.

"I bet she's grown."

Millie nodded, her eyes shining with love for her child. That love made her all the more beautiful.

"I'll just go and . . ." Sylvie sidled toward the door, letting herself out quietly, but Henry couldn't take his eyes from Millie.

Nor she him.

Did that mean she had missed him as much as he missed her?

"I should go—" she started, gesturing toward the door through which her aunt had just disappeared.

"No!" Henry hadn't meant to shout, but his emotions were running high, nearly drowning him in their intensity. "No," he said, much more quietly. "Please stay. Talk to me." Seeing her again made it all so clear. He needed her. He had been kidding himself to believe that he could live without her. He needed her in his life. She was his life. And he had to do whatever he could to win her love once again. His voice cracked, but he pressed on. "Tell me what's happening. If you can't tell me what's wrong, how can I fix it?"

* * *

His words nearly choked her. Her breath caught in her throat. Her hands trembled and she felt the tears sting at the back of her eyes.

"I told you what was wrong and you can't fix it. No one can." She had come to terms with the fact that she would never have any more children. Why couldn't he see this was for the best? That she was doing this for him?

He shook his head. "Why do you have the only say in this?"

"Because you're a good man, Henry King."

"I don't understand," he said with a frown.

Tears spilled over her lower lids, trekking down her cheeks. She hadn't wanted to cry. She had told herself that she had cried enough. But here the tears were once again. "You would never walk away from me and Linda Beth."

"Of course not."

"So I did it for you. I released you from our agreement." She sighed. "I told you all this." And it was even harder to say a second time. Why hadn't it gotten easier? It should have become a part of her in these last few weeks; it should have settled in and made itself at home. But the idea seemed as foreign and strange to her today as it had the day she had told him.

Why?

Because she hadn't wanted to release him.

There. She admitted it to herself. But instead of making her feel better, the words made her feel selfish and self-serving.

"This is not easy for me," she said.

"Good," he returned. "Then quit it. Go the easy route."

She shook her head. "I can't do that. Your happiness is at stake."

"Why don't you let me worry about that?"

"But—" she started, but he cut her off after the one word.

"No buts. You think you'll make me happy in the future, but how can my future have any happiness in it if you aren't there?"

She stopped, tried not to absorb his words, but they were already becoming a part of her. Why was he making sense all of a sudden?

"You and Linda Beth." He walked toward her slowly, as if approaching a skittish fawn. That was how she felt, as fragile and wobbly as a newborn baby deer. "When Anna Kate told me that she was moving to Belize, I only thought I was heartbroken. I moped around and even drank a little—don't tell Dat . . . or Dawdi." He smiled, and her heart grew warm with the sight. "Then I met you and I realized that the happiness I thought I had lost had been waiting for me all along. Even more happiness," he said, "because I not only got you, but a precious baby girl who is as beautiful as her mother and so special in every way." He reached her then, stopped inches from her. So close she could smell the detergent from his clothes and the scent of outdoors that he had picked up on the buggy ride over. "Why do you think I need anything more?" he asked. "Anything else?"

"But—" Why did that seem like the only word she could say?

"No buts," he said again. Then he reached out, slowly, giving her plenty of time to object. Or maybe it was plenty of time to accept the fact that he was going to kiss her. She should have protested. She should have told him to stop, that he couldn't kiss her because if he did, she wouldn't be able to send him away again.

But the truth was, she already knew that she wouldn't be able to refuse him now. She couldn't deny the love she felt for him. The longing she had for him. The happiness she had wanted to share with him. The fact that she was so, so tired of fighting against it.

He cupped one hand under her chin and tilted her face toward his.

His lips on hers were sweet, chaste, and the best thing she had ever felt.

She sighed as he pulled away.

"See?" he said simply. He didn't even have to say what. She knew. They would be good together. They belonged together.

But the weight of it all still bore down on her.

"You don't have to answer now," he said. "But know this: I am coming back here every day until you say yes."

She might have said yes right then had the air around them not been rent with the screeching wail of a siren.

"What's that?" Henry said, a frown puckering his brow.

"Fire truck," she replied. "I think."

Just then, Sylvie bustled back in cradling Linda Beth in her arms. "The siren woke her," she explained. "I think she needs to eat." She shot Henry an apologetic grimace.

And Millie knew for certain that she had been set up. "Time to go, Henry." She had been given a reprieve. She had to do this. For Henry. She and Linda Beth would be fine on their own, but Henry . . . he deserved more.

Thank you, Lord, she silently prayed. She didn't look at him again as she took the baby from her aunt and made her way upstairs. Now if she could just be this strong come tomorrow.

"I can't believe you were in town gorging yourself on desserts at Sylvie's while my life was in danger."

Henry tried to look ashamed, but mostly he was concerned.

There had been a moment this afternoon when he had believed just for a bit that Millie was about to cave, that she was going to drop her façade and admit that she loved him. That she needed him, that she wanted him. Then the fire truck and her aunt and feeding the baby and the moment had been shattered. So he had left with his vow to return every day until she said yes. And he meant it too. Then he drove back out to his *dawdi*'s farm only to discover the fire truck parked in their yard.

"How did you catch the kitchen on fire anyway?" he asked, watching as the firemen wound up their hoses and prepared to leave. Water still dripped from the roof of the house and into the cavern that had once been the kitchen. A small white-and-tan dog bounded around, barking and growling at the men who implicitly ignored him.

As far as fires went, this one hadn't been completely devastating. The kitchen was destroyed and the two of them would have to stay at the inn until they could have repairs made. Henry was something of an amateur carpenter, but this was beyond his skills by far. Appliances would have to be replaced, walls rebuilt, the floor . . . well, there was no floor any longer. All of that would have to be repaired.

Vern popped open the container of desserts he had

rescued from the buggy when Henry pulled into the drive. They had led their gelding out of harm's way and used their own water system to hose down the barn and other outbuildings lest the fire jump from one to another while the firemen extinguished the flames licking upward from what used to be the kitchen.

"I just wanted something to eat," he grumbled.

Henry sighed. "And did you get it?"

Vern held up the container of treats from Sylvie. "*Jah*."

"So you nearly burned down the house and didn't even get something to eat?" Henry asked.

"I put on a can of soup. I really am tired of eating stuff from a can, you know. Then I heard this barking."

That explained the dog.

"I guess I had the stove up too high," he said. "Because I started playing fetch with the pup and the next thing I knew, I smelled smoke."

Or his father was right and Vern really was starting to get forgetful.

Henry hadn't seen it up until now. Oh, Vern might have been a little absentminded, misplacing his glasses or walking into a room and forgetting why he was there. But that was normal forgetfulness. At least that was what Henry had thought.

He looked over to the ruined kitchen. The house itself wasn't a total loss. But he was certain that everything inside had either smoke or water damage.

And he knew as sure as he was named after his other *dawdi* that his father would be there by the end of the week, demanding that they all move back to Oklahoma.

"Maybe he's right." Vern looked to the dripping, charred remains of the kitchen.

"Who?" Henry asked.

"Dale. Maybe he's right."

Henry turned to study his *dawdi*. "What do you mean?" He had never seen his grandfather look so solemn, not in all the time he had been in Missouri.

"Maybe I do need a keeper."

"Dat said that?"

Vern shook his head. "Not in so many words, but I knew what he meant."

Henry frowned. "You don't need a keeper." Or maybe more had been going on that Henry didn't know about. His father hadn't sent him there to observe. He had sent him there to make sure Vern got his crops in and to help him get the house ready to sell. Then he was supposed to hire a truck, pack up his *dawdi*'s belongings, and move it all to Wells Landing.

"Take care, Vern," one of the firemen said, tipping his thick fire helmet in Vern's direction before hopping onto the back of the truck. He slapped the flat of his hand against the side panel a couple of times and the big engine roared to life.

The fireman knew Vern's name. But that really didn't say a lot. Paradise Springs wasn't a big town. Even if you added in all of the valley, it wasn't what anyone would consider large. So it stood to reason that his grandfather would know just about everyone in town, including the firemen.

But there was the new paint in Vern's bedroom . . . paint Henry hadn't applied.

"This isn't the first fire you've started, is it?" he asked.

Vern shook his head, his chin dropped in shame. "I told myself that I would be more careful. That I was just being lazy." He shrugged one shoulder. "That's not the right word, but you know what I mean."

Henry did. Distracted. That's what his grandfather was. Completely distracted. "And that's why Dat thinks you need to move down to Oklahoma." It wasn't quite a question.

"*Jah.*"

"What about Joy and her family?"

"She can't keep track of me and her entire brood. Not since Johnny B's accident."

"But if you move, she'll be the only King left here in Paradise Springs." Now why did that make him feel strangely nostalgic? He hadn't grown up there. He couldn't remember living there at all, though they told him he was born there and lived in Missouri for the first three or so years of his life.

Vern shrugged again. "I don't reckon that's something Dale concerns himself with."

Henry bit back a sigh. He supposed his grandfather was right about that one.

"It's settled," Henry said as they picked through their closets and tried to find clothes that didn't smell too much like smoke. The washing machine had been in the small room off the kitchen and had perished in the fire. He could only hope that Sylvie and Millie would take pity on two bachelors and wash their things for them. Otherwise they were going to walk around for days smelling like a hamburger grill . . . without the hamburgers.

"It's settled," Vern grumbled.

The man was stubborn, Henry'd give him that, but they couldn't stay in the house until a lot of repair work had been done. It simply wasn't possible. The only place he figured they could stay was the Motel 9 out off the highway or the Paradise B&B. As far as he was concerned, it was no choice at all. Millie was at the B&B, and he would use this as just one more step toward gaining back her love.

No, that wasn't it exactly. He had a feeling her love was still there. He just had to break down these silly walls she had constructed and get to the real heart of the matter. That she felt like she couldn't give him his dreams. Truth was, she *was* his dreams. All of them wrapped up in an apron and a prayer covering. Everything he could want. And a baby to boot.

There wasn't a man alive who could ask for more.

But his grandfather's reluctance to leave the house . . .

"Are you afraid that if you leave the house, my *dat* won't let you return?" They had already talked, and both agreed that Dale would be there by the end of the week. Though Vern had said Saturday, Henry had countered with Friday. They had a bucket of gourmet popcorn on the line, but Henry was confident. His father would be knocking on their door as soon as he could. And there was no way they could move back into the house before Friday, or even Saturday.

"*Jah*," Vern answered. Though a little quickly.

"What?" Henry asked.

"No. Nothing. That's it. That's exactly why I don't want to leave the house and move into the B&B. Are you sure you don't want to stay at the Motel 9?"

Henry was glad the gelding knew the way into town by heart. The reins loosened in his hands as he turned toward his grandfather. "You don't want to stay at the B&B," he said, the idea just coming to him. "Why?"

"Well," his *dawdi* blustered. "It's not that at all."

"Then what is it?" He watched Vern for a moment, then turned his attention back to the road. The gelding was still on the right path, but he thought his grandfather needed a little time to gather himself.

"Sylvie," he finally admitted.

"What about Sylvie?"

"She told me that if I couldn't get the two of you together—you and Millie—then I wasn't to come back until I did."

Henry half turned in his seat, his driving forgotten once again. "When was this?"

"A week or so ago. Maybe two," he miserably admitted.

"A couple of weeks ago? Why am I just hearing about this now?"

He shrugged. "She fed me French doughnuts and tried to get me to come up with a plan to get you and Millie together. When I couldn't think of one right away, she said Christmas was going to be awkward, and I said I didn't think I would be here for Christmas—and now I really don't—then she got mad and told me to leave."

And two weeks later she invited Henry over. Another attempt to get them together.

"Why do you suppose that is?" Henry asked.

Vern shrugged. "I suppose because she's mad."

"No," Henry said as patiently as he could. He had always heard that women thought men were clueless. He had never known why until now. "She likes you."

"What?" Vern stroked his beard, as if the idea was foreign, but he might could get used to it real quick.

"She likes you." And it all made perfect sense.

They were almost to town and Henry pulled the buggy down one of the tractor tracks at the side of the road. "If she likes you, she wants you to stay as well. And if I stay, you're staying . . ." Perfect sense.

"So what do we do?"

Henry smiled. "I've got a plan. I need to make one stop and then we'll go to the inn," he said. "And then . . ."

Chapter Twenty-Seven

Henry could never have predicted the scene that met his eyes as he walked into the B&B forty minutes later.

He had been playing it out in his head the entire time he was explaining his plan to his grandfather and the whole of the time he spent in the library printing out even more documents with the librarian's help.

Most of these plans consisted of him walking in and sweeping Millie off her feet—in a figurative sense—telling her that he loved her, he wasn't giving up, and she might as well agree to marry him. In those thoughts he was calm and confident. He was brave and steady.

But in reality he was quaking like the last leaf of fall.

And it didn't help that the inn was in complete chaos.

A crying child, screaming women, and a squalling baby.

Linda Beth was in the little baby daybed in the front sitting room, red-faced and seriously unhappy as Sylvie rushed around with a fishing net, swatting at a gray, unidentifiable mass that darted under furniture and up the stairs.

It paused on the landing long enough for Henry to see

that it was a squirrel, but the women were carrying on as if a true monster was among them.

Well, the English women were. Sylvie was chasing it, obviously trying to capture it, and Millie was trying to calm everyone else down. Everyone else being a grandmother, a mother, and a young daughter. The daughter was crying almost as loudly as Linda Beth, while the mother and grandmother squealed whenever the squirrel came too close, which seemed to be about every thirty seconds. The squirrel would dart up the stairs and onto the landing. Then he would swing over onto the light fixture and scurry down the curtains used to partition off the dining area when it wasn't being used. Then the women would carry on, the squirrel would dart up the stairs trying to get away from them, and the whole process would start all over again.

As they came into the inn, Millie looked up, a smile lighting her harried features as she spotted the two of them. "Thank heavens," she said. "Please do something."

But Vern was already in motion. He pulled Linda Beth from the daybed like a seasoned pro, sticking the tip of his little finger into her mouth and in seconds quietening the unhappy baby. Henry didn't know much about children, but he didn't think that would appease the infant for long, but it gave him just enough quiet to think. He watched the squirrel as he scampered down the fabric partition and the women screamed once again. The squirrel spotted them, but not him. The little rodent darted back toward the staircase, but Henry was there. He dropped his hat on the animal, smartly stopping the little creature and trapping him for a moment before the hat started moving across the hardwood floor.

The women screamed again.

"Here." Sylvie handed him the fishing net.

Using his hat as a guide, Henry scooped the vermin into the net and carried it out onto the porch and set it free. The squirrel scampered away, no doubt relieved to be outside once again.

"Thank you! Thank you!" The two English women rushed toward him, throwing their arms around him and hugging him in their grateful excitement.

Henry wasn't sure what to do, so he stood there and let them embrace him. The exchange didn't last long. Mainly because the little girl was still crying. When the mom showed her daughter that the squirrel had been caught, she gave a great sniff, and the entire inn fell silent.

The quiet was almost deafening after all the noise.

"Thank you again," the mom said, nodding to all of them in turn.

Then the three women headed for the door.

"Remember," said Sylvie, "the popcorn shop is just down on Main a couple of blocks. You can't miss it."

"Poppin' Paradise," the mother repeated.

"I'm going to get dill-pickle-flavored," the little girl warned, her eyes still watery and red.

The grandmother shook her head. "I won't be eating any of that," she promised. And the trio disappeared out the front door and into the evening sunshine. It was almost seven and the sun would be going down soon, but until then . . .

"Nice save," Sylvie told Henry.

He handed her back her fishing net. "Thanks. But I think the real credit goes to Dawdi."

Vern looked up from the baby he cradled in his arms

to the two women who watched him in amazement. "What?" he asked. "I've held my share of babies."

"I suppose so," Sylvie murmured.

"But I think she would rather have her *mamm*," he said, making his way toward Millie as he spoke. Linda Beth was just starting to get fussy. Most likely time to eat again.

And Henry wondered if all babies had such poor timing.

Millie glanced up at him, then down at the baby. "I'll just . . ." She didn't finish that thought. Merely carried the baby up the staircase and down the hall, disappearing from view. A moment later Henry heard the door slam. How long would it be before the baby was content and asleep again?

He had told Millie that he would be back every day and this was his second time at the inn since he'd made that promise. And he was determined to make the most of it.

"I'll just . . . wait," he finished, walking over to the bottom of the stairs and easing down on the first step. She would have to come out of her room eventually, and when she did, he would be waiting for her.

"Sylvie Yoder," Vern started, his voice booming in the hollowness of the foyer.

Sylvie stopped, and Henry wondered if he was going to do this right there. It seemed he was.

"I set fire to my house. I'm forgetful and sometimes distracted." He half turned toward Henry. "That's the word I was looking for."

Henry hid his smile and nodded.

"But I'm not moving to Oklahoma."

Sylvie blinked at him, and Henry had to wonder what

was going on behind her hooded eyes. "*Jah*," she said. "Okay."

"Furthermore," Vern continued. "I think I love you and I want to see where that goes."

She propped her hands on her hips and eyed him closely. "You think?"

He cleared his throat, his face turning the same color as the geraniums that Henry's mother used to plant in the old flower bed around their mailbox back home. "I know. I know I'm in love with you, and I've been wondering if you would do me the favor of being my wife."

"*Jah*," she said, her face turning as pink as Vern's. "Yes! *Jah*!"

Henry watched with a smile as the pair came closer. Mindful of their audience, they stopped about a foot apart, holding hands and staring into each other's eyes.

Third wheel. Wasn't that what it was called when a couple plus one was in a room together? That's what he was, the third wheel, though he had no place to go. Or maybe he was refusing to go. He was sitting on that step until Millie came down those stairs and agreed to marry him. And that was all there was to it.

Once Linda Beth was quiet and sleeping again with a full belly and a sweet kiss from her *mamm*, Millie knew she had to go back downstairs. Vern and Henry hadn't said why they had come back to the inn again so soon, but she could imagine. Her aunt had set her up once today, and Vern had been in on the plan from the start. The plan to get her and Henry together. She could only suspect that this trip was part of the plan as well.

She sighed. She could stay up in her room for a while, but it wouldn't be long before someone came to get her. Sylvie of course, stating she needed help with one thing or another, and Millie would be forced into going downstairs.

And there he would be. Henry King. The man who had stolen her heart even before she had known she'd had it back. The man who deserved more than a barren wife and a child from another man.

That wasn't fair, she knew. There were a great many blended families in their community. Couples had children, spouses died, those left behind remarried. These families had troubles as all families did, but they got through them together. She just wanted more for Henry. She wanted all his dreams to come true, not him accepting what had been handed to him.

But isn't that what you're doing?

She tried to push that voice aside, but it stubbornly refused.

Jah, she could admit that she had accepted what had been handed to her. God's plan for her. So why couldn't all this—being married to her and all that it brought with it and all that it didn't—be part of God's plan for Henry?

She looked over to where Linda Beth was sleeping. He would love her as his own. She knew that much. And Linda Beth would grow up to be a better woman from having been raised by Henry King. Millie herself would be happier if she allowed her love to be matched by his.

So why was she so reluctant?

"For I know the plans I have for you," declares the Lord, "plans to prosper you and not to harm you, plans to give you hope and a future."

Jeremiah 29:11. She had learned the verse after Joshua died and she found out that she was carrying their child. She had wondered then as she was wondering now what God's plan for her could be.

Maybe it was already there.

Perhaps you were created for a time such as this.

It was a paraphrase, but she knew that verse as well. Esther 4:14.

And in that moment she knew she was being ridiculous. She was only bringing heartache to the both of them. He was right. She loved him, and she had to allow him to decide what he wanted for his dreams.

Her heart constricted in her chest as she cast one look at Linda Beth, sleeping so peacefully in her crib. She turned on the baby monitor and grabbed the remote. She preferred to have the baby close to her, but she was adjusting.

"Never fear, little one," she said softly. "I'll go get your daddy."

She made her way down the stairs, her mouth dry, her hands sweaty, her everything trembling. She was so nervous. What if he had changed his mind? What if he had only come to the inn to bring Vern by? Was there another sink messed up somewhere?

But she found Henry sitting at the foot of the stairs just . . . waiting.

She cleared her throat, and that coupled with the creak of the last step had Henry on his feet, spinning around to face her in a flash.

"Millie," he said, though her name on his lips was like a breath of prayer.

"Henry." She nodded. Now that she was down here with him, she didn't know what to say. How to start. "I—"

He shook his head and held up one hand. "No. Hear me out. I love you. I think I have from the very start. I understand that you are having a hard time, but believe me, having you and Linda Beth is all I need in this life. Marry me, Millie. Let me spend the rest of my days proving that to you."

"Okay," she said simply. It was an easy out, just agreeing with him and letting him do the hard part, all the talking and explaining, but it seemed as if he had been stewing in these feelings for a while now.

"Before you tell me no, listen to me. I love you," he said again. "You're all I need. I would never have imagined it to be so, but things change. Haven't we both learned that one the hard way?"

"*Jah*," she said. "I'll marry you."

"I mean, sometimes God's plan for us differs from what we imagined, but that doesn't make it less than what it is. God's plan. And who are we to argue with God?"

"Henry," she started, but he was on a roll.

"Well, sometimes it's hard not to; we are only human after all. But I love you, Millie; that's one part of His plan that I won't fuss about. Not if you agree to marry me."

She opened her mouth to speak, but he plowed on ahead.

"And I went to the library today. Look." He held up papers that looked as if they had been printed from a computer. "There's all sorts of options we can use to have more children. Get more children," he corrected. "We can adopt a baby from here, or a child from another country, or even foster. That's when they come to live with you for a while, then go on to different homes. I'm not sure how I'd feel about that, but if that's what you want, we can do it. Whatever you need, Millie."

"I need you." She laughed, then came the rest of the way down the stairs to where he waited for her. "You silly man," she said, cupping his chin in one hand. "I've said yes three times."

His eyes grew bright. "You have?" he asked. "You'll marry me?"

"If you'll still have me," she said. "I'm sorry I've been so afraid, it's just—" but it wasn't *just* anything. She *was* only human.

But that was just fine, because he didn't let her finish that sentence anyway. Instead he pulled her close and kissed her once more, letting her know without a doubt that God's plan for the two of them—for the three of them and any more to come however they were achieved—was for them to be together as a family.

Now and always.

Epilogue

As expected, Dale King, father to Henry and son to Vern, arrived on Friday. Now it was Monday, and Vern was still upset over having to buy Henry an extra-large bucket of popcorn. Cheddar and caramel mixed. Vern's favorite. But the worst part was that Henry would only share it with Millie.

The best part was they looked so happy together. It might be a while before they actually got married, but there were plans being made. For him and Sylvie too.

That was the funny thing about life. What was the saying, man plans and God laughs? He was sure the good Lord was having quite a chuckle over this one.

"Let me get this straight," Dale said once again. "You're not moving, but the house isn't livable, and I'm supposed to accept that."

"That's about it," Henry said, tossing back a big bite of the popcorn. "But we've got someone coming to look at it tomorrow. It's the third estimate, but I think he's going to be our man to fix the damage."

"And then you're going to move into the house with

Millie and the baby, and you," Dale turned to Vern, "are moving into the inn here with Sylvie."

"That's right," Vern said with a confident nod.

Dale shook his head. He was a stubborn boy, always had been. But Vern knew that stubborn could carry a man long and far as long as he wasn't directing that obstinance toward the Lord. Or His plans for a body. "And I'm . . ."

"Going back to Oklahoma tomorrow," Vern supplied.

Before Dale could say anything more, a cry rent the air, coming from the little white speaker Henry had placed on the side table next to his chair.

The women were gone and the men had gathered in the front sitting area eating through whatever snacks they could find in the kitchen.

"That's for me." Henry was on his feet in a second, wiping his sticky cheddar hands on a damp napkin before loping up the stairs to Millie's room, where Linda Beth had been sleeping peacefully.

The women had headed out to visit with Joy and help her start getting her house ready for church. Soon it would be her turn to host and a great many of the ladies were pitching in to help her. It was the way it was supposed to be, neighbor helping neighbor. That was the Amish way. And Joy needed more help than ever since Johnny B's accident. Frankly Vern was relieved to be staying in Missouri to help her. And now that he had Millie and Sylvie enlisted as new family members . . . they would all get along just fine. He knew it as sure as the heavens above.

"I thought you said she baked whoopie pies." Dale looked over at the many containers of desserts Vern had brought out. Mini pineapple upside-down cakes, no-bake chocolate oatmeal cookies, some chewy something that looked like it was made with peanut butter and cornflakes, and sugar cookies with orange-flavored icing. "These are mighty fine, but I don't see any whoopie pies."

That was the one thing Vern hadn't managed to iron out, but he knew it would happen in time. Sylvie had taken quite a blow to her ego, but he figured once they were married, he could start a full-time campaign to get her back to baking what really mattered most—whoopie pies.

"In time, my boy."

Dale chose one of the treats as Henry came down the stairs gingerly cradling the baby to him. He looked like he was holding a squirming cactus that might bite.

Vern bit back a chuckle. His grandson would learn soon enough. Babies were more resilient than they looked.

"And this is my new, soon-to-be granddaughter?" Dale asked.

Henry nodded. "Dat, meet Linda Beth."

Dale smiled and peered over into the bundle Henry held. "I'm not sure I'm ready to be a *dawdi* again," Dale said, but he was still smiling when he said it. And he still wore that slightly dazed look of a grandpa who sees his grandchild for the first time.

Well, he had seen her before, but never after finding out that he was to be her grandfather. The look on his face was priceless, and Vern filed it away for those times when Dale grew too stubborn in the future, for he knew those times would come.

Until then, he was content. Happy. Content and happy to just be a man in love.

He looked up and caught Henry's amazed gaze. And Vern knew his grandson felt the same. Two men in love with two very special women—three counting little Linda Beth—and that was all they ever wanted to be.

Please turn the page
for some delicious recipes
from Paradise Valley!

Sylvie Yoder's Baked Beignets

Ingredients:

¾ cup lukewarm water
¼ cup extra-fine sugar*
1½ teaspoon active dry yeast
3 tablespoons melted butter
1 large egg, beaten
½ cup buttermilk
½ teaspoon salt
2 teaspoons vanilla extract
3¾ cups flour
⅛ cup milk
1 tablespoon melted butter (for finishing)
¼ cup powdered sugar (for finishing)

Instructions:

Preheat oven to 200°F. (For speed-rising directions, skip this step if allowing to naturally rise.)

Line 3 baking sheets with parchment paper. Set aside.

In a large mixing bowl, whisk together water, sugar, and yeast to combine. Let stand for about 10 minutes or until it starts to get a foamy surface.

Then add 3 tablespoons of melted butter, egg, buttermilk, salt, and vanilla. Whisk to combine.

Slowly add in the flour and stir until the dough begins to pull from the sides of the bowl. If needed, add in additional flour one tablespoon at a time until the dough pulls away from the bowl.

Knead dough on floured surface for 5 minutes. Transfer dough to a lightly greased oven-safe bowl. Allow to rise for 1 hour or . . . turn off preheated oven and place bowl in the oven with the door slightly ajar. Be sure to cover bowl with a towel. DO NOT allow it to touch the heating elements of the oven. Allow to rise for 15 minutes.

Remove bowl from the oven, close the door, and re-preheat to 200°F.

On a lightly floured surface, roll dough out into a rectangle about ¼-inch thick.

Cut 2-inch squares with a butter knife or pizza cutter.

Place dough on the prepared baking sheets. Cover with plastic wrap that has been coated with baking spray on the underside.

Turn off preheated oven and place the baking sheets in the oven with the door slightly ajar. Allow to rise for another 30 minutes.

Remove baking sheets from oven and preheat to 375°F.

Remove plastic wrap and brush the tops lightly with milk.

Bake individual baking sheets for 10–12 minutes or until golden brown. Let cool for about 5 minutes.

Brush the beignets' tops lightly with melted butter, then dust liberally with powdered sugar.

Enjoy!

Notes:

Beignets should be eaten warm and fresh.

If you plan to eat them the next day, skip the finishing steps until ready to enjoy.

* To make granulated sugar extra fine, run through a clean, standard coffee grinder a couple of times. Not too many rounds or you'll end up with powdered sugar.

Millie's Favorite
Vanilla Whoopie Pies

Cake:

> ½ cup shortening
> 3 large eggs
> 2 teaspoons vanilla
> 1 cup sugar
> ½ cup hot water
> 2 cups flour
> ½ teaspoon salt
> 1 teaspoon baking soda
> ½ teaspoon baking powder

Icing:

> 1 cup shortening
> 4 cups powdered sugar
> 4 tablespoons water
> 2 tablespoons heavy cream

Instructions:

Preheat oven to 350° F.

In a large bowl, whisk together shortening, eggs, and vanilla.

In medium bowl, combine sugar, flour, salt, baking soda, and baking powder.

Slowly add dry ingredients to wet ingredients and mix well.

Line a baking sheet with parchment paper.

Use a cookie scoop to drop dough onto prepared baking sheets about 1 inch apart.

Bake 10–12 minutes (or use the toothpick method to check doneness).

Remove from the oven and cool for about 5 minutes. Transfer to wire racks and cool completely.

Filling:

In a large bowl, beat butter and 1 tablespoon of the heavy cream until creamy.

Add powdered sugar and vanilla. Beat just until smooth. (Here you'll have to judge the stiffness of your icing. If it is too thick carefully and slowly add more of the cream. If it is too runny, you can add more sugar or place in the fridge until it firms up a bit.)

Add icing to a pastry piping bag.

Assemble:

Turn half of the cooled cookies upside down. Pipe filling onto the flat side of overturned cookies.

Place a second cookie, flat side down, on top of filling. Press down slightly so that filling spreads to cookie edges.

Repeat until all cookies are used.

Enjoy!

Sadie Yoder's Award-Winning Brownie Whoopie Pies
with Salted Caramel Buttercream Filling

The "English" Instructions

Brownie Cookie

- ½ cup semisweet, mini chocolate chips
- ½ cup butter
- 3 large eggs
- ¼ cup brown sugar
- 1 cup granulated sugar
- 1 tablespoon vanilla extract
- ½ teaspoon baking powder
- ½ teaspoon salt
- ¾ cup all-purpose flour
- ¼ cup unsweetened cocoa powder
- 1 cup pecans or walnuts
- 12 oz. bittersweet chocolate chips

Instructions:

Preheat oven to 350 F.

Melt chocolate chips and butter in a saucepan on low heat. Stir constantly until completely melted and well-combined. Remove from heat. Set aside.

With a mixer, beat the eggs, brown sugar, granulated sugar, vanilla, baking powder, and salt on high for 5 minutes. (Set a kitchen timer to ensure that it's a full 5 minutes.)

Reduce the speed to low and mix in the melted chocolate-butter mixture until well-combined.

Stir in flour and cocoa powder just until mixed.

Add nuts and mini chocolate chips. Stir.

Cover the batter and chill for 30 minutes.

Line two baking sheets with parchment paper.

Using a cookie scoop, drop batter onto the prepared cookie sheets about 2 inches apart. (A cookie scoop will ensure your cookies come out roughly the same size.)

Bake cookies 8–10 minutes. The cookies will look set at the edges but still be a little doughy-looking in the center. Don't overbake.

The shiny, crackly crust will begin to show as the cookies cool on the baking sheet.

Allow to fully cool before assembling.

Salted Caramel Buttercream

Ingredients:

    ½ cup unsalted butter, room temperature
    1½–2 cups powdered sugar
    ⅓ cup homemade salted caramel (recipe on next page)
    ¼ teaspoon vanilla extract
    Sifted powdered sugar (set aside)

Instructions:

Place butter in a large bowl. Mix on medium high until creamy, for about 30 seconds.

Add 1½ cups of the powdered sugar. Mix on low until incorporated.

Slowly add the caramel sauce while raising speed to medium-high. Cream for 1 minute until creamy and smooth. Add vanilla. If the mixture is too runny, add more sugar.

Place frosting in a piping bag.

To assemble:

Pipe some of the salted caramel filling onto the bottom of one cooled cookie. Top with another cookie.

Pies should be stored in the fridge.

Makes 18 whoopie pies

Salted Caramel Sauce

Ingredients:

½ cup sugar
¼ cup heavy cream
½ teaspoon kosher salt
3 tablespoons unsalted butter

Instructions:

Place sugar in a medium saucepan.

Bring to a boil over medium heat. Stir constantly so sugar melts evenly.

Once the mixture is a golden amber color, remove from the heat.

Carefully and slowly add cream and salt. The mixture will rise to the top of the pan but will subside. Gently whisk mixture until combined.

Gently add butter. The mixture will once again rise, so go slowly.

Whisk until combined.

Bring mixture to a quick boil, while constantly whisking.

Let it boil for a few seconds, remove from heat.

Wait a couple of minutes for caramel to cool slightly.

Pour into a glass jar. Let cool completely before use.